HOLD
Me

COURTNEY MILAN

This is a work of fiction. Names, characters, and incidents are the product of the author's imagination or are used fictitiously. Any resemblance to actual people, living or dead, or companies or products, is purely coincidental.

*For everyone who thinks
that tone comes across just fine
on the internet*

1.

September

*G*abriel was supposed to be here ten minutes ago.

Instead, my brother is running late—no surprise, as he plays the role of absentminded scientist a little too well. He double-booked dinner tonight. He forgot that he was supposed to find me after my class. And when he sent directions to the place where I'm supposed to meet his friend...

Go to the chemistry complex, he said. *The lab's in the basement,* he said.

Ha.

There are multiple buildings, each with their own basement. Some have two. After a brief, maddening trip down a rabbit hole of cement walls, metal doors, and blue-green paint, I ascend for air—or, rather, cellular signal—to look up room numbers and a map.

If I didn't love my brother so much, I might be pissed.

But I've finally found the right place, a mere ten minutes late. I'm not even slightly miffed about the number of stairs I've had to tackle in heels. After all,

Gabe is not a distant Skype call at odd hours coming from half the globe away. He's in Berkeley. He's *here*.

At least, he'll be here soon. For now, he's directed me to ask for his friend Jay and wait.

I eye the door I've found with skepticism. A little placard to the side designates it as the Thalang Group. The door itself is festooned with warnings of impending death.

DANGER, says a sign in giant red letters. VISIBLE AND/OR INVISIBLE LASER RADIATION. Another sheet of laminated paper lists every chemical in the room that could kill me. It's a long list.

Possible fatality. Just how I like to start all my evenings.

I knock hard enough to bruise my knuckles, but the fireproof door makes only the slightest, most muffled thump in response. That's when I notice the tiny piece of paper duct-taped to the door. *Ring bell for entry.*

I ring.

I wait.

I'm not sure what to expect from a chemistry death lab, but my imagination has always been excellent. Radioactive bees? Radioactive nanobots? Radioactive mind-controlled soldiers? The possibilities are endless.

The door opens.

Damn. The room beyond looks painfully prosaic—desks, bookshelves, and a couch are visible from here. There are no super-soldiers equipped with prosthetic lasers, intent on world domination. There is no aquarium filled with radioactive spiders. There aren't spiders of any kind.

There's just a man standing at the door, frowning at me. He's almost exactly as tall as I am in these heels, which makes him pretty darned tall. He's almost as brown as I am, even though he can't get much sun down here.

He takes one look at me, tilts his head, and narrows his eyes. His eyebrows are thick and set in determined lines; he folds his arms in front of his chest. I'm pretty sure a super-soldier would be less intimidating.

I saw a photo of Professor Aroon na Thalang, the principal investigator of this group, on the website five minutes ago when I looked up the location of his lab. In that picture, he was thumbnail-sized and serious. Between the tiny image and the CV highlights listed beneath—an impressive acronym soup composed of a PhD from Cambridge, an NSF CAREER grant, and funding from DARPA—I had assumed he was twenty years older than me.

He's not. He looks about twenty-three. It has to be the Asian genes. He's kind of hot, in a glowering, grumpy scientist kind of way.

"You're incredibly late," he says. He has a hint of an accent. A *British* accent, to be precise, enough to remind me of that Cambridge PhD.

"Um." I bite my lip and curse my brother. "I'm sorry?"

"You're sorry, question mark." His eyes narrow as he says this, like I've committed some kind of cardinal sin, and his accent becomes more marked. "Either you're not sure you're sorry, in which case you shouldn't be apologizing, or you're sorry, period, and you need to work on your inflection. Which is it?"

This is going well. I try again. "I'm Maria—"

"I don't care. Group meeting finished an hour ago." He looks even more annoyed. "If you want to work in my lab—"

"I don't want to work in your lab. I'm here to meet Jay."

His glower deepens. Shit. I waved off the fact that I didn't see a Jay listed on the group website. It's September, the start of a new academic year. Groups change; I figured the listing was out of date. Now I'm wondering if Gabe gave me the wrong group name. Or the wrong department.

"So sorry." He delivers the word with a period at the end. A *sarcastic* period, since we are arguing punctuation, the kind that says he's not sorry at all. "I don't know you, and I don't have time for…" He squints at me and gives me another look, this one a little more pointed. "What are you selling, anyway? Lab supplies? Amway?"

Other people's stupid assumptions shouldn't bother me.

But they do. I don't know him, but he just decided it was more likely I was selling makeup than any of the other much more likely possibilities.

I know what I look like. I'm pretty. I should be; I work hard for it. I *like* being pretty. I like wearing skirts and heels and makeup. I'm not going to apologize for doing my hair or knowing how to contour foundation or any of the other tiny skills I've invested years in learning.

I'm going to get judged for caring about how I look. But I would get judged for *not* caring. I might as well dress exactly how I want.

Rationally, it shouldn't matter that a complete stranger has decided that I'm an airhead. His judgment still stings.

"I'm not selling anything," I say.

"So you *are* a grad student." He rubs his hair, making it stick up in little black spikes. "Let me make this easy: I'm looking for three-sigma students. Not people who arrive two hours late, who interrupt a perfectly good discussion with my postdoc, and who stare at me like they're deer losing brain cells in headlights. There's no point wasting each other's time."

My pulse pounds thickly.

"I'm...sorry?" I hear that question mark again and wince, just as his eyebrow rises. I try again. "I'm not sorry," I say, "but if you would just tell Jay I'm here—"

"Don't be sorry," he says. "Just join another group."

I inhale. "I think you misunderstood. I'm—"

"Nope," he says. "Sorry. I've got things to do."

Before I can say anything else, he shuts the lab door on me. Great. I contemplate the buzzer and wonder what he would do if I rang it again. Given the degree of asshole he just displayed, and the fact that he said he was in the middle of a perfectly good work session, he'd probably just get mad at the hapless Jay, who is likely the postdoc he mentioned.

Fine.

I exhale, take out my phone, and...dammit. Still no signal. There is a single flickering bar of campus wifi, though. I connect and message my brother.

Are you sure you told me the right place? The Thalang Group in chemistry? Did you mean biology?

His response comes seconds later. *Yep. Almost there.*

I frown dubiously at my phone. *The Aroon na Thalang Group? There's no Jay listed on the group page.*

That's him, my brother texts back. *Jay. It's a nickname. Nobody calls him Aroon.*

I consider hitting my head against the cement wall in front of me.

Yay. Gabe's friend—the one who just shut the door in my face, the one I'm supposed to have dinner with—is a dick.

Yes, he jumped to conclusions. Yes, I'm sure he'll make all the right pretend apologies when Gabe clues him in. But he still looked at me and decided I was a lab-supply salesperson, and didn't let me get a word in edgewise.

Great.

It doesn't help that I'm staring at a poster of his lab's work. I noticed these in the hallways earlier as I was looking for this place. They're essentially advertisements for all the research groups that are recruiting new graduate students.

I've seen badly Photoshopped versions representing various groups as X-Men or the Avengers. Here, someone has pasted Jay's face on the massive, genetically enhanced dinosaur that wreaked havoc on a fictional theme park. I recognize the rest of the group from the picture as velociraptors.

"Apt," I mutter.

Strangely, though, this reminder of fictional mayhem calms me down. Most people, when they're feeling a little upset, take deep breaths and think good thoughts.

I'm Maria Lopez. *I* take deep breaths and think about the end of the world.

Literally. These basement chemistry laboratories are an apocalyptic filmmaker's wet dream. I am not far from the room where plutonium was discovered. If there's a catastrophe waiting to happen in some scientist's experiment, it could be close by. Behind that fire door, someone may well be tinkering with some nanotechnological device that will spell the end of civilization as we know it.

So far, despite humanity's best efforts, civilization has persisted.

I know all about apocalypses that don't happen. The apocalypse is nothing more than shitty things that happen to you instead of someone else. The apocalypse has been fiction for me, and fiction it will remain.

Life goes on. I can handle one dinner with an asshole. I've dealt with worse.

Almost there, Gabe texts. *Sorry!*

It's okay, I answer. *I didn't expect you to be on time.*

He texts me a face with its tongue sticking out.

Gabe and I have lived in different cities since I was twelve and my parents kicked me out of the house. Even back then, he used to pick me up from school twenty or thirty minutes after class let out. In the years since, he's been late for Skype calls and the occasional dinner when our paths intersect. It's not just me; this is a perpetual habit. He was late for his own PhD commencement ceremony. His advisor walked onstage alone with Gabe's hood and gave the crowd a shrug.

I didn't think things would be any different now that we're living a mile apart. After everything we've been through together, I can spot him fifteen minutes.

The fire door to my right opens, and Gabriel walks through. He has medium brown hair—like me, except his is a uniform, shaggy brown, because he also forgets to get haircuts for months on end. His jaw is a little more square, and he's about an inch shorter than I am. Which is why I hug him and say...

"Hello, *little* brother." He's three years older than I am. Before I went through my growth spurt, he used to give me noogies and say, "That's what you get for being so small."

Biology is a bitch, and so are younger sisters. I give him a noogie.

"Gah." He pulls away. "It's not fair."

That was *my* line when we were kids. I stick my tongue out at him.

"I need to invent time travel and punch my teenage self in the face." He turns to the door and presses the bell. "You're going to really like Jay. He's a good guy."

I grimace at his back.

It's not the first time I've played nice with one of his "good guy" friends, and it won't be the last. There are a lot of reasons for guys to be a dick to me, and I've experienced them all.

We wait.

Professor Thalang opens the door again. Now that I know he's Jay, and my brother's friend, his age is a little easier to discern. He's probably a few years older than I am—three, five?—but no more. I remember the intimidating alphabet soup of his CV. Damn. He has been busy with his life.

His eyes land on my brother and his face lights up. He grabs Gabe by the shoulders, slapping him on the back.

"Look at you," Jay says. "You survived Switzerland. Almost. Too bad about the *other* thing."

Gabe laughs. "Dude. Don't give me shit about the *other* thing until you meet Jutta. She's the greatest."

My lip curls slightly at this exchange.

Yeah, that little crack is about par for the "good guy" course, in my experience. My brother spent the last two years in Switzerland. He had a postdoctoral position at CERN. He worked with some of the brightest scientists in the world at the world's most powerful supercollider. He published two papers about elementary particles. But all of that is equivalent to *almost* surviving Switzerland, because while Gabe was there, he got engaged to a lovely, smart computational scientist. Surely a fate worse than death.

I might as well be invisible. Jay—Professor Thalang—I'm not sure *how* I should think of him—steps back and grins. "How have you been, man?"

"Oh, you know. Busy on that revision for *JACR* still."

I don't remember what journal that acronym stands for. I suspect that if I don't say anything, the two of them will descend into science. Which I don't mind, but I want Jay to squirm.

"Gabe." I touch my brother's arm.

That's when Professor Thalang notices me. He literally didn't see me before now. He frowns in my direction, turning away from my brother. "Hey."

Gabe doesn't notice the look on his face. "Right. Jay, I forgot to mention that my little sister is coming to dinner with us. Her name's Maria."

I look Jay in the eye and decide to annoy him. "Hi?" I let my voice go up at the end intentionally, making the word into a question.

He grimaces. "Oh."

Oh indeed.

"Shit." He looks into my eyes and inhales. His eyes are dark brown and piercing, and the effect of his thick eyebrows is that he looks fierce…and not at all apologetic.

"Maria," Gabe says, not noticing the ratcheting tension, "this is Jay. He was a postdoc at Harvard when I was there. He does work on—"

"I read his lab posters in the hall after he shut the door in my face," I say sweetly. "I know what he does."

Gabe frowns. Even he can't avoid noticing this anvil of a clue indicating that all is not well.

Jay doesn't quite roll his eyes. "You read my poster," he says with a hint of disbelief. "You know what I do. *Sure.*" His accent becomes just a little more pronounced, almost pretentiously British.

That emphasis on *sure*, the way he looks at me… He doesn't believe I *could* understand. He thinks I'm stupid.

Like I said. It's not the first time someone's made assumptions about me, and it won't be the last. The good thing is, if he's not going to even pretend to be nice, I don't have to, either.

"I understand everything," I say, turning to Gabe. "Did you know Jay's working on a top secret project for the Department of Defense? He uses invisible radiation to turn himself into an asshole."

Gabe looks at me, then at his friend, then back at me. "I'm missing something."

"Don't worry, little brother." I pat Gabe's shoulder. "His terrible transformation only happens around women. You're safe."

2.

JAY

*T*here's something about Gabriel's younger sister that makes me feel incredibly restless. No, it's not the fact that I've already pissed her off. It's not even the fact that she implied I was a sexist. After two female postdocs, three female grad students, six female coauthors, and countless friends, my record speaks for itself. Someone who's known me for all of fifteen seconds isn't going to send me into a crisis of self-doubt.

I try to put my finger on what's bothering me as we walk to the restaurant.

One: Maria Lopez doesn't talk to me.

And yes, I get it—my response to her earlier left much to be desired. But she doesn't address me at all. She chatters to her brother about their grandmother, who apparently lives nearby, some band they both like, and—of all things—his *wedding* plans.

"No," Gabe says bemusedly. "I *don't* have a venue yet, but we're not getting married for thirteen months. There's plenty of time."

"Sorry." Maria doesn't sound apologetic. "But Jutta will kill me if I let you drop the ball on this one."

The second thing that annoys me about Maria is *what* she is saying. I'm not sure how serious, thoughtful

Gabe ended up with a sister who is bugging him about wedding plans in one breath, then asking him about some movie in the next. She's like a pond skater, flitting from topic to topic, scarcely touching the surface and skimming away without delving into any depth.

I'm not participating in the conversation, and she's already driving me nuts.

Three: I can't stop looking at her.

No, it's not that I find her overwhelmingly attractive. I stopped letting my little head do all the thinking back when I was in high school. Pretty is a dime a dozen.

But Maria Lopez isn't *pretty* to look at. Neither is the *Mona Lisa,* if it comes down to it. No, Maria is something far more invasive. She's *interesting* to look at.

Her nose is sharp and pronounced; her eyes are soft and smoky. Her hair is dark, except where it glints with gold and red. She's a combination of elements that should not go together—inviting lips, forbidding eyebrows that narrow in my direction when she catches me looking at her. She draws my eye as if a graphic artist designed her for that express purpose. No matter how I try to look away, I keep turning back.

The fourth thing that annoys me about Maria is her shoes. I'm aware the entire length of the walk to the restaurant—almost a mile—that she's keeping up with the brisk pace that I'm setting.

In heels. Pink heels, and not the short stubby kind either. She doesn't complain, and she probably should. Her heels have bright silver studs in them, and they keep reflecting little flashes of light as she walks.

And that means I keep looking down at her shoes. And her calves. And the six inches of thigh visible below her skirt. From there, it's not hard for my gaze to slide to the shift of her hips as she's walking, the tensing muscles of her behind.

And fuck me, but here is number five: Gabe is a really good friend of mine, and the last thing I want is for him to realize that I keep checking out his sister's ass.

We finally arrive at the Italian place I've picked out and are shown to a table in back.

Both Gabe and Maria head to the restroom to wash up.

Item six: Maria's the first one to come back. If there were any fairness to the universe, she would have taken an extra five minutes to redo her lipstick, or whatever women like her do. But no.

She approaches the table warily. We make eye contact as if we are a pair of strange wolves, growling over who will be alpha of this restaurant.

She sits stiff-leggedly. A spray of plastic flowers separates us. It's not enough of a barrier.

Here's the seventh reason why Maria is incredibly annoying: I was really looking forward to having Gabe around for a year.

Nobody tells you the dirty secret of academia until it's too late. It should be obvious. In reality, you only realize what's happening once you're committed.

I spent all my university years making friends—good friends—who scattered to the wind when we graduated. That's to be expected. I made more friends when I was getting my doctoral degree. There were labmates, postdocs, some professors. There were people

I met at short classes and conferences. In other words, I found my people, and then watched them disappear from my life. Multiply by the absent friends acquired during my postdoc years and more scientific conferences.

Nobody tells you when you decide to be a scientist that you will spend the rest of your life having your forty closest friends live at a distance.

I'm not lonely. I'm too busy to be lonely. What I am is bloody annoyed that I spent ten minutes listening to one of those friends argue with his little sister about Taylor Swift. I'm annoyed that she's here at this table right now, and Gabe is not.

And maybe that's why I look at Maria—who is pretending to find the unlit candle on the table more interesting than me—and say these words: "I'll make you a deal."

Her eyebrows scrunch together suspiciously. She sets the candle down. "What kind of deal?"

"I'll apologize to you for being a jerk earlier if you'll stop distracting your brother."

Her head tilts slightly; the dim lights of the restaurant catch a light gold strand of her hair. "How am *I* distracting my brother?"

She doesn't even know. Her cluelessness is item eight. I hold her gaze. "This is the most important year of his life. He needs to continue to turn the last two years of his work into papers, all while impressing his current principal investigator. He needs to come up with a viable research agenda and practice defending it. Gabe has a shot at the holy grail of a tenure-track job. He doesn't need to waste his time thinking about Britney Spears."

It wasn't Britney Spears. She doesn't correct me. "You think a few minutes talking about music will kill his job prospects?"

"Sunday dinner every week?" I hold up a finger. "A trip to Santa Monica to hear some music that you can stream for free while doing work?" A second finger. "And on top of that, you expect him to put together a full wedding? That's not even everything I heard in the last twenty minutes. Yes, you're distracting him."

Her jaw shifts and squares, but she doesn't say anything.

"I'm just saying, he's not in high school anymore. You can't act like he's your personal chauffeur."

She bites her lip. "So that's the deal you're offering. You'll apologize to me, and I'll go off and do my own thing."

"Pretty much."

"Okay." She leans down and opens her purse. To my great annoyance, she takes out a mirrored compact and a tube of lipstick, which she proceeds to apply.

"You're not even going to answer?"

"Mmm." She's like a parakeet, entranced with her own reflection. "If I have to bargain for your apology, it doesn't really mean anything, does it?"

I frown at her.

"Also, what my brother and I talk about is really not your business. You don't know me or my relationship with my brother. You don't get a vote."

"I'm rather more of an expert on the academic market than you are."

She closes her mirror with a snap. "Congratulations."

"And look at you. You took a *selfie* with your brother. You're a girly-girl. You care about your hair and clothes and pop culture. I've seen too many of my good friends struggle to get jobs. You don't know this market."

"How sweet." Her lipstick glistens, catching the light. "I'm average, and you only respect people three standard deviations above the mean. I don't make the cut."

"I didn't say that."

"Sure you did, Three Sigma. Back in your lab, right as you were throwing me out."

I grimace.

"This dinner must be incredibly weird for you," she continues smoothly. "Forced social interaction with people who like popular things? Oooh. Awkward."

"I definitely didn't say that."

I just thought it. And she heard it anyway. It's like she heard the entire list I've been making in my head, because she tosses back her hair with a practiced flick that a wind machine couldn't improve, and crosses her legs, pointing one toe of those outrageous pink heels in my direction. The posture is defiantly, femininely rude.

"Let me help you hate me," she says in a low, silky voice. "I also read romance novels. I watched every part of *Twilight* in the theater even though I was Team Jacob. If you think that girly-girl is an *insult* to me, you're wrong. I *am* a girl, and I am proud of it."

I exhale. "I don't have a problem with women. Just you."

"You know what you *do* have a problem with? You're not my brother's boss. You're not his owner. You're his friend. If he wants to come with me to every Britney Spears concert in the country, it's none of your business. You don't get to come between us. That's not your place, now or ever. So take your ninety-nine point seventh percentile intelligence and shove it."

"Jesus," says a voice behind me. It's Gabe. He's come up to the table. "Jay, what did you *say?* You made *Maria* mad?"

She turns her head and tosses her hair, and...

Fuck.

Here's the thing. Rationally, I know she's pissed at me. Rationally, I know that we would never, ever, in a million years get along. Rationally, I'm aware that even if I had been nice from the beginning, I would get shot down hard if I made a play for her.

Not that Maria is out of my league. It's more that the very concept of a league makes no sense, because we're not playing the same sport. I'm more of a pickup basketball kind of guy, and she's... Well, she's into whatever game you play with a French manicure and Louboutins. The game she's playing sucks, the players are mean, and I want nothing to do with it or them.

Nothing, except... My stupid lizard brain wouldn't mind watching her play. The light catches her hair—a high-gloss counterpoint that draws my eye—and it's so perfect that I can't help but wonder if she planned it.

My teeth grind together. Maybe I could collapse reasons one through eight into this: Maria reminds me of Clio. It's not anything so obvious as her looks—Clio was blond and about six inches shorter—so much as a vague impression. Clio had that same air of polished perfection. That same awareness in her eyes when she caught me looking. *Go ahead.* I can see that final message in my mind's eye. *No one cares.*

Including me. I won't care, and I don't want anything to do with Maria or the memories she brings up.

I turn to Gabe. "Let's talk particle physics."

He frowns at me. He glances at Maria. He shakes his head, then sits down. "Dude," he finally says. "Don't be mean to my sister, okay?"

"Don't bother," Maria says smoothly. "He's too busy to be reprimanded." She glances in my direction and smiles sweetly. "And I don't mind."

Striking, yes. Eye-catching, yes. And was I mean to her? I consider everything I've said. Yes, that was probably over the top. I have too many memories of where playing nice with girls like her gets me.

The last thing I need at this point is to spend more time looking at her. The less we like each other, the better.

---

*I*t's nine at night, half an hour after I abandoned Gabe, his sister, and the world's most painful dinner. I'm reading through my grant proposal one last time, sitting in bed in sweats, trying to pretend I'm not waiting…

Ding. My phone chirps beside me, and I smile. *Smile* isn't the right word for what I do. My whole body lights up, the way I know it shouldn't, not for someone I've never met. Not for someone I've never *seen*.

I pick up my phone and open the chat app.

There's a message. It's from Em. *I'm sorry. I know I promised I was going to get this post up in the next hour, but I'm not finishing it tonight.*

I don't even hesitate before typing back. *Do you need to work something out? It's not like my grant deadline is tomorrow or anything.*

My grant deadline is tomorrow.

I can be a sounding board, I write.

Her response is immediate and dismissive. *It's not that at all. I need soup.*

Oh. Shit. Stop everything! We have a soup emergency here. Do you have any soup in the house?

There's a pause before her response comes through. *Soup. In the house. I must have misheard. Did you say soup in the house?*

There's a longer pause. It's weird how colloquialisms play out on the internet. It's not like she could actually mishear me; my words are right there, and they aren't changing.

She goes on: *You are, perhaps, referring to the abomination known as soup in a can? What kind of a monster do you take me for? Soup in a can is not soup. The vegetables get soggy. The noodles turn to mush. SOUP IN A CAN IS NOT REAL SOUP, OKAY?*

I have a goofy grin on my face as I shut my laptop. I don't take a lot of breaks; my tenure clock has effectively three years left before I have to put the final application together. I'm not about to screw around. But relationships ebb and flow differently in real life versus online. The friend I played pool with three times a week at university now posts happy birthday on my Facebook wall once a year. By contrast, Vithika Chaudhary and I never started talking quantum algorithms until six months after we ended up at a physics course in the French Alps together. Now we talk twice a week and make plans to cross paths as often as two people on opposite sides of the world can.

As for Em? I have no idea who she is.

We found each other by accident, when Vithika forwarded me a link to her blog a few years ago. We started talking some months later when I left a comment critiquing her physics, and we somehow never stopped.

I grin as I type. *Uh. Em. I'm pretty sure canned soup is actually soup. There's an entire series of paintings about it.*

She sends me a skull-and-crossbones emoji. *FUCK WARHOL. I AM SERIOUS ABOUT SOUP.*

Whoa, I type. *Em. Calm down.*

IF YOU ARE GOING TO BE FLIPPANT ABOUT SOUP, THIS CONVERSATION IS OVER.

I know she's joking the way I know Rayleigh scattering explains why the sky is blue: immediately and without thinking. Over the past eighteen months, I've come to know her pretty well.

That's why I play along. *I apologize. Clearly I have failed to take soup with the seriousness that soup deserves. All hail the mighty soup. Ave, soup. Morituri te salutant.*

I can almost feel the suspicion roiling off my phone. Three little dots appear, indicating that she's typing. Then: *What are you talking about?*

It's not often I manage to stump her. Reading comics in my misspent youth has given me *some* useful ammunition. *It's what ancient gladiators would say to Caesar before they did battle. Except the soup part. It means something like, "We who are about to die salute you." One can't get more serious about soup than a death match in its honor.*

I can almost imagine her smiling. *I detect sarcasm on your part. Whatever. I'll circle back to this later. I have to run out for soup before the good restaurants close. I have about a two-block radius.*

What's in two blocks? I ask, before I think better of the question.

Pretty much everything. Chinese. Korean. Vietnamese. Thai. I am not sure which soup I will get, but there will be soup.

I bite my lip.

Here's the thing. I grew up spending afternoons at Cyclone Technologies, the computer company where my mother worked. Basic online safety was drummed into me from an early age. *Always use a pseudonym if you can. Never tell people who you are or where you live. Never drop clues.*

It's a good idea for all minors; it's an absolute necessity for a teenager messing around on a computer hooked to the network of one of the largest computer manufacturers in the world. Black-hat hackers would have loved to infect our machines.

As an adult with a ridiculously Googleable name, I've learned it's best to adhere to those rules. People discover who my parents are, and things get weird.

Em knows me as my online pseudonym—Actual Physicist—and I know her as Em. And after eighteen months of chatting, I've realized that layer of pseudonymity is important. Necessary, even.

I shake my head and type. *Okay, not that I want to be crazy stalker guy, but that was a slip. If I *were* crazy stalker* *guy, you realize that you just told me a lot of stuff about yourself, right?*

I haven't mentioned Em to my other friends. Or my parents. Or my colleagues. For one, I'm not sure how I would classify her. We are friends, yes. We flirt, yes. I talk to her a lot, because she's fun to talk to, and I'm so busy being not-lonely that someone interesting who I've never met fits perfectly into my life.

This isn't really weird. I've written papers with people on the other side of the globe, people I've never met. I'm *used* to relationships that don't involve phone conversations or the exchange of pictures. I don't need to think of her as anything except the little avatar she uses—a globe of the earth, rotating silently in space, blue and green and brown and glowing with pulsating radioactivity.

Shit, she says. *What did I say?*

I bite my lip.

Not to freak you out or anything, but if restaurants are just now closing, that pretty much told me you're on the West Coast. And you've listed four separate ethnicities in a two-block radius, so you're in a major urban center. So Seattle/Portland/Bay Area/LA Basin. I think for a moment, and then add: *Scratch the LA Basin, because you can't really walk anywhere in LA. Sorry, Em. I try not to think about these things. But I can't help it. My mind just doesn't shut up.*

This is a lie. I think about her all the time. I have a mental image of her that I cannot get rid of, no matter how many times I tell myself she's just an avatar. Em, in my mind, is self-conscious. I suspect she's a little hesitant in real life. She's short, and she shies away from eye contact. She wears jeans and hoodies, and she doesn't smile often, but when she does…

Dammit. I wipe the image from my head.

Thanks, she types. *I didn't even think before typing. My need for soup is dire. Please don't sell my personal information to the Haters of the Great Zombie Schism. It would not make this day better.*

It's the second time she's mentioned having a rough day. I contemplate asking. That not-lonely-but-maybe part of me wants to know. My forefinger hovers over the onscreen keyboard.

Em rarely complains, and today is no exception.

I don't really want to say more, because otherwise you'll figure out that you forgot Sacramento in your list of population centers.

Jokes are good. The last thing I want is us comparing locations or agreeing to meet. I'm too aware of the way I smile when she messages me. Starting a long-distance relationship while my tenure clock is ticking is the worst idea I can think of.

Besides, she's as careful as I am, and I respect that. Em is—in her own way—a minor celebrity.

She has a blog. The basic premise is that her blog is written by someone from the future, someone known only by the initials "MCL." In MCL's future, the human race is on the verge of dying due to some catastrophic mistake that our generation is making. As a last-ditch effort, her society invents a way to send instructions back in time about how to prevent that catastrophe.

Invariably, history is rewritten, disaster is avoided… And MCL comes back the next week, to explain how a *different* screwup now threatens to wipe out humanity.

She's funny and playful, and my email loops amusedly share links when she touches on our subject matter. She protects her identity. I protect my time. It works for both of us.

So I play into the joke. *Everyone forgets Sacramento. Even you would. Even if you were living in it.*

True, she shoots back. *There's also Davis. I could live in Davis. Anywhere there's a college town, you can find some walkable bits. Okay. Have arrived. Am ordering soup.*

I halfheartedly reopen my laptop. Read through the objectives of my grant proposal. I imagine Em blowing on a spoonful of soup, with steam obscuring her glasses, before I catch myself daydreaming.

I don't know why I'm sure that Em wears glasses, but I am.

After five minutes, I text again. *Is it helping?*

Soup *always* helps, comes the reply. *My grandmother used to have soup with me when I was in high school and shit sucked.*

I don't say anything. She's never mentioned her family before, and I don't know if I should stop her again. But Em is careful—so careful, that even now, eighteen months after we first started talking, I'm just learning that she was close to her grandmother. That she *went* to high school. I'm not surprised high school sucked for her.

Yay, soup, I say instead.

Yay, soup, she agrees. *I feel substantially less embarrassed and substantially more enraged. I have decided I was not wrong. The other guy was at fault.*

I smile. *I'm sure he was. What a dick.*

You don't even know any details. You're quick to take my side.

I don't need to think before I type. *I don't need details. My money is on you in any death match you choose to participate in. Ave Em, morituri te salutant.*

And that's it for personal exchanges, thankfully. She starts telling me the idea she has for her next blogpost, and I offer my comments and answer a few questions. For the next forty-five minutes, I don't think about graduate students or my grant proposal or anything except soup and someone who makes me smile. We say our good-byes a few minutes later.

I finish looking over the final draft of this Chaudhary/Thalang proposal one last time. Vithika signed off on it already, but I can't let go. It's twenty pages on quantum entanglement and evaluation. Even after six times through, I still find myself smoothing methodology here, notes about future work there.

Friendship with Em is like bite-sized smiles I can fit anywhere in my day. I can ignore messages when I need to, and pick them up when I have a few spare moments. It's the beauty of the internet—she can be anyone, anywhere, and so can I. The fact that I sometimes find myself wondering where she lives, and what she looks like, is proof that I shouldn't try for any more.

I already put off my never-ending pile of work for her. I can't imagine what it would be like if I actually had a picture to obsess over.

I shake my head, finish my review of the proposal, and   hit   send.

3.

MARIA

---

*T*he week after that terrible dinner, it feels like I see Jay na Thalang everywhere. In line with me at the coffee shop. Talking to a gray-haired professor as they stroll along the banks of the little redwood-lined stream that runs through campus. He even passes me once as I'm waiting for a bus.

The first time we see each other, our eyes meet. I feel awkward, trying to figure out if I should wave and nod or pretend I don't know him.

I breathe a sigh of relief when he looks away. We're going to pretend we don't know each other. Thank god.

It gets easier to ignore him every time I see him.

Until the day he runs into me. *Literally* runs into me. It's noon, and I'm crossing Sproul Plaza along with a crowd of other students intent on lunch. The trees lining the walkway have started to drop yellow leaves, and the crowd around me presses shoulder to shoulder.

I'm texting Tina, my best friend and housemate. *You done with your project yet?*

Ugh, she types back. *One last bug. I think. Can we skip lunch today?*

No, I type severely. If one can type severely. *We can skip having lunch together, but you have to eat. I'm bringing you something.*

My housemate has always been a goody two-shoes. *OMG Maria,* she responds. *Can't eat in computer lab.*

I shake my head. **Shouldn't* eat in computer lab. Completely possible to do so.*

But I know she won't. I sigh. *I'll bring you something in an hour and you can eat on your way to class. But you have to eat.*

Her text comes a minute later. *Yes, Mom.*

I smile, looking at my phone. That's when someone rams into my left arm hard, spinning me around. I drop my bag involuntarily and tubes of lipstick spill on the pavement.

"Shit," a voice says.

I turn around, my shoulder still stinging.

"Sorry." The man who ran into me leans down to help me get my stuff.

It's Jay. He looks at me, blinking, his eyes widening in recognition. The concerned expression on his face fades. He freezes, half-crouching.

He can't pretend I'm invisible now. This is the first time I've seen him up close in daylight. He's wearing a blue shirt with lines and arrows on it. Big white letters say: PUMPED, EXCITED, INVERTED, AND STIMULATED.

Oh look. Dirty jokes about lasers. That seems just like him.

I don't want to notice that he has nice arms, but I do. He has biceps. Like, *real* biceps. And he's tattooed— his arms are covered with a dark geometric design, starting from his hands and disappearing into his sleeves.

He reaches for my compact. "Watch where you're going," he says. "What were you doing, taking a selfie?"

Oh, for god's sake.

"Taking six," I snap at him. "Gotta make sure my profile picture is perfect, after all. Do I look okay?"

I mean it as something of a barbed joke. But he pauses where he is, one knee on the ground before me. His fingers are half-closed around my compact, and he looks up. For a second, his expression goes utterly blank.

I know the answer to the question I just asked him. I look more than okay. I'm wearing a pink sundress with black patent leather sandals—thick, glossy lines that crisscross my feet. I've added a little silver charm that dangles over my ankle. I can feel his gaze sliding up. He starts from the pale blue of my toenail polish. His gaze slides up the lines of my sandals, up my legs. He eventually gets to my eyes. It's a long eventually.

He doesn't need to answer my question. By his total lack of response, I look more than okay. He blows out a breath and shakes his head, as if the fact that I look more than okay pisses him off.

He swallows. "Beauty standards are shit, anyway."

I lean down and grab the compact from him. Our hands brush.

Here's the other thing: He is not ugly. For just one second, our eyes meet again. Even this much proximity makes me uncomfortably aware of him.

"Beauty standards are shit," I say in one hundred percent agreement. Then I straighten, compact in hand. "Apparently, so are manners."

He looks at me for a second. Slowly, he clambers to his feet.

"'Sorry I bumped into you' would have been another way to respond," I tell him. "Just FYI."

He dusts off his hands. "Happy to oblige. I'm sorry every time I bump into you." His accent comes through more markedly on those words, posh and British. I think I may hate him.

"Have a nice life," I say.

"Have a nice cliché."

I roll my eyes and turn away. Because there is absolutely no justice in the world, I think of all the things I could have said instead of that stupid "have a nice life" as soon as he is out of my sight.

The asshole police aren't working today. You won't get a ticket if you exceed the minimum levels of human decency.

Maybe. Except…

Would the asshole police ticket people for *being* an asshole or *not* being one? I'm not really clear on the job description.

Not that I need to be. It's an insult, not an invitation to revisit the system of carceral punishment. *This* is why I am a better blogger than a public speaker.

"Maria?"

I'm overthinking the insult I no longer have the opportunity to deliver so much that at first, I don't hear my name.

Then the word sounds again, closer this time. "Maria?"

I turn twenty degrees and see a figure coming toward me through the crowd. It's Angela Choi. She's tall and willow thin, with just a hint of muscle, which I can see because she's wearing a tank top even though it's sixty degrees out. She has a flannel shirt tied around her waist, and her hair is glossy black and stick straight. It hits just above her shoulders. She gives me a tentative smile.

I'm older than the average college senior, and my best friends tend to be people who aren't typical college students away from home for the first time. Anj is no exception. She's a biology graduate student. She's smart, funny, independent, rich, and a complete mess.

Three years ago, Anj was one of my best friends. We shared an apartment with a third friend for the space of a school year, and it was hell.

The latter experience is the reason her smile is tentative, and why my answering smile feels just a little forced. I'm not mad at her. It's not that we actually *stopped* being friends. But some friends were not made to live together, and that was basically me and Anj.

It is, to be honest, ninety-eight percent of the world's population and Anj. She's funny, hilarious, bubbly, exuberant, outgoing, and over the top. She's the lynchpin of the trans community here, and everyone loves her, because she hasn't met a big dream she can't make enormous.

Those same things that make her an incredible person—the passion, the focus, the over-the-top desire to change the world—also made her the world's most terrible housemate. It was a relief when our household broke up because she had to go to Montana for some work she was doing on her thesis.

We hug despite the awkwardness.

"We haven't talked in forever," she says when we pull away.

Six months, unless you count a brief exchange on Facebook. It's been awkward. Everyone loves Anj; they kept asking me when she was coming back.

"I know. It sucks."

She looks over at me, bites her lip, and wrinkles her nose. "I don't suppose you have time to get lunch?"

I think about all the reasons I was shamefully relieved she had to go out of town.

They are myriad. She only eats cereal. When she's focused on a project—which is all the time—she leaves her cereal bowls, half-full of milk, wherever she finishes eating. She keeps four snakes, seven lizards, and a hundred-gallon saltwater aquarium for her glow-in-the-dark shark, even though our lease specifically said that no pets were allowed. ("They're not pets," Anj explained, "they're projects.") Also, Anj thinks it is perfectly fine to raise mealworms for said lizards in the living room. She fought incessantly with our third roommate about all of these things, and I hid as much as I could while they argued. Anj is a mess to live with and she knows it.

There are huge differences between us, and I don't just mean the cereal bowls and the lizards. When we first agreed to get a place together, I had no idea how rich she was. She doesn't *act* like she's rich. She sure doesn't *dress* like she's rich.

But Anj just could not understand why the thought of losing my deposit stressed me out. The imminent possibility of eviction hung over my head, and Anj only understood vaguely that I was upset. She'd try to make me feel better with some effusive gesture like taking me out to dinner at an extremely fancy restaurant.

She would eat nothing, because they didn't serve cereal. Then we would come home to our seven lizards and our geometrically expanding mealworm population.

"I'd love to get lunch," I say. I can get something for Tina to go, and it'll wash the memory of Jay and his three-sigma asshole police out of my mind.

We walk down Shattuck and find a crepe place. It's crowded, and I can barely hear her. We're shoved together at the end of a bench in the lunch hour crush.

"Are you still rooming with…" She pauses. "What's her name, your little friend?"

"Tina?" I say pointedly.

"Right. Her."

Tina and I studied for organic chemistry together probably fifty times when Anj and I shared an apartment. Anj really should know her name. But Anj isn't the kind of person who pretends to forget someone's name to be snooty. Anj's memory is reserved for the scientific names of thousands of extinct species. "Tina Chen" is not Latin enough for her to recall.

"Yes," I say. "We're sharing a house." I pause. "With her boyfriend."

Anj wrinkles her nose. "Ugh," she says. "I'm sorry. At least she's discreet, right? She's good at making herself invisible."

I feel my hackles rise at this, in part because… Well, it's true. Or at least, it used to be.

I turn to Anj and lean in. "Okay, look. I live on a totally separate level of the house, right? So…I don't hear anything, I don't see anything. But her boyfriend…"

How to say this.

Anj shakes her head. "Is he completely disgusting? Because men." She shakes her head on that last word, as if that phrase—*because men*—explains everything.

He doesn't leave half-empty bowls of congealing cereal on the floor.

I sigh. "*Because men* doesn't even come close to explaining it. He's Blake Reynolds."

I don't have to say anything more. She knows who Blake is. Even though Anj doesn't know Tina's name after having met her repeatedly, Blake Reynolds is essentially Silicon Valley royalty. His father, Adam Reynolds, founded Cyclone Technologies, one of the primary producers of consumer gadgetry in the world.

Anj knows about Blake because *everyone* knows him. She also knows him because she's a form of Silicon Valley royalty herself. Her father runs one of the VC firms that dumps a ridiculous amount of money into startups.

Anj's face clears. "Oh, him," she says casually. "He's actually not bad for a cis man. But he's still such a cis dude."

From her, this is incredibly high praise.

I wrinkle my nose. "Do I even want to know?"

"Yeah, my dad dumped something like fifteen mil into Cyclone before it went public?" She shrugs, as if this is a completely normal thing to happen. And it is, for her. "He was on the board of directors for ten years or something, so Blake and I got shoved together a lot when we were kids. We played with dinosaurs." She glances over at me. "Just ask him about his dimetrodon someday."

I look over at her and shake my head. This is the thing about Anj: You would never know what her background was until she'd randomly mention having lunch with some CEO, or complain about one of her own startups, or casually refer to getting into childhood fights with Blake fucking Reynolds while their parents were off deciding the future of the personal computer. She drops the bit about dimetrodons with a waggle of her eyebrows as if it's really a euphemism. This being Anj, I'm pretty sure she means actual dimetrodons.

"What about his dimetrodon?"

"A dimetrodon is not a dinosaur," Anj explains patiently. "Tell him I'm still waiting for my apology from his mansplaining ass."

"Okay," I say. "Wait." I pull out my phone and text Blake.

Angela Choi wants me to tell you a dimetrodon is not a dinosaur. She's waiting for an apology.

The answer comes back swiftly. *NO. *Chip* is a dinosaur. A dinosaur that has not yet been discovered in the fossil record. And happens to look like a dimetrodon. BUT HE IS NOT A DIMETRODON. CHIP IS A DINOSAUR.*

I hold up the phone so Anj can read this. Anj grins broadly. "Go show him, Maria," she says.

Anj is right, I type. *You're a mansplainer.*

There's a long pause. *A what?*

A man. Who explains. More specifically, a man who explains things to women that the women know better than the man.

Another long pause. *I am *not*.*

Anj shakes her head beside him. "He so is."

I type a response. *Are you seriously telling me you know prehistoric biology better than Angela Choi?*

I can almost see him sighing. *I feel very strongly about Chip,* he writes. *VERY STRONGLY. Pass on this heartfelt apology to Anj: FUCK YOU, ANJ. CHIP IS A DINOSAUR.*

She laughs. "As you can see," she says, "we're good friends. Actually, we got dumped together so often we're more like brother and sister. We used to fight a lot."

"I have never seen Blake fight with *anyone.*"

Her smile weakens. She looks away. "I seem to have that effect on…everyone who gets to know me."

There's some truth to that. For instance, I've known Blake Reynolds for a while now, and he's pretty even-keeled. He has to be; he works with his dad, who is terrible. Blake earned the praise, "not bad for a cis man" from Anj, which is basically her version of nominating him for the Nobel Peace Prize. I've never seen him lose his temper. Not until *FUCK YOU, ANJ.*

"Hey." I set my hand on her arm. "Don't be ridiculous. Everyone loves you. Everyone."

She looks over at me. She doesn't say anything for a long time. "Yeah?" she finally says. "Then why are you mad at me?"

Her eyes are dark and just a little cutting, and I feel myself freeze in place.

It's one thing to tell Jay and the asshole police to fuck off; it's another entirely to say that to one of my best friends.

I don't care if Jay hates me. I care what Anj thinks, though. I care a lot.

"I'm not mad at you," I say slowly. And it's true. I was never mad at her. It was just a shitty, mismatched situation.

"You sure?" she asks. "Because I just got this sense..." She shakes her head. "Never mind. Maybe I'm just overreacting. I'm in my vulnerable bitch phase right now. Vee and I broke up."

"Oh, honey. I'm sorry."

"It's okay," she says. "Really. It makes me twitchy, that's all. Vee said I was overbearing and selfish."

I shake my head. "Selfish people don't worry about being selfish. You're not selfish. You're just focused."

"Maybe."

"And I know you're going to miss them. But I think they were..." I search for words. "Maybe just a little clingier than you, okay?"

"So what you're saying," she says, "is that I'm arrogant and overbearing, so I need to find someone who is disdainful and doesn't want my company."

"No," I say slowly. "What I'm saying is that if I were arranging your marriage, I would find someone who was as fiercely independent and committed to something as you are. You're not a babysitter. Some people need babysitters."

She looks over at me and narrows her eyes. "So you're going to tell me that I was the most considerate housemate in the world?"

I may have lost my temper. Somewhere at the end. I still regret that.

"No," I say calmly. "But we both learned something from that. Next time, you'll tell someone *before* they move in that you're going to be raising sharks."

"One shark!" Anj says. "A baby shark! She was just seven inches long. Besides, who is going to object to a GFP shark? She is the only genetically altered biofluorescent shark in existence."

I look at her. I don't say anything at first. "Anj," I finally manage, "most people don't splice fluorescent proteins into sharks to begin with."

"Sure, but…"

"And they don't name them Lisa and talk to them in high-pitched baby talk and tell them they're a good little glowing shark."

"But most people don't *have* glowing sharks," Anj says, "and Lisa *is* the best glowing shark in the world."

I don't sigh. The worst part of rooming with Anj was this: It was almost impossible to properly complain to other people. Disagreements about pets are common among roommates. People understand if you complain about an illicit kitten or an unruly dog. But every time I tried to vent a little steam with other friends, they tended to get stuck on "genetically engineered shark named Lisa."

I look at Anj. She is making puppy-dog eyes. There is no point fighting with her about her damned anxiety-inducing pet shark. There was *never* any point. She didn't even get rid of Lisa when the *landlord* told her to.

I give up. "You see?" I say. "Who could possibly object?"

She winces.

"And if there's any fault there, it's on me for not asking," I continue. "It's on my list of good tenant questions from here on out. 'How fast does the hot water start running? How many sharks do you plan on keeping?'"

She shakes her head. "I feel awful. Vee left. You stopped talking to me. Am I that terrible?"

"No. I've just been busy. So have you." It's mostly true. "You're wonderful. You're my favorite Anj of all the Anjs in the world, and I missed you."

"Fine." She exhales. "But you'd tell me if anything were really wrong, right?"

I ignore this. "Have lunch with me again. Like this. Like we used to."

"Yeah." She smiles at me. "That'll be good. You can tell me about the boys you're dating, and I'll say, 'Ugh, boys.'"

"And you can tell me about the people you're dating and ask me if it's too soon to introduce them to Leia." Leia is her boa constrictor.

"Oooh." She sits up straight. "Did I tell you I got an alligator?"

"Anj."

"You'll like her," she says cheerily. "She doesn't even glow."

"What are you *doing* with the poor thing?"

"Oh," she says unconvincingly, "nothing really."

I'll believe that when I see it. Which, hopefully, I will never have to do.

I'm waiting outside Soda Hall when Tina emerges into the afternoon sunlight, blinking blearily.

"Here." I hand her the crepe I got as we were leaving the restaurant. "Eat. Starving is bad for you."

She takes it. "Thank you. I owe you."

I shrug.

"I'll make dinner tonight, okay?"

Tina and I have been roommates for over a year, but this year has been night-and-day different from last one. Last year, we shared an unheated garage because Tina couldn't afford to pay for anything else.

This year, we're living in her boyfriend's massive house in the Berkeley Hills. It's huge and nice and…weird. Tina's no longer working in the library. But she's been busier than ever.

"Did you know Anj knows Blake?"

She stops to take a bite of her crepe. She chews while contemplating this. "No. But doesn't everyone?"

"Not like this. They knew each other as kids."

"Huh." She shrugs. "Cyclone nightcare?"

It's my turn to look at her dubiously.

"There were a bunch of kids at Cyclone who got stuck together when their parents were on deadline. Blake refers to them as the Cyclone nightcare crowd. Like daycare, except at night. He describes it as *Lord of the Flies,* except with computers. Also, nobody got killed. Blake said it was a lot of fun."

"Uh, okay."

Everything I hear about Cyclone gives me pause. I used to be able to tell Tina anything. But she and Blake have been together for something like seven months now, and it's beginning to feel serious. So serious that Tina has begun to accept things like *Lord-of-the-Flies-but-with-Computers* as part of her new normal.

Don't get me wrong. I like Blake. I'm sharing a house with him, and he's genuinely a decent guy.

But you never like a friend's boyfriend the way you love your friend. I don't believe in unconditional love under the best of circumstances. I don't even believe in unconditional *like*. The friendship I have with my best friend's boyfriend is both reluctant and conditional. *We will be cool as long as you treat her well, but screw that up, and I will cut you to shreds.*

Blake is fine, but I'm Team Tina all the way. Especially because Team Blake happens to be Team Lord-of-the-Flies-but-with-Computers.

"I don't think so," I say dubiously. "Anj said something about her dad being on the Board of Directors."

"Of course. She's too important for anything else."

I make a face. Anj and Tina don't precisely *not* get along. They would actually do just *fine* if they ever got over their initial animosity. And if Anj managed to remember Tina's name. They're both scientists. They're both—

No, not Chinese. I can almost see Anj rolling her eyes and grimacing. *I'm* Taiwanese, *Maria. It matters.*

They both have a dry sense of humor. Tina tends to be careful, though, and Anj hasn't met a barrier she doesn't want to kick down. I stopped trying to get them to like each other when Anj left for Montana.

Maybe now it'll work better.

Ha.

"Never mind. I shouldn't have said that." Tina swallows another giant bite. "I have rich people baggage with Anj. She kept inviting me to shit I couldn't afford, then I never accepted…" She looks at the last bit of her crepe. "Also, she takes you for granted."

"She doesn't."

"She totally does," Tina says. "She never even noticed how much you did for her. But if you're okay with her now, I'm not going to complain."

We've reached the building where her class takes place.

"Thanks," Tina says. "I was starving. I owe you."

I wave good-bye to her. It's a beautiful day, and I find a patch of sunlight on the grass. I have work to do before my next class, after all.

For the first two years of my college life, I worked in the bookstore like a schlub. But the summer before my junior year, my blog took off. Mentions everywhere—*Popular Science, Asimov Magazine, Wired*—and my subscriber count went from thousands to tens of thousands, then hundreds of thousands. I get ad revenue, referral fees, and income from the occasional product link.

It isn't a lot, in the sense that I couldn't live on it once I graduate, but I make more than I did in the bookstore. It's also a lot more work. It's *fun* work, yes, but it's work.

Right now, I'm working on a mathematical model of the apocalypse. I took one introductory programming class in high school, enough to manage super-kludgy code.

I check the test results I ran this morning—correct, correct, correct, finally—and then set my Monte Carlo plague simulator up for a longer run.

While I watch the output being written to a file, I pull out my phone and find my chat with Actual Physicist from last night and start writing. *It's working! I think it's working! Although I shouldn't count my postapocalyptic chickens until they properly die of the plague.*

I'm never sure if he'll be around during the day. Sometimes it takes him hours to get back to me. Today, though, it takes him thirty seconds to reply.

Awesome. A pox be on you!

I smile. *A pox be on everyone!* I consider this, and then offer this careful amendment. *Actually, the simulator starts off with a 48% survival rate. So really, only one of us should statistically be poxed.*

Right now, I'm examining a very important question, for certain values of *important*. Most post-plague apocalypse fiction assumes that the transportation network—the trucks that bring food into cities, the warehousing and distribution facilities—will break down, but that the amount of excess food remaining—cans, boxes, and so forth—will feed the remaining population for years to come.

This is actually a really bad assumption. Most grocery stores have high turnover in shelved goods. Our cities don't have much more than a few weeks to a month or so of food stored in them. I'm trying to figure out what percentage of people have to die so that the network of food deliveries breaks down, but the remaining population is large enough that they run through the excess food capacity and start rioting.

I get paid for this.

Hmm, A writes. *That's a 23% chance both of us survive.*

I think he is flirting. It would take a giant dork to flirt with, "I hope we both survive a super-flu infection," but since his screen name is "Actual Physicist," odds are that he is a giant dork.

Because I am also a giant dork, this is how I flirt back: *27% chance we both die. Until 5 minutes from now, when I rerun the simulation with a 46% survival rate.*

That's about as specific as we usually get. Except this time…

Promise me that if there's ever an apocalypse, you'll let me join your roving band of survivors?

He would never be able to find me. He doesn't know my name. Doesn't have my picture. We only ever talk about meeting in the most hypothetical of senses.

Maybe, I type in return. *Do you have any useful skills? Hunting, gathering, cage-fighting?*

…Feynman diagrams?

I laugh out loud. *Both tasty and calorically dense, I'm sure.*

He doesn't say anything for another ten minutes, and I check my guesses against the results as they come in.

Then I get this: *You know the instant you post this, someone is going to make a list of everyone who's ever published a paper on Monte Carlo simulations of network effects?*

I know. They've done it before. My super-fans have a list of people I could be.

I'm not on it. I'm not anywhere near it. The forums on my site have heavy odds on a thirty-seven-year-old computer science professor in Iowa, who constantly claims he's not me, and a fifty-year-old dude in Stanford's Management and Engineering Science Program. Daniel van Tijn (the Stanford guy) actually sent me (or, rather MCL) an email when the argument over who I was got especially fierce one afternoon.

Hey MCL—

Love your blog. No idea who you are. If you ever want to coauthor a piece on quasi-state authorities in cybersecurity, hit me up.

It's frankly flattering that anyone thinks I could be either one of them.

I started my blog when I was eighteen and fresh out of high school. I'd planned to take a few years off before starting college to make enough money for surgery and hormones. My high-school chemistry teacher told me to be careful, that if I got out of the habit of learning, I'd lose the knack.

"People *say* they'll go to college eventually," he told me, "but they get comfortable, and then they don't."

I started my blog as a promise to myself that I wasn't going to stop learning.

The first four years weren't my best. I was fresh out of high school and had a lot to learn. I made a lot of stupid mistakes. The consensus is that someone else must have been running the blog back then.

But I *did* learn, and I *did* get better, and even if what I do is silly now, I'm proud of the fact that it's *sound* silliness.

So sound that people mistake my silliness for intelligence.

I started my blog as a promise that I wasn't going to stop learning, and maybe that's why my final year before I graduate seems so bittersweet. I need a job—an actual job that pays adult bills—and people who hire actuaries are notoriously stodgy. I'm graduating this year, and student loans and health insurance won't pay for themselves. I'm not sure I'll miss the arguments over my identity, or the occasional dustups when climate change deniers decide I'm a political shill.

But I'll miss making network models of flu infection.

Let them make their list, I tell Actual Physicist. *I'll just smile mysteriously.*

I close my laptop and shut my eyes, letting the breeze play on my face. I know I'll have to shutter my blog when I graduate. I won't have time to work and do all of this. I'm going to miss talking to him about science.

Sure, I tell myself mockingly. Science. That's all this is.

Actual Physicist doesn't want to know who I am, and that's fine by me. Tina says I give everyone four chances to fuck up before I really trust them. She's joking—I think—but I *really* don't believe in unconditional anything. I only believe in conditions I have yet to discover.

I *like* Actual Physicist. I like talking to him. I like our casual, hypothetical flirtation. I'm not in any hurry to discover what his conditions will be.

4.

J A Y

Two weeks later

"*G*osh. Is that rap?"

I look up from my desk. There are multiple faculty offices in this hall, and I've made the mistake of leaving my door open and the *Hamilton* soundtrack on.

Eric Llewellyn is one of the older faculty—*much* older. He's one of those guys who was around in the somewhat early days of quantum mechanics, back when, "but how can anything be both a *particle* and a *wave?*" was a question that real people with real doctoral degrees still asked in confusion.

For a moment, I imagine trying to explain to Eric precisely where in the musical lexicon *Hamilton* sits. Except someone who still thinks of wave-particle duality as a fundamental breakthrough instead of a fact of life will undoubtedly freak over the melding of hip-hop and Broadway musical.

"Yes," I say instead. "It is."

"Weird," he muses. "I thought Asians didn't like black people."

"Uh." I have no response to this. It is wrong on so many levels that I don't even know where to start. The wrongness expands upon examination into more wrongness. The boundaries of his wrongness are infinite and fractal.

But he isn't finished. "I like rap. One of my students showed me MC Hawking."

"Uh." This is apparently the only word I will manage. MC Hawking is a parody. Someone thought a synthetic voice sounded like Stephen Hawking's computerized text-to-speech program, and proceeded to make an album about science. The only way this conversation could get worse would be if…

He strikes a pose and flashes an awkward hand signal. "E equals MC! E equals MC Hawking, motherfuckers!"

…Yeah. That would do it. It's much worse when Eric starts rapping.

I turn off my music.

"Oh. Right." He snaps his fingers. "Ryan and Dave wanted to know if you wanted to hit up Kerr for lunch tomorrow."

No, I want to say, *I'm good.* But I don't have tenure, and I can't afford to alienate people.

My graduate advisor gave me a lot of advice when I started. Things like: *Publish amazing work. Do capable service. Nobody cares about your teaching.* But also: *Be friendly. Let everyone feel like you're on their side.*

"Sure," I say instead.

"Groovy, dude." He exaggerates the last word. He probably thinks this is how people my age actually talk. "See you at the physical seminar."

"Yeah. Dude."

He makes finger guns at me and leaves. I consider banging my head against the wall.

I'm not lonely, I remind myself. I'm too busy to be fucking lonely. I have tons of friends. I keep in touch with them as best as I can. We have dinner together when we end up in the same place. Sometimes, as it has with Gabe, my path intersects one of theirs for a year or two.

In real life, I mostly have students and colleagues. I'm *friendly* with my graduate students—we work together after all—but I'd be an idiot to ignore the power dynamics at play. I control how long they labor at a scarcely livable wage. I pass judgment on their work. I'm going to be their primary reference for at least a decade. It doesn't matter that I'm only five years older. We can be friendly, but we can't really be *friends*.

As for colleagues? Colleagues can be friends, and some of them are, never mind the politics of them voting on my tenure application in a handful of years. We all speak the same language—science—and that forms bonds, MC Eric Llewellyn notwithstanding.

But the demographics of university professorship are skewed against anything more than a mild acquaintance. Aging baby boomers occupy most of the tenured slots, and open faculty lines have a half-life close to Fermium-252. I'm the youngest professor by far in an aging department, and I feel it.

We're an odd social mix. Half of my colleagues are old enough that the concept of a *faculty wife* was a part of the reality they grew up with. The generation that follows is mostly married to each other or other scientists who work up the hill. Their worst nightmare is what they call the nearly insoluble two-body problem—the difficulty of finding two academic jobs in the same geographic location.

Then there's my generation. Half my friends have cobbled together postdoc after postdoc, or collected adjunct positions into some shambling sense of security. Never mind finding two *jobs* in the same place; I know people, good people, *smart* people, people with PhDs from Harvard, who would kill for *one* job with health insurance.

I'm the lucky one, the one that gets held up as the shiny example of *you, too, could achieve this*. Except we all know that we can't. The jobs just don't exist.

You, too, can win the right to slowly lose touch with your friends. To gradually watch your life undergo an order-to-disorder transition while you scramble to keep on top of a shifting pile of sand.

Sometimes I think about my friend Lillian who went to work for industry. She leaves her job at Merck at five every night. Lucky bastard.

Not that working outside academia is any guarantee of a reasonable schedule. I have only to look at my own mother to see how industry work can turn out.

I *am* the lucky one. I know that. I'm lucky, and I'll stay lucky as long as I don't stop moving.

I shake my head. I don't have time for maudlin thoughts or self-comparisons.

My phone dings, and I turn it over.

Quick question, Em says. *Do you know anything about carcinogens, or should I ping someone else?*

I know almost nothing about carcinogens. Still, I find myself replying. *Chemical, radiation, or something else?*

I'm looking for a chemical the government can put in the water, she says. *Maybe a carcinogen. Maybe a mutagen. It feels kinda fake to just make up something like 1,3-trans-dimethyl-cyclohexane. If I do, someone will grab the MSDS and make me look like an idiot.*

Yeah. Once we get into materials safety data sheets, we're over my head. *Not my thing,* I tell her. *You need a chemist.*

But I'm reluctant to jump back into work. Maybe because I'm thinking of her. Maybe because the encounter with Eric left me feeling unmoored from my work. I know, quite literally, a hundred people who have the capability to be here, and some days, I'm still not sure why it's me instead.

So I add this: *Did you pull 1,3-trans-dimethyl-cyclohexane out of a hat, or does it have some special meaning?*

Inside joke, she shoots back. *I have a tattoo of 1,3-trans-dimethyl-cyclohexane. It started because—oh shit, sorry, can't talk. I have a presentation to give in an hour. Dammit.*

Em and I rarely talk about our day jobs. I suspect she's somewhere in industry. She has to have figured that I'm in academia.

You ready?

No, she responds a few moments later. *I can't find my fuck-off shoes.*

I blink at my phone.

You got me, I write, *I know what fuck-me shoes are. What are fuck-off shoes?*

My mind is already coming up with options: combat boots, maybe. Or thick-soled steel-toed trainers.

What she writes is this: *Er, so. I make shoes.*

I wasn't expecting that.

Or, I mean, I decorate them. I buy old designer shoes at thrift stores and bling them up. Then I classify them by mood. Fuck-off shoes are the same concept as fuck-me shoes, but with one subtle distinction. Fuck-off shoes are kind of a combination "you wish you could get with this" + "look what I am, I'm not backing down" + "I'm killing it and you can't stop me."

Not steel-toed trainers, then.

There's this guy I've known for a couple of years, she continues, *and he hates me. Thinks I'm a freak and I do not belong. And we keep crossing paths. So I'm wearing the shoes to my presentation just for him.*

Lucky guy.

I don't want to examine that thought as it drifts through my head, and so I don't.

Found them! Wanna see?

Sure, I say before I think better of it.

A minute later, she sends me a picture. My idle curiosity… Holy shit. Everything goes up in flames. I'm not an expert in women's shoes. I wouldn't know one designer from another.

Oh look, those are shoes, is the extent of my usual commentary. Right now, all I can think is this: Holy Shit. Those are *shoes.*

Her shoes are arranged on a light hardwood floor. The cherry-red leather gleams in some warm overhead light. I can almost imagine her reflection in the surface. Maybe that dark blob is her phone.

Nothing says "fuck off" quite like red, strappy stilettos with three-inch heels. Twin stylized gold butterflies are wired to each buckle, and Swarovski crystals are affixed to the straps. It's not enough bling to make them gaudy. Instead, it's enough to glitter, to draw attention to their obvious femininity.

These are her take-no-prisoners shoes? No kidding. I would surrender. Gladly.

My mental image of Em always placed her firmly on the shy spectrum. I've imagined her with long, untamable hair that was the bane of her existence.

I know enough about the issues of women in STEM to be able to imagine exactly why some asshole man would think she was a freak who didn't belong. I doubt she gets enough credit for her intelligence where she works. Vithika told me that she started talking to me because I *didn't* interrupt her, and if there's a shittier indictment of our profession, I don't know it.

I can imagine Em taking off her usual sneakers and replacing them with those heels. They would be her quiet way of saying, I'm a woman, and you can't ignore me. Fuck you; I do *so* belong.

I swallow hard. I can't take my eyes off her shoes.

I know exactly why I like Em—and I'm all too aware how tame the word *like* is for how I feel. She's funny, clever, and smart.

I've lived in Berkeley for three years. No matter how hard I work, no matter how good a job I do at staying in touch with distant friends, deep down I'm hungry for human contact. I should have held the line here. Drawn firmer boundaries. Not let this slip.

Because right now? I want to know more. I want to see Em in those shoes.

Fuck me.

She's written more. *In some way, my fuck-off shoes are about everything everyone ever told me. I wear them to remind myself that everyone who said that people like me couldn't wear shoes like this was wrong. I am feminine. I am pretty. I can wear heels, and I don't care if it makes me 6'2". It's a fuck off to the voices I heard all my childhood, telling me that I couldn't.*

I've never had so clear a picture of Em as a child. My mental image rearranges slightly. She's no longer short; she's tall, gawky, and ungainly. Teased by everyone around her. She had to dig deep inside herself for a validation that nobody gave her, and she found it anyway. She trots it out daily, because she never gets enough credit from the people around her.

Yep, I write slowly. *Those sure are shoes.*

I make myself face the truth. I like Em. I like her way too much. I haven't met her. I don't know her name. I've never seen her picture.

And I'm the lucky one, the one with the one-in-a-million opportunity that my best friends would kill to have. I'm the one with something to prove, and dammit, I am going to prove it.

Even if it means not asking more about the shoes.

Definitely shoes, I say again. And because I can't help myself, I add this: *Good luck on your presentation.*

I go back to my work, but those shoes linger in my mind   for   far   too   long.

5.

October

The moment I see who's calling, my heart sinks. I know why she's calling. I know what she wants. And I realize that I've fucked up. Again.

I pick up. "Hi, Mom."

"Jay, you told me to call you in early October. Here we are."

Crap.

It sounds terrible to say that I forget about my parents. I never really forget about my parents. Every time I think about them, I feel a tinge of guilt.

Which is why I tend to put my parents out of my mind as long as I can. They live an hour away when the traffic's good, which means it's more like three hours most of the time.

It's October, and we haven't seen each other since February.

"So," my mother says, "we were saving this weekend for you to visit. How are things looking for you?"

To the uninitiated, my mother's accent is hard to place. She was born in Thailand, moved to Hong Kong when she was nine, got her undergraduate degree from Oxford, a master's from Stanford, and has worked at Cyclone Technologies ever since, a job that has taken her around the globe.

She sounds like a linear combination of British and American, with a liberal dose of swearing that is all her own.

Looking at my calendar is a total pretense. She can't see me do it, and I already know what it will show.

"So. Um. About this weekend. It's not great. What about next?"

"Mmm." She doesn't sound terribly disappointed. "Next weekend, *I'm* traveling. We're having one of our Cyclone software summits, and I promised our localization support in London I'd be with them this time around."

In most families, landing a tenure-track position at a research one university would be considered a signal success. For me? Not so much. My mom's the baby of her family. She's also the vice president of software engineering at Cyclone. My aunts and uncles—a swarm of nine, all related, but not really *aunts* or *uncles* the way Americans would mean those words—range from executives in Singapore to cutting-edge doctors in France. There's Lung Wat, who does large-scale art installations where he covers skyscrapers in fabric.

In that company, I don't even make the average mark. My cousins and I—all nineteen of us—used to complain in our private Facebook group about the impossible bar our parents had set. Back when we had time.

"The week after that?" she asks hopefully.

"Uh." I *do* have to look at my calendar now. "Also…not great."

There's a long pause before she speaks again. "After that, things get a little hairy on our end. My fault; I was going to remind you before now, but I never see you on c-chat anymore."

C-chat is the messaging system built into all Cyclone computers. I look at the computer in front of me and feel another pang of guilt. "That's because I don't have Cyclone machines at work."

Once, Mom wouldn't have accepted so transparent an excuse. *Aren't you in charge of purchasing for your lab?* she'd grumble. Or, once she figured out the problem: *What do you mean, your laser doesn't have a driver for Cyclone systems? Your cousin Philippe wrote his own device driver for his PCR machine, and he doesn't have half your experience.*

Instead she's quiet for a moment. "Ah. I should have realized. I wasn't calling to play Cyclone salesperson anyway. Let's go back to this weekend. What about a few hours? Your father and I could come up."

I exhale slowly. "Mom, I picked up two graduate students this year, and I already have a theory of quantum computation session set up for Saturday. I'm taking them out after."

Once she would have said something about that. *You're taking out your graduate students instead of seeing your own parents?*

Now…

She clicks her tongue. "Brunch Sunday? Early Sunday, if you can."

"I've got a call with Vithika."

She doesn't say anything, but I still feel the need to explain why a call with my collaborator takes precedence over brunch with my parents.

"She lives in Australia. It really is the only time our schedules overlap for three weeks—her husband is at a conference, and so she has the kids in the evening—and we have to go over the final revisions on our paper."

"It's okay," she says.

These days, it's always okay.

"It's just, your father's book comes out after that, and he'll be on tour. You know how it is."

I do.

My father writes literary fiction. Every few years, he produces a book to moderate critical acclaim.

I haven't read his last book. Or the book before it. Or... Or any book of his at all, not since I was nineteen. I'm too chicken to admit that I'm afraid of what I'll find.

I look upward. "I'm sorry. We'll work something out when Dad gets back, okay? When we all have some time."

My mother is tiny and filled with energy. She's always fidgeting, except when she's upset. I can imagine her now, momentarily still.

"I'm sorry," I say. And I am.

She brushes me off. "Not your fault. My schedule was hell until we got the beta out, and you can't help that your summer is all conferences. Now it's your dad's turn. Don't worry; we'll figure it out."

It *is* my fault. When we touched base frantically in June—me preparing a poster for a conference in Spain, Mom going over her schedule for the Cyclone

Developer's Conference—we'd agreed to get together in October.

It is entirely my fault, and it doesn't matter that she doesn't blame me. The thing about being a perfectionist workaholic is that you bring your own guilt with you.

"Fine," she says again. "Maybe later this month, then. But since I have you now, set aside December fifth, okay? Don't forget that Saints and Dinosaurs is that weekend."

Saints and Dinosaurs is a party my mom throws for the Cyclone employees who work under her. It has also become my parents' excuse to have something to occupy themselves during that time of year.

I shut my eyes. "Of course. I'll come down. It might not be right at the start of the shindig, but I'll spend the night. We can talk in the morning."

"Good. Now talk to your dad. Here."

I hear the rustle of them handing off the phone.

"Hi, Dad."

"Jay." My dad's voice is deep and entirely unlike my mother's—more California surfer than anything else.

I fumble for a topic of conversation—any topic. "How's the new book going? Are you going to finish it before your tour?"

He makes a little sound in his throat—a weird, growling noise. "Never ask that question. I think I killed the wrong person. The book is terrible. Everything is terrible."

I almost smile. My father writes serious books that he does not take seriously.

"Maybe you could kill two people," I suggest mildly. "Salvage what you have."

"That would mess with my authorial signature. One person dying is a tragedy. Two? That's bordering on thriller territory. It would be off-brand."

"Ha." I smile despite myself.

"Did you finish your grant proposal for DARPA?"

"Last night. Seven whole hours early."

"My punctual son," he says drily. "Wherever did you get that skill?"

"Try being on time. Once. You might like it."

"No good. My editor would die of shock, and we have an excellent working relationship. It would be inconvenient to have to find someone else at this juncture."

"I bet." I stare at my desk. The pause lingers as I shuffle papers around.

I can imagine him running his hand through his hair—still mostly dark, with a few white threads—and looking upward, trying to think of something to say. Small talk can only carry a conversation so far.

My father is an author. My mother is the VP of one of the world's biggest corporations. I come by my workaholic tendencies honestly.

My parents used to expect a lot of me. Now? Now it's all awkward pauses and excuses.

I never worry that I'll disappoint them these days. You can't disappoint people who have no expectations.

"So," my dad finally says. "Saints and Dinosaurs is on the schedule. First Saturday in December. Think you can make it?"

That's what I get these days. *Think you can make it?* It used to be: *Attendance is mandatory; do not think of escaping.*

I blow out a breath. "Mom already told me. Is she going to draft me to help?"

I wish she would. Saints and Dinosaurs is a party, but it's also a competition. Ostensibly, it started as type-A bluster. Twelve years ago, in the midst of some epic shit-talking battle between Mom and her boss, Mom claimed she was a better cook.

Did it matter that nobody in the upper echelons of Cyclone ever cooked beyond microwaving Hot Pockets? No. A challenge had been made; it had to be answered.

Thirty minutes later, their outrageous claims had morphed into a dessert-off between the two of them. Five hundred and some Cyclone employees were enlisted as the judges, and an excuse for a party at the end of the year was born.

"You are safe," Dad says. "I am her sole sous chef in this matter."

I fix my gaze on a point across the room. Of course. They don't even expect me to help any longer.

"Come in the evening, when you have time. Spend the night after we get rid of the hoi polloi. We'll have breakfast in the morning. If you can, that is?"

"You know, Dad." I swallow, pitching my voice to sarcastic so he won't know how serious I am. "You *are* allowed to expect me to show up for family events."

"We don't want to be a bother. We know you're busy."

That's the way it always goes. *We don't expect anything of you, Jay.* I rub my forehead.

"It's okay," Dad says again. "We get it. You have a lot to do. I'll let you go. I've a book to write."

"Same," I say. "Except it's a paper."

Yeah. There's more than one reason why I might disappoint them.

I glance at my shelves, where his last three books stand next to a giant orange text on applied mathematics. I've spent all my time with the math.

"Love you," I whisper. But he's already hung up.

Dad's most successful book to date came out when I was a junior in college. It's a thick volume with a maroon cover, and it's followed me around from dorm room to apartment, from one office to another. It never gathers dust. I pull it out and look at the cover every couple of weeks and tell myself that I'll read it. Next month. When I have time.

I glance at it now and vow that I'll read it before December.

It's a lie. I don't even have expectations of myself. His book is about a man who lost his child. I read the dedication the day it came out and put it down. Ever since, I've been too busy to read any further. I've made sure of it. I've filled every hour as full as I possibly can.

It sounds stupid to say I forget about my parents. But I try hard not to remember my family, and mostly I succeed.

I haven't precisely managed to forget by that night, and I've been trying. Trying so hard, that I don't even realize it's almost ten and I'm still in my office until my phone pings.

Hey, A., Em writes. *Is everything okay?*

It's fine. I frown. *Why?*

Because you weren't the first person to question me about radioactive half-lives. Just checking in.

Shit. I look at the time. I pull up her blog. And— after seven straight hours of working—I recognize that maybe, maybe I have an issue. My eyes hurt. My back is cramped. My mouth is dry.

I sit at my desk and look at the deserted courtyard below, shadows and concrete barely visible through my window. I roll my shoulders, feeling my muscles complain. I am so busy that someone I don't even know is checking in on me.

Nothing unusual, I write with a grimace. *Just coping with generalized guilt at my inability to accomplish things.*

Writing those words in the dark of my office makes them real. The generalized guilt settles on me more specifically, enveloping me like a heavy parka.

Let me guess, Em writes. *You're still in your office.*

I frown at my surroundings and type very slowly. *Heh.*

Well? comes her response. *What are you waiting for? Get out.*

But, I start to type. I don't get a chance to finish my thought.

Is there anything that must urgently be done by tomorrow morning?

I backspace. *Not really, but—*

She must be at a keyboard, because she's typing ten times faster than I can on my phone. *It's never a good idea to give in to guilt.*

I give up and backspace again.

Fine. But you're walking home with me. I hit send before I can think better of it.

She doesn't respond immediately, and I know just how fast she can type.

I stand up. I put my pencils back in the drawer, file the stray papers and lesson plans for tomorrow, and find my messenger bag.

She still hasn't responded by the time I've finished.

I tap my foot almost impatiently.

Her answer finally comes. *You mean virtually?*

I roll my eyes. *No, Em. I mean in real life. I'm not leaving my office until you get on a plane and meet me here. I have three Clif Bars and a blood-orange San Pelligrino, so I assure you, I can wait a long time.*

Her only response is an emoji of a person sticking her tongue out.

I slip out of my office door and type as I go down the hall. *And they say tone doesn't come across on the internet.*

People do say that, and I guess I can see why. If you aren't familiar with the ways that sarcasm or fancifulness or humor are typically signaled, internet conversations must seem like a confusion of lies.

Em and I are on the same wavelength tonight. *Who are these people who are magically understood by all in real life?* she asks.

I think, I say, *they're...normal?* It's been a long time since I spent any time with someone who could be called that. The last time was probably...Gabe's sister, Maria. Pretty because she tried to be. All too aware of the reaction I had to her. As annoyed by me as I was by her.

I don't think normal exists, Em says. *I think it's a myth, like the rational economic man. The only question is if we see "normal" as something to aspire to.*

Ha.

I've been trying not to think of my conversation with my parents all day, but it comes rushing back at that.

I type a little more slowly. *When I was a freshman in high school, I got an A- in Spanish.*

To anyone else, this would look like a total non sequitur. Not to Em. Tone comes through on the internet for her. Campus is dark, but not truly empty. I can hear the strains of music playing, the shout of someone laughing and drunk off in the shadows.

Watching the screen of my phone ruins my night vision, but I don't care.

My mom, I write, *took one look at the grade and shook her head.*

You monster, Em replies. *An A-.*

My dad was worse. He said, "Well, let's be reasonable. Maybe that's the best he can do." And he looked at me and asked: "Is that really the best you can do?"

Oh dear, she responds. *Your parents are cruel.*

I nod in semi-agreement even though she can't see me. I'm off campus now, trudging through the first few blocks of restaurants and grungy apartments.

Yep. My mom would insert the knife; Dad would twist it and ask if I was bleeding.

And you've been trying to meet their unreasonable expectations ever since, Em says.

I've told this story before. It's recognizable. It's normal. It's another variant of the "Oh my god, my Asian parents" story that half my friends can tell.

It's the truth. It's just not the full truth. Maybe that's why I tell her the part I've always left off.

No. I send this single word out. The air is cool against my fingers, and I take my time measuring out my next words. *My senior year, I fucked up. Really badly.*

Beyond all forgiveness.

After that, I type, *they stopped having any expectations of me at all.*

Tone shouldn't come through on the internet, least of all in silence, but it does. There's a comfort to the way she doesn't respond, as if she's letting me pick my words, think my thoughts through.

So, I say, *I've had to make my own unreasonable expectations ever since. I figured if I make them big enough, maybe one day they'll believe in me again.*

Oh, A., she writes. *I'm sorry.*

I shake my head. I don't want her pity. I want to fix this. It's taken me this long, and dammit, I'm not letting up.

But Em is still typing. *There was a point in my life,* she writes, *where I really needed to hear these words: You are enough, just as you are. So I'm going to say them to you. You are enough, just as you are.*

I stop walking. I look at my phone. The concept just doesn't make sense.

Worse; it feels dangerous on this dark night. *Enough* means being ungrateful for my million-in-one tenure-track job. *Enough* means ignoring what I did to my parents, my brother. Enough is selfish. I'm not enough, not now. Maybe one day I will be, but it will never happen, not if I let myself believe...this.

Yeah, I type. *This is why I prefer not knowing anything about each other. I don't want you to make me feel better or to badger me to leave the office. I'm fine.*

They're mean words. The instant I hit send, I want to take them back. She was trying to be nice; it wasn't her fault I didn't want her comfort.

But maybe my tone comes through too well on the internet, because she hears it—not just the sarcastic dismissal I sent, but the hurt behind it.

Sure, big guy, she writes. *Just remember that those words are here any time you want them.*

Streets quiet as we go farther from campus. I head uphill a few blocks. Find my house. Take out my keys.

My chest feels weird. My throat feels hoarse from the conversation, and I haven't said a word.

It's one thing to flirt with someone you've never met. But these? These are actual feelings. I'm not sure what they mean or what to do with them.

I think about asking her something personal. Something like...her name. Her location. I want to know what shoes she's wearing now. I want to call her, to hear her voice.

But I don't have her number, thankfully—just her ID on this messaging app we use. And I can't stop moving. I can't.

So I put my phone on the charger and ignore her the rest of the evening.

6.

MARIA

*S*unday dinner is a tradition in many families besides ours. I have vague memories of it from my preteen years. I know the mythology of it from TV—a big table where people gather around home-cooked food. They pass rolls and salad around the table. There's usually apple pie for dessert.

I'm not opposed to the idea in principle. In practice, though, when it comes to my grandmother, the traditional Sunday dinner is a nonstarter. God forbid that Camilla Hernandez Garcia *cook*.

"I don't want to do it," Nana told me once. "*You* don't want me to do it. I am done with that."

This is why my brother and I have decamped with her to an Italian restaurant, where someone else is in charge of not burning the rolls, and the markup on red wine isn't terrible if you know what to order.

"So," my grandmother says. "You're both looking for jobs this year. How is that going?"

"Well—" Gabe starts to say, but she holds up a hand.

"No, wait. Let me guess." She puts her fingers to her temples. "Maria, you've sent out fifty résumés. You have three contingency plans and a spreadsheet. Gabe…" She shakes her head at him. "Ha."

Gabe mock-frowns as he adds Parmesan from a shaker to his pasta. "That's not fair. I'm not disorganized. The academic job market just sucks."

Nana ignores this. "That birth order stuff skipped you two."

"Hey!" My brother points a finger at her. "I don't know what you're talking about. I'm the *perfect* older child. I have a PhD in physics from Harvard. And—"

"Did you buy your plane tickets to Portland yet?" I ask sweetly.

Gabe blows out a breath. "Whatever."

I turn to my grandmother. "He has an interview there in a month."

"They just called me a week ago! I have plenty of time to get tickets."

"Did you turn in your reimbursements from North Dakota yet? Because you told me—"

Gabe picks up his glass of wine and moves his chair six inches away from me. "I don't know why I even come, when the two of you just make fun of me."

"Free spaghetti," I deadpan.

"Oh. Right." Our eyes meet; there's a glint of humor in his.

Gabe and I argue. Especially when we are around family. I don't know why we do it; there's just something about being around each other that makes us both revert to childhood. The first time Jutta, his fiancée, observed it, she nearly died of embarrassment. We had to stop mid-argument and explain to her that we weren't serious, and the goal was to make the other person laugh.

"So what are your three options, Maria?"

"It's not really three. The company I interned at last summer wants to hire me full-time."

They were offering something that would look like a decent salary if they weren't based in San Francisco. On the other hand, they had decent healthcare benefits. The job is, to put it bluntly, incredibly boring. But…health insurance.

"That's really the only one I've put on my spreadsheet so far. I've applied to a handful of consulting firms—"

My brother guffaws. "Actuarial *consultants?* Who needs an actuarial consultant? That's not a real thing."

I fold my arms and glare at him. "Okay, dude who worked at the literal Hadron collider on a project designed to figure out if the universe is covered by an indetectable field. You would be the expert on things that are not real."

"It's not indetectable, it's—"

"Oh, excuse me. You might be able to prove it exists if you can find your God particle. I stand corrected."

"Don't call it that." But he snorts, on the verge of cracking up.

I shrug. "Have it your way. *Actuarial consultants* don't exist. I mean, they just have webpages and business cards."

Nana shakes her head in mock dismay. "Children, children. Behave yourselves."

Gabe points at me. "She started it!"

"Did not!"

Nana glares at us. "Children who argue about Higgs bosons over dinner don't get dessert."

"Who says?" Gabe turns to her.

"Sorry, kids. It's the law. San Francisco municipal code section 415.1. If I saw the restaurant violating it, I'd have to shut them down, and it's my *favorite* restaurant."

Gabe and I meet each other's eyes across the table, and we both crack up.

She raises her arms in victory. "I win!"

"Fine," I grumble. "Be that way."

"And Maria was telling us about her possibilities," Nana says. "What's number three?"

"Number three..." Number three is not even an offer. It's a non-possibility.

But it arrived in my email—MCL's email, that is—two days ago. It was from a microchip company that sourced supplies globally. They'd read my post about the collapse of western civilization after the great helium shortage of 2028. I had, apparently, correctly predicted some of their supply chain vulnerabilities and freaked out their upper management. Why their upper management was not freaked before, I do not know. All of the information I used was public domain.

Still, they wanted to hire me to do a risk assessment at an hourly rate that staggered me. Two weeks of work would have paid off my student loans.

But I've seen the arguments about who I am online. There are several people who are convinced I'm a professor at some university. They think I have *credentials*. I can't imagine how they'd react to *me* in person.

Hi. I'm still an undergrad.

Yeah. That would go over really well.

I'd declined; they had written back and told me the offer was open indefinitely.

I can daydream as much as the next person. A part of me loves the idea of doing worldwide risk consultations and getting paid for it.

It's just a part of me. I learned long ago to avoid the mountaintops of life. Sure, it's fun to get to the top. But storms come and lightning strikes, and it's no fun being exposed on top of the world in those moments. Daydreams are great, but an established salary and health benefits have to come first, thank you.

So I just smile. "Number three is nonexistent. The job market sucks everywhere. And Gabe? I'm sorry I made fun of your God particle. I'm sure you won't destroy the universe."

"Thanks."

"Yet," I add, and he glares at me.

"We die," Tina says, "we live to fight another day."

We're sitting at the granite island in the kitchen, sharing barbecue pork buns and talking shit about... Well, technically, we are talking shit about her parents.

"It won't be that bad." I promise her. "I mean, I know your mom is indiscreet, but..."

She shakes her head. "Oh my god, Maria. She's terrible. It's not that she's indiscreet. She's seriously collecting *articles* on Cyclone's business in China and highlighting portions. She has the scrapbook of shit-talking that she is saving for Adam Reynolds. She prints things off the internet. 'Just in case I forget.'"

"It'll work out," I promise. I don't know that this is true, but Blake is pretty easygoing, and even though his dad is an asshole, it's worked so far.

My phone dings. I look down at the notification.

In conclusion, A. has written, *I am a horrible fraud, so give me more grant money.*

It's been a few weeks since I argued him out of his office. We've fallen back into our friendship after he snapped at me, but it feels like there's an edge to it. Still, I find myself smiling in spite of myself. I tap out a quick response: *Yay, you finished!*

I set the phone down and look up at Tina, who is watching me with one raised eyebrow.

"Sorry," I say. "But look—as long as your parents *don't* meet, you're going to be dreading worst-case scenarios, and from experience, that's—"

My phone dings again, and I look down.

I have a bad case of impostor syndrome, A. writes. *Grant writing makes it worse. It's always YES, MY RESEARCH WILL CURE CANCER. In reality, ha.*

I look up. Tina is eyeing me. She points at my phone. "Do you need to get that?"

"No," I say guiltily. "No. I'm listening. I swear." I try to remember what I was saying. Something something something her parents? Dang it.

"You're smiling," she says.

I cross my legs primly on the barstool. "Listening and smiling are not incompatible."

"Who are you texting?"

"I'm not texting anyone." I look her in the eye and manage to keep the silly smile off my face. "I'm using a chat application that *simulates* texting so I don't have to give out my number."

"Oh, well." She matches my tone. "That's *completely* different."

We look at each other, twin expressions of innocence on our faces. I break first, laughing, and she follows suit.

"Seriously, who are you texting?"

"Some physicist," I toss off.

"Ooh, a *physicist*. Is he hot?"

I don't look at her. "I wouldn't know. We just talk science."

"Does this physicist have a *name?*"

"I'm sure he does," I say. "He just hasn't told me yet. He comments on my blog sometimes."

"So it's no big deal." Tina looks at me suspiciously.

"I met him through my blog. We mostly talk about plagues and nuclear explosions."

I'm not lying, not really. I'm just not telling her the complete truth.

She indicates my phone. "Are you going to answer?"

"It can wait."

"No, no." Tina smiles. "This is way better than stressing myself out. Are you going to answer? How long have you been not-texting this physicist anyway?"

"Some months," I say vaguely, counting back.

Tina, however, has detected blood in the water. Her eyebrow goes up at this evasiveness. "*Some* months, huh?" Her fingers tap on the kitchen counter. "Would that be a few months? A couple of months? A half-dozen months?"

Crap. Busted.

"Nineteen months." I give her a brief glare, pick up my phone, and type.

I didn't realize that physicists cured cancer, I say. *Isn't that more of a medical thing?*

"You've been talking to him for nineteen months and you don't know his name?"

"It's not like that." I flip my phone around and hand it to Tina. "We're talking about his grant proposal. It's all totally science. I consult him about physics problems and in exchange, I console him about how much time he spends at work. There's nothing to see here."

Nothing I know how to examine, that is.

As I'm talking his reply appears. *You know how all science is either physics or stamp-collecting?*

"Oh, he's one of *those.*" Tina rolls her eyes.

In grant proposals, A. continues, *there are really only two choices. Either it's MOAR CANCER, ARR, RADIATION FOR EVERYONE. Or you're saving the world from those of us who irradiate everything.*

"Maria," Tina says slowly, "are you flirting with this poor boy about radiation?"

"Would I do that?"

Actual Physicist has no idea the conversation is being observed, because he continues.

And then there's the supreme dunderheaded confidence required to write the requisite papers: MY COMPLETE FAILURE OF A PROJECT PROVIDES IMPORTANT INFORMATION ABOUT SCIENTIFIC FAILURE, PART 19.

"He's cute," Tina says. "I feel weird eavesdropping." She hands my phone back to me.

I shake my head. *I don't get the impression you fail often, Actual Physicist.*

No. But that just makes the pressure worse. Inevitable reversion to the mean = I'm cruisin' for a bruisin'.

"You're not eavesdropping," I say. "Seriously. Look. Reversion to the mean. We talk statistics."

She shakes her head. "Maria, that is not talking about statistics. That is using the language of statistics to talk about life. You know that's not the same thing, right?"

I wave my hand airily. "If I can't lie to my best friend, who *can* I lie to?"

"How long has this guy been low-key flirting with you using math?"

I bite my lip. "Maybe...eighteen of the last nineteen months?"

"And how long have you been flirting back?"

"About the same."

"And he's never asked your name? Never wanted to see a picture? Never suggested you webcam?"

"He said his family is weird and kind of Googleable, and he prefers pseudonyms."

Tina looks at me, and I feel my cheeks heat.

"And I'm fine not giving out personal information to—"

"To someone who flirts with you for a year and a half?" She shakes her head. "Have you considered the possibility that he's catfishing you?"

"How?" I throw up my arms. "He hasn't given me a name. Or a photo or a Facebook page. You can't catfish someone if you never tell them anything."

Tina sighs.

"Or are you thinking that he's maybe not a man?" I ask this more pointedly.

"I didn't say that."

"Good," I say. "Because I asked his pronouns when we first started chatting, and a, he didn't think it was a weird question, and b, he said he/him. That's good enough for me. If it turns out that reality is more complicated than that, I can cope with complicated."

"Fair enough." She shakes her head apologetically. "You're right. I shouldn't have interrupted your dorky flirtation. I just don't want you to get hurt."

I stick out my tongue at her. "You can't get hurt if you don't know anything."

She raises one eyebrow. Neither of us believe that. But she doesn't push the matter. "I'll let you get back to it."

She leaves. The kitchen seems larger without her, and maybe a little colder. Yeah. I look back at my phone and feel a fluttering in my stomach. Shit.

Sorry, I type slowly. *My housemate caught me smiling at the phone, and she accused me of flirting with math.*

Oh, god. Why did I hit send? Why isn't there a take-back button on this app? Flirting is one thing. *Labeling* my dorky flirtation as flirtation is another. The label strips the entire conversation of plausible deniability. Up until now, I could pretend. *What, me? I just like math jokes.*

But I just made it real. Reality makes me vulnerable. My hands feel cold; I try not to stare at my screen, waiting for his response.

Nonsense, A. types. My heart sinks. *You weren't flirting with math. You were flirting with statistics.*

I exhale slowly. That *you*... It feels very singular. Almost exclusionary. *We* would have been fine. *You* makes me feel like I'm all alone in this.

Hell, maybe I am. I shake my head and try not to sound bothered. *Hate to break it to you, but statistics are a form of math.*

Do we live in the days of Gauss? he writes back. *What is the point of treating interdisciplinary study as a lesser endeavor if we don't separate our disciplines?*

Here's the thing: Admitting I'm flirting is a big step for me. I don't want to be ignored. It hurts, like I'm being told that it's just me. That *I'm* flirting, and he's just handing out equations.

But if it's a big step for me, it probably is for him as well. If he doesn't want to give what we do a label, fine.

I exhale. *I see. You're a purist.*

I'm a physicist, he responds. *I'm pure as the driven snow. But you can corrupt me with biology if you want.*

I stare at those words, my nose wrinkling. He doesn't have to tell me his name. Or send a picture. Or friend me on Facebook. But I do have limits. He can't flirt and pretend it's only me doing it.

Corrupt your own damned self, I suggest. *The rest of us have work to do.* I slap my phone down.

7.

November

*R*ain is falling in slashing fits, and the backsplash against the pavement is soaking my ankles. Even though we're high up in the Berkeley Hills, the clouds obscure any hint of a view. Beside me, Rachel, my postdoc, is swathed in a giant blue nylon raincoat, huddling under my umbrella. None of this helps. By the time we make it from the parking lot to the building a few hundred yards away, we're soaked.

The rain seemed like an annoyance down on campus; up here in the hills where the Lawrence Berkeley National Laboratory is nestled, water lashes down with nothing to stop it.

It's six o'clock, and the clouds outside make the cement hallways gloomy. But Gabe's office on the third floor—one he shares with a grad student and another postdoc—is warm and smells like something savory.

I'm suddenly starving. Cold and starving.

"Hey," Gabriel greets me as I come in. "Thanks for coming by. I know you had to run after my practice job talk, and I appreciate your taking time to talk this through."

"Dude. It's what I'm here for." I set my umbrella outside the hall. "This is Rachel. I told you about her."

"Yeah." Gabe reaches out and shakes her hand. "Rachel. You're on the market next year, right?"

Rachel shakes out her giant raincoat and nods. "I read your slides. And your paper."

Gabe nods. "Okay. So I was thinking that everyone keeps asking me about quantum coherence. And—"

"Seriously?" says a voice behind us. "Gabe. I'm sitting right here."

I haven't seen Maria Lopez in almost two months. I still recognize her voice. I feel the hair on the back of my neck stand on end as I turn around.

She's seated in an oversized armchair, probably donated to the office when some previous occupant moved across country a decade ago. She's wearing a skirt with sparkly patterns and a light blue blouse. There's no evidence that she even knows about the rain outdoors; she's dry, and her hair is blown perfectly straight.

I bet the rain doesn't dare fall on her. Gold hoop earrings sparkle in the fluorescent lights. The way she's sitting makes me think she could sell that chair in any magazine.

She has a pile of paper on her lap, and she's frowning at me. At all of us.

"What?" asks her brother.

"First, they're dripping wet. At least offer them… I don't know, a towel or something."

Gabe looks at her with a frown. "I don't have a towel. Do you, um…" He looks around the room wildly. "Do you want some Kleenex? Or a napkin?"

Maria looks at me. I can tell she is thinking about the time we ran into each other out on the plaza. About the shit I said to her. Her jaw works. Then she sets her papers aside, stands, and pulls a black bag out from under a desk.

"Here." I hear the noise of a zipper; she brandishes a bright yellow towel. "Unused. I didn't get to the gym today."

Of *course* Maria Lopez goes to the gym on a regular basis. I don't say this.

She holds it out to Rachel, pointedly not looking at me. "Hi," she says. "I'm Maria, Gabe's big sister."

Gabe makes a noise in his throat. "She's my *younger* sister."

"And you're shorter than me," Maria says, "so suck it up, little brother."

Rachel takes it. "Thanks. You're a real hoopy frood." She wipes water off her face, and then hands it to me. For a second, I consider not using Maria's towel. But umbrella or no, I'm drenched. I don't say anything as I rub my hair dry.

She takes the towel from me with thumb and forefinger when I hand it back, dropping it into a plastic grocery bag like it needs to be quarantined and disinfected. Apparently, I have cooties.

"What's your field?" Rachel asks Maria.

"Actuarial math." Maria gives Rachel a friendly smile. "This is not exactly my ball game here, but I muddle along."

Rachel lights up. "Oh, yay! That means we have a chance for science-free conversation."

"Good luck." Maria zips her gym bag and lets it fall to the floor with a thump. "Have you *met* my brother? Or this guy?"

"I'm *this guy?*"

Maria doesn't skip a beat. "Have you *met* Professor Thalang?"

I roll my eyes at her. "Are you in my quantum class?"

"No."

"Then you aren't going to call me Professor Thalang. That's weird."

"You know what's weird?" Rachel interjects. "I don't know if you're Professor Thalang or Professor na Thalang. I mean, I always figured it was the latter. But then it says Thalang Group on our lab door…" She trails off. "God, that sounds really dumb. Sorry to interrupt."

I don't really want to go into details right now, but I also don't want to brush her off.

"Both right," I say after a pause. "Long story short. When my grandfather came to the US fifty years ago, immigration recorded *Thalang* as his last name, and *na* as a middle name. He thought it was funny, and besides, he didn't expect to stay after he finished college, so he never bothered to change it. Now it's a family joke. *Na* is legally my middle name, but actually it shouldn't be."

I don't look at Maria. Still, I can see her wrinkling her nose out of the corner of my eye.

"You were born in the US?" She doesn't wait for my answer. "Of course. I should have known your accent was a put-on. The pretentiousness fits you."

There's an uneasy silence, broken only by Gabe's sigh.

"Oh," Rachel says with a determined smile. "That's, um, really interesting, Jay. We can be non-middle-name twins. People think that Ramirez is my middle name all the time. But we're getting distracted. We were going to go over Gabe's job talk."

We start in on Gabe's slides.

The thing that surprises me is that Maria participates.

"This should be r-squared," she points out on the second slide, indicating one equation. And then, two slides later—"This should be h-bar here, unless you dropped a factor of two pi earlier."

I glance at her, this time for a little longer.

She sees me looking at her. For a second, our eyes meet. The lights glint off the hoops in her ears, which are the brightest things in the room.

"Don't make anything of it," she says with a half smile. "You're not going to have to reevaluate your world order, Three Sigma. I'm mostly average. I just happen to be an equation proofreading savant."

It takes me a moment to remember why she's calling me "Three Sigma"—that stupid conversation when we first met, when I implied that she wasn't extraordinary enough to work with me.

Gabe winces. The sarcasm in her voice cuts sharper than a diamond blade. "You're more than that," he mutters.

"True," Maria says brightly. "I'm also a towel service. And pizza delivery girl."

"Oh my god," Rachel says. "Pizza. Is that what I'm smelling?"

There is pizza. Apparently, Maria brought pizza for us.

Halfway through, Gabe calls a short dinner break. We find paper towels. The pizza is mushroom and green pepper, which likely means that Gabe told Maria that I don't like meat on pizza, and she was nice enough to comply.

Maria being nice to me, even if in so limited a fashion, makes me feel like more of a dick than ever.

Gabe takes a slice and sits on the desk. "Rachel, did I hear you promising to talk about nonscience stuff for fifteen minutes?"

"Yes," she says. "We can do it! Go team!"

Maria glances at me, as if she expects me to blame her for this development. "Don't let me stop you," Maria says. "Talk about whatever you want."

"No." I sit down. "Please. We all know how *important* it is to be well-rounded. Come to think of it, Maria, I don't remember where you are in grad school. Are you past the qualifying exam stage, or…?"

She looks at her brother in annoyance. Then she looks back at me. "I'm a senior. My major is officially statistics and international relations, but I'm studying for actuarial exams."

There's a long pause. I try to calculate her age. This involves me staring at her. Into her eyes. Medium brown, sparkling with a malicious humor, winged in black liquid lines.

I swallow. "A senior." My words come slowly. "As in, you don't have a bachelor's yet?" I look at her, then at her brother. "I didn't realize there was that large an age difference between the two of you. What is that, nine years?"

She flushes. "Three years. I'm twenty-four."

"I see." I look up. "You're just slow."

Rachel frowns and shakes her head. "Seriously? Why are you being so cold? Gabe, I work for him. You have to kick his ass."

Gabriel shrugs and looks at his sister, who shakes her head. "Maria can take care of herself. She'll let me know if she needs to tap out."

"I had some stuff I wanted to do before I started university," Maria says. "It's none of your business."

"Trying to get your modeling career off the ground," I guess. "I'm actually shocked that it failed."

Rachel blows out a breath. "Hey," she says with a forced smile. "So speaking of none of my business, how long did it take you to get your PhD, Jay?"

I let her change the subject. "Three and a half years."

Maria blinks. "Are you serious? I'm not sure you're an actual human being."

"I'm human." I fold my arms. "I'm just focused. Directed. Laser-like."

She purses her lips. "Laser-like."

"Yes." I raise an eyebrow in her direction. "You know. My actions tend to be in phase with each other. I don't dillydally all over the place."

"I wasn't disagreeing." She's almost smirking. In fact, she looks amused. "I was just trying the idea on. Laser-like is actually a really appropriate description for you."

"Oh?"

"Sure." She shrugs. "First, you're an unnatural phenomenon."

I tilt my head. "Unnatural." I consider this. "Sure. Civilization is unnatural in the first place."

"Second, you only manage to be as coherent as you are by dumping an abnormally large amount of energy into the system."

"His nickname at Harvard," Gabe puts in, "was Negative Temperature."

I ignore this. "Okay," I say to Maria. "Sure. I've had less favorable descriptions."

"Which," Maria continues, "means that system-wise—what is it that laser stands for again?"

"Light Amplification by Stimulated Emission of Radiation," Rachel chimes in helpfully.

She snaps her fingers. "Right. It means you end up in a near-perpetually excited state, and the only way you know how to deal with it is by stimulated emission."

Rachel's mouth falls open a fraction. Gabe coughs into his fist. I look at Maria, feeling utterly blank. It's not…entirely untrue. I do have hookups when I have the time, but…yes, stimulated emission is often easier and more effective.

I'm surprised for a more basic reason. Maria knows what a laser is. And not just the sci-fi version of a laser beam. She knows how a laser *works*.

Gabriel blows out a breath. "Burn."

Rachel slides lower in her chair. "Sick burn."

"Hey," Maria says, with a shrug. "I'm not dissing stimulated emission."

I haven't looked away from her. "Bullshit you aren't."

"I'm not," she says. "But you called me slow. What exactly was your course?"

"Graduated college at twenty," I say. "PhD by twenty-three. Tenure-track position at twenty-five. And the department will recommend me for tenure by the time I'm thirty-one."

"So what's the rush?" she asks me.

I lick my lips.

"I mean it. What would have happened if it had taken you four and a half years to finish your PhD instead of three and a half? What will happen if you don't make full professor by thirty-five?"

I take a bite of pizza so I have an excuse not to answer. For some reason, my conversation with Em a month ago comes back. *Is there anything that must urgently be done?* And then: *You are enough.* I shake my head to dispel the idea.

Maria persists. "What are you going to miss out on?"

"I suppose I can ask the opposite question. What's the point of doing anything if you're not all in? I mean, let's take...you, for instance."

She raises her eyebrows.

I continue.

"Actuarial math? Seriously? What are you going to do, make risk tables for insurance companies for the rest of your life? Let me guess. You're a dabbler. You like a little bit of everything. You don't go deep."

"Well, you know how it is." She doesn't flinch. "Endless repetition without variation does tend to chafe." Her eyes meet mine. "Or, wait—maybe you *don't* know that? It would explain why you work all the time and rely on stimulated emission."

I smile despite myself.

She shrugs. "But it's okay. It takes all types."

"Now *there's* a true but useless platitude. 'It takes all types.' The ocean needs both plankton and whales to be a functioning ecosystem, but nobody wants to be plankton. It's better farther up the food chain."

She meets my eyes levelly. "Well, that's a shitty analogy." She shifts forward. "It's more like the difference between omnivores and carnivores. Some of us are grizzlies. We eat anything. Salmon. Blueberries."

"Bicycle chains," I put in.

She tilts her head at me.

"I read it in *National Geographic*. There was a grizzly once who was bothering everyone, and they pumped its stomach..." I trail off. "But go ahead. Make the case for indiscriminate consumption. I'm waiting."

"Some of us," she continues, ignoring this, "are pandas. We're screwed without our bamboo. We only eat the same damned thing over and over."

I look at her. "I'm the panda, I take it? That's a crappy insult. You're saying I'm sweet, majestic, and lovable."

"I'm saying you're completely dysfunctional outside your ecosystem."

"Sure." I nod. "I'll grant you that. But I'm a panda with a laser. You're a grizzly with an actuarial statistics table. Who do you think is going to win?"

Rachel speaks up. "Oh, now *this* is a fun game. It's like Rock/Paper/Scissors, but with Actuarial

Table/Laser..." She frowns, considering. "Okay, what's the third thing?"

"Grant proposal," Gabe puts in. "Laser shreds actuarial table. Actuarial table defeats grant proposal. Grant proposal defeats laser."

Maria is watching me throughout all of this with a half smile on her face.

"Long story short," I say, "I still win."

"Fine," she says. "But we're going best two out of three."

I make a show of glancing at my watch. "Rain check on the next two rounds. We have a shitload of bamboo here, and it's not eating itself. And you..." I look over at her. "You have, what? A bachelor's degree to work on?"

She just shakes her head.

I sit back in my seat. For a moment, I feel self-satisfied. I made my point.

It doesn't last long. First, I can tell that Rachel is uncomfortable. Some people don't like conflict, and...well, apparently, she's one of them. It occurs to me that she's been trying to keep us from tearing each other's throats out every time we spoke, and failing. Shit.

Second, Maria sits back in her chair and takes a bite of her pizza. Her eyes meet mine.

Here's the thing: Maria is fucking hot, and she knows it. She knows it so well that she probably knows to the electron-volt how much expectant energy zings through me when she licks her thumb clean of an errant bit of pizza sauce. She knows that my eyes linger on her mouth.

Fuck me. I don't want anything to do with anyone who knows how to be as hot as she does.

Third occurs to me like a punch to the gut. I made some assumptions about Maria when we first met. She was hot. She knew it. She talked about concerts and...dammit, dammit, dammit.

For all that she taunted me about being average before, it's obvious that she's not. Maria is smart—almost as smart as she is hot—and she knows it.

"Is something wrong, Three Sigma?" she asks pointedly.

I manage to look away. But Maria is like the sun—even after I stop staring at her, I can almost see her imprinted on my eyelids.

"Guys." Rachel shakes her head. "Guys, bad news. We totally failed."

Maria turns to her. "Failed how?"

"We were going to not talk about science over dinner. But...lasers, ecosystems, grant proposals." She shakes her head sadly. "The score stands at us, three. Conversation, zero."

"Oh." Maria glances at me sidelong and smiles once more. "Are we all on the same team? I didn't notice."

MARIA

After dinner, Rachel excuses herself. Jay and I both stay, going through my brother's slides. I listen to Jay talk strategy. I *am* an omnivore, whether he respects it or not, and every detail of academic life is something I might be able to slide into a future post at some point.

But my brother still has work to do, and when they finish their discussion and the clock strikes nine-thirty, Gabe asks Jay if he can take me down.

LBL is a government-run lab; I'm technically only here as Gabe's visitor, and I'm not allowed to go running around on my own. Jay and I exchange dubious glances.

"Fine," he says shortly.

I have no excuse. We're stuck together.

He doesn't look at me as we walk down the hallway. He opens the first fire door for me, but it's an automatic response, not any form of chivalry, and he doesn't say anything when I open the outside door for him.

I don't like him, but he's friends with my brother, and he's giving Gabe valuable advice. I can tolerate him for that.

I open my umbrella. It's not raining as hard as it was earlier, but it's still drizzling.

He doesn't touch his umbrella. One of those kinds of people, I guess.

We go down the building stairs together. "I drove," he says curtly. "Want me to take you back to campus?"

I don't really have a choice. "Sure."

I get in his car. The car reminds me of him. It's a practical compact hybrid. There are no errant papers on the front seat, no extra Starbucks cups left in the cup holder. It smells like some generic flavor of sweet air freshener.

Campus is mostly dark below us, lit by little globes of lights. Eucalyptus trees block the view intermittently as he makes his way down the wet asphalt.

The entire situation is weird. For one, Jay is a professor. It doesn't feel like it to me, because I met him through Gabe instead of in a class. But he is most definitely a professor. He's also only five years older than I am.

He probably has students who are twice his age.

He doesn't say anything as he drives to campus. He doesn't offer to drive me home. He just parks in the north lot and unlocks the doors.

I get out. "Thanks for the ride. Us plankton have a hard time getting around."

He doesn't say anything immediately. Instead, he pulls the parking brake and gets out. The yellow globe of the streetlight paints his face with dark shadows. He folds his arms and looks at me.

"Fine." He speaks as if the words have been reluctantly drawn from him. "I owe you an apology."

The dim light of the overhead lamp shouldn't be flattering to anyone. It is to him, giving his face mysterious planes, deepening the color of his skin. His eyes are enigmatic. He looks fierce and forbidding, not apologetic.

"What for?"

He frowns. "You were right. I made a lot of assumptions about you."

"Did you?" I stare flatly at him. "I *am* a girly-girl. I love heels. I do my hair. I watch makeup tutorials on YouTube, and I do a better smoky eye than you could dream of."

"Yes, but I didn't realize…" He makes a frustrated sound.

"That I *also* knew math?" I tilt my head in his direction. "That my brother wrote his dissertation on second-order nonlinear optical processes, and in the course of talking to him every week on Skype, I somehow learned the basics of how a laser worked?"

He gives me a single nod.

All my latent annoyance boils over. "You're apologizing for the wrong thing."

"Am I?"

"You're a goddamned *professor*. If you assume your female students who care about their appearance don't know math, you're doing them an incredible disservice."

He doesn't say anything.

"That's sexist and gross, and I have friends in STEM and—" And I'm not going on that rant. I can hear myself breathing heavily, even though I've done nothing more strenuous than sit in his car. I inhale long and slow, willing my heart rate to come down.

He folds his arms. The drizzle is collecting on him, beading on his skin. "Are you done?"

"No," I say. "Because it shouldn't matter. Saying, 'I didn't know you knew math, so I'm sorry I treated you like a nonperson' is also fucked up. People who don't know math *also* deserve respect."

He looks at me for a long time. "Of course," he says coldly.

Laser-like doesn't begin to describe him. I feel like he's laying me bare. Like he knows everything about me.

He folds his arms. "My apology stands as given. I don't take back anything else I said last time. I think you're distracting your brother."

"Thanks," I manage.

"I'm serious," Jay says. "Your brother needs to focus. Let him fucking digest his bamboo."

"Criticism noted. My answer still applies."

"That being said," Jay continues, "I should..." He hesitates, and then looks down. "Fine, whatever. You're right about two things. I...have some thinking to do about...stuff." He frowns as he says this. "Second, that plankton shit today was uncalled for. I play to win, but that was unfair on my part."

"You mean I'm slightly more developed than protozoa?" I look over at him.

His eyes dip down, briefly. Momentarily. My throat tightens.

"Yes," he says. "You are. It doesn't mean I like you."

Our eyes meet briefly. I know he doesn't like me. I know it the way I know he can't look away. I know it the way I can see his lip curl when his gaze dips down to my shoes—sensible flats with a filmy bow, my late-night get-work-done shoes.

"Fuck you," I say calmly. "Fuck your apology. And fuck your holier-than-thou fake British accent."

He shakes his head.

"I'm not the one you need to apologize to, anyway," I tell him. "You know who you really messed with back there? Rachel."

His eyes narrow. "Bullshit."

"Because you just sent her a really clear message, Three Sigma. She's going to wonder if you'll turn on her if she shows up to lab looking nice because she has a date. She spent an hour and a half listening to you make fun of another Latina, and she was so upset that she left halfway through. She has to work with you. How is she ever supposed to trust you again?"

His expression doesn't change. He stares at me as if he were carved from a block of ice, before finally he shakes his head. "I'm out of here. I have research to go over. Grant proposals to write."

"Be careful. Actuarial tables defeat grant proposals."

His eyes don't move, but I still have the impression that he's taking me in. All of me, from head to toe. I have the distinct feeling that if he let himself, he'd take a step toward me.

Maybe he thinks the same thing, because he rolls his eyes. "No shit. You're not just distracting your brother."

With that, he gets in his car and pulls away.

Maybe it's wishful thinking, but part of me *wants* him to be distracted by me. Not because I'm attracted to him in anything other than an abstract, physical sense.

No, my desire is much crueler. I want him to want me because I want him to not have me. I want him to know that I'm completely, utterly out of his league. That there's nothing he can do that will ever make things better.

I want to distract him from science by existing without him.

I want him to regret being a jerk to me. I want him to beg me for forgiveness for misjudging me.

And when he does, I want to squash him like the cockroach that he is and walk out of his life.

I swipe the rain out of my eyes and head home. On foot.

8.

MARIA

I park my car in the driveway, my thoughts boiling. I don't like what just happened with Maria. I don't like it at all. Right now, I just want to talk to someone who will tell me that I'm okay. That I haven't fucked up.

Em comes to mind. *You're enough just as you are,* she told me. And I still haven't forgotten.

I get out my phone in front of my house and type. *How does this soup thing work? I think I need soup.*

The neighborhood seems silent and still.

I don't know if Em's around right now. She goes out, after all. But a half-minute later, three little dots appear.

Are you okay? she asks.

I'm fine. I just fucked up, is all, and I hate fucking up.

She doesn't ask for details, and I don't provide them. I don't really want to have to explain to Em that someone I didn't want to respect just pointed out that I was a dick. I hate even more that Maria was right.

I have always considered myself... I don't know, one of the good guys. My first grad student was female. My study groups always had women in them. My perpetual coauthor had to cancel our last in-person work session because her daughter got pneumonia, and that's just the way things are. My mom has a master's in computer science, and I've seen all the bullshit she went through to get to the top of her field. I believe in birth control and expanding the STEM pipeline, and dammit, I think of myself as a feminist.

Except apparently, I'm not as good as I thought I was. I knew that Rachel was upset, but until Maria said those words, I didn't realize *how* upset.

I feel like shit.

Sorry, I type. *Just a case of wanting cookies I don't deserve.*

She sends back one character: *?*

You know. I feel even worse explaining this to her. *Cookies. The praise people expect for being a basically decent human being. Except apparently I've been awarding myself cookies and doing it wrong.*

I know what cookies are. I just didn't think you did.

I frown, and type. *Why?*

Not to stereotype, but cookies are usually transparent to men. Men think they always deserve them.

I'm frustrated. Unhappy. My sentences come out choppy. *Yeah. Probably. I fucked up.*

I don't realize how much I was hoping for Em to forgive me until she doesn't.

I'm not really in a mood to offer soup or cookies to men who fuck up right now, she writes. *I know I should be a good friend or something and tell you that it's okay, but you know what? Maybe it isn't okay, and maybe it's your fault, and maybe I'm not going to be your magical female scientist friend right now. If you fucked up, don't whine to me about it. Do better next time.*

Now I feel shittier than ever, because that is exactly what I wanted her to do—make me feel better.

I grimace. *You know what? You're right. I'm just going to shut up.*

I should...read papers or something before I go to sleep, but I can't. When I got out my phone, I had this image of texting Em. Of her offering support. Telling me that I'm not that bad, that one little mistake doesn't make me a bad person.

And it doesn't. But the truth is, this is not a *little* mistake. I keep thinking of the look on Rachel's face when she left. I keep hearing Maria's voice. *How is she ever supposed to trust you again?* I can still see the curl in Maria's lip. *People who don't know math also deserve respect.*

I hate that Maria is right. I hate it. I hate that I'm not as good as I believed myself to be, and I hate that I let Rachel down. I hate that it's going to take me months to build up trust again. I fucked up, and I hate it.

MARIA

*I*t's almost eleven, and I'm home and in bed and warm, before I get out my phone again. The guilt hasn't gone away, which means...dammit. I text an apology.

Hey. I'm sorry about earlier. I snapped at you because I was upset about something else.

I'm sitting on my bed. I have an eight AM class. Still, I haven't been able to wind down for the night yet. I don't know if Actual Physicist is awake still, but...

Heh. His response is almost immediate. *I was just about to apologize to you. You implied you were upset earlier. I ignored it because I was mad about discovering I was imperfect.*

I don't say anything for a little while. I don't like fighting with him, not like this. It's stupid to care what a pseudonymous physicist hidden somewhere in the world thinks of me, but I do.

I was a dick, he says. *You basically told me someone was a jerk to you, and I kept going on about me. Are you okay?*

There are so many things I can say to that. I start typing, and delete, and start again three times.

I keep waiting to discover the conditions on our friendship, I type. I don't hit send.

I delete a fourth time and try again. *There aren't many people who know me well,* I type instead. *I usually don't let myself get too angry with people I care about.*

I don't realize what I've said until the words are contained in a little green bubble, with no way to call them back.

The words are meaningless enough. "I care about you" doesn't specify how much. It doesn't tell him that his texts make me smile. That I've been worrying about him snapping at me or not writing back or…

I'm going to say something terribly selfish, he says in response.

My heart gives a wild thump.

I was upset earlier. Because you were right and I was afraid you'd think badly of me, and also, if I told you the whole story, you would absolutely think badly of me. It took me an hour to realize that instead of worrying about how to tell a story so I looked like I wasn't a prick, I should just stop doing things that would make you think badly of me.

It's stupid. Sometimes—more than sometimes—I wonder what he looks like. I've kind of imagined him as a rail-thin guy with glasses and messy hair, sarcastic and funny and just a little self-deprecating.

We've flirted before. Not seriously. It's all been *friendly* flirting. But there's been just that edge.

This, though? This isn't casual internet flirtation. Not for the first time, I think about asking him something stupid. Something like, *where do you live?*

I'm glad I don't know you, he types, *because if this were real, I'd be so embarrassed I'd never be able to talk to you again.*

If this were real. I exhale. Shut my eyes.

Fine. That's fine. I tell him I care about him and he reminds me that I'm not real. Message received loud and clear, Actual Physicist.

Yeah, well. My sarcasm comes out a little. *I'll take my fake self off to fake bed.*

Sorry. I didn't mean it that way.

I shake my head, tired all over again. *It's okay. I know what you meant.*

And I do. He knows I'm real. He just doesn't want me to be real to *him*.

9.

MARIA

Late November

"lake."

I'm sitting in our kitchen at a barstool on the kitchen island, frowning at my computer. Tina's ten feet away at the table, two monitors hooked up to her one Cyclone laptop. Blake sits across from her. He's reading something—I suspect *not* schoolwork, because Blake never seems to do schoolwork—on a tablet. "Hey, Blake."

He looks up the second time she speaks. "Hmm?"

"Can you play cybersecurity specialist for a sec?"

He gestures to his monitors. "I'm playing cybersecurity specialist right now, genius."

"I mean for me."

He gives her a look. It's a long, steady, heated look. His voice drops a few notes. "You mean in the bedroom?"

TMI. I bite my lip and look away. When I first agreed to live with them, Blake and Tina were still traversing new territory, and it felt like solidarity to be here for Tina if—when—they broke up.

But that *when* doesn't seem to be materializing any time soon. And I feel more and more like an interloper in what should be my space, too.

"No. It's not that. Let me show you this." She unplugs her laptop and pushes it across the table to him. "Does this mean someone's trying to hack into my account?" She points to the screen.

He frowns.

"Unless you mistyped your password ten times and don't remember doing it? I'd say yes."

"Crap. Should I do something?"

Blake bites his lip. "Do you really want to hear this?"

"Of course I do."

He sighs. "Okay. So. Your password is sc3nturion, spelled with an s, 3 swapped for the e."

I can see the blood draining from her face. I can't pretend I'm not paying attention any longer. Slowly, we both turn to face him.

She exhales heavily. "How exactly do you know that?"

He shrugs. "Because I've seen you typing it in. You don't bother to hide your fingers when you put in your password. I figured it out like five months ago. I wasn't going to say anything. Most people have insecure passwords. If I told everyone every time I figured out their password, I'd always be explaining myself."

"Um." Tina's hand goes to her hip.

Maybe he can sense us both watching him incredulously, because he looks around slowly. "What?" He seems honestly surprised. "It's not like I used it or anything."

It takes me a moment to figure out what to think. Truth is, it's incredibly easy to forget that Blake is anything other than a regular college student who barely cares about his grades. He's disarmingly nice. He doesn't flaunt his wealth. He doesn't remind everyone that his father used to run one of the most powerful companies in the world. When he agreed to share a house with Tina and me, he took to a chore rotation and a dinner list without complaint, even though I doubt he's cleaned a bathroom in his life.

He blinked when we told him it made no sense to throw out empty plastic tubs of cream cheese, but he accepted the idea of reusing them as makeshift Tupperware with relative ease.

Still, every once in a while, he does something so baffling that I'm reminded he is not normal.

"Do you typically figure people's passwords out?" Tina asks.

He has the grace to finally look chagrined. "Well. So. Maybe? Sort of?"

"Maybe?" Tina's foot starts tapping. "Sort of?"

"Okay, all the time," he admits. "When I was a kid, and we were at Cyclone late at night, we used to play these games."

"Oh god." Tina winces. "How did I know this was going to turn into a fucked-up Cyclone nightcare story?"

"I swear to god, this isn't one of the fucked-up stories," Blake says. "These were just red team/blue team games. You know."

I don't know. "Red team/blue team?" I ask. "Like, team sports?"

"Exactly. It's basically capture the flag, except we played it on Cyclone servers. First team to hack into the other team's enclave won. You got glory if you won. And if you found an actual Cyclone vulnerability and told the security team, you'd get a share of Cyclone stock. So, um. Old habits die hard."

Tina and I both look at him. He returns our stares with an innocent, unblinking gaze.

"That's weird," I finally say.

Tina shakes her head. "Let me see if I understand this. Your dad used child labor to find bugs?"

"No," Blake says smoothly. "Not my dad. He wasn't the computer security expert. The internal bug-bounty program was run by Cyclone's CFO."

"That's *so* much better."

It's like he can't even hear my sarcasm. He goes on. "A good password is like a secret. You don't think about it. You don't remember it. You put it in muscle memory—a series of keystrokes that only your fingers know. I don't even know my own passwords."

Tina and I exchange glances. *Brief* glances. Here's the thing—she doesn't tell me a lot about her boyfriend, but we are on the same dinner rotation. He told me—in that same *this messed-up thing is incredibly normal* tone—that he had issues in the past with not eating. And also running too much. Given what I know about him, *you put your secrets in muscle memory* is kind of a screwed-up thing for him to say.

But hey. At least he has good password security and Cyclone stock.

"Or," Tina says, "you could use a password aggregator and generator."

"Well, but that means—" He cuts himself off, looking at us. "Right. Yeah. Do that."

Tina goes over to sit next to him. She takes his hand, and I look away. I don't want to hear their conversation. Trying not to overhear two people talking from four feet away is almost impossible.

"It's not that weird," Blake says to her. "Is it?"

"It's a little weird," she says. "But weird is not bad."

"I know. I just forget that normal people can have passwords based on real words. Hackers try to break into my account all the time."

I almost feel sorry for him.

"And this," Tina says, "is why no thank you, I don't want anything to do with Cyclone, or Cyclone subsidiaries, or non-Cyclone non-subsidiaries that are owned by Cyclone people. It's bad enough as it is. Is it so weird to want a separate life?"

He shakes his head. "No. Trust me. Nobody understands that as well as I do."

I should leave. I'm not sure if it would be more awkward if I do, or if I don't.

I should talk to Tina about it.

But she's holding hands with her boyfriend, and dammit, I don't want to make her uncomfortable.

"That reminds me," Blake says. "Speaking of normal people. Maria, do you want to come to Saints and Dinosaurs?"

Now I have to pretend I'm listening again. I look up. "What?"

"It's this Cyclone thing," he explains earnestly. "It started a while back. Long story short, hundreds of Cyclone employees and friends and family come. My dad makes dessert. So does the head of programming. Employees vote on which one's better."

"Um." I look over at Tina. "It sounds…"

It sounds awful. Cyclone people are all inherently suspect. They work with his dad, for one, and Blake's dad is, as far as I can tell, King Asshole of Asshole County. Plus, Cyclone people are programmers. They skew male. They have lots of stock options, and tend to think that makes them far more attractive than they actually are. Spending time around Cyclone programmers sounds about as fun as slapping myself in the face with a porcupine.

But Tina is giving me puppy-dog eyes. "Please come," she says. "Blake has to abandon me to help his dad. That leaves me to be eaten by the wolves. Pretty please."

I look down at my computer. "Wolves. How enticing."

"Anj will be there," she says coaxingly. "You'll have fun. Sorta."

I look over at Tina. I look back at Blake.

"Fine," I say. "I think I have some extra wolf spray around here somewhere."

11:47 AM

Good news: I have experimentally verified that there is, in fact, a difference between drowning in twelve feet of water and drowning in fifty. Spoiler alert: The extra water pressure crushes you faster.

11:48 AM

Am I supposed to feel sorry for you, Actual Physicist?

11:49 AM
*As long as you die slowly enough,
you'll get another publication out of it.
That's got to count for something.*

11:50 AM
:P

11:53 AM
*Speaking of drowning. I just agreed to go to this thing with
my friend. I am going to be surrounded by...dudes.
Dudes who will explain everything I know to me the entire
time. I will have to smile and nod and not correct them. I do not
know why I agreed to this.*

11:54 AM
I suspect it is because you are a genuinely nice person.

11:57 AM
*It's cool. I can handle a little mild social interaction.
Probably.
And look at me, hijacking your conversation.
What went wrong on your end?*

11:59 AM
*I just heard back on the last of my grant proposals and I am so
fucked.*

12:01 PM
Oh no!

Did it not go well?

12:03 PM
Define "well."
"You get maybe 20% of your proposals funded," my old PI told me. "If you want funding for two projects, submit ten proposals." Fuck me. I thought at five I was maybe undercutting it?

12:04 PM
Oh dear. Was five not enough? Is it too late to send out another round?

12:08 PM
Alas. That is not the problem I have. I can't even complain about the problem I have to my friends, because I try not to be a complete dick. I am suffering from the crushing burden of success. I am five for five. Now how am I supposed to get all this research done?

12:09 PM
Poor Actual Physicist.
Having to do Actual Physics.

12:09 PM
I detect sarcasm.

12:10 PM
Poor baby. It'll be okay.
We can talk again in three years, when you have time.

12:10 PM
You're mean.

12:10 PM

You're busy.

JAY

$\mathcal{A}$ rap on my office door interrupts the conversation.

"Jay. Yo. Are you in there?"

I'm jolted away from the messages on my phone. I shake my head and look around my office. My papers are in order on my desk. It's fifteen minutes past noon, and...holy shit, I'm starving. I had no idea.

Fuck. I didn't realize how effectively Em had distracted me. I hadn't even noticed how hungry I was. I stand up and open my office door.

Gabriel Lopez is standing in front of me. He's gotten a haircut since last I saw him, probably proof that the job search is on in earnest. His dark eyes are furrowed in worry.

I blink at him in utter confusion.

"We were going to do lunch today, remember? I've been waiting for like ten minutes."

"Shit." I run my hand through my hair. "Dammit. I'm sorry. I was just in the middle of something. I forgot."

He glances at my desk. There's no evidence of Em in my office, just a few papers filled with my doodles of a quantum circuit.

"We were going to talk about your paper over lunch." I read the abstract. "Let me grab it."

He rolls his eyes. "You work too much. Fuck my paper. You obviously need a break."

I blink. I'm meeting with my grad students in forty-five minutes. Plus, I'm finishing my final so that my graduate student instructor can take it and make sure that all the problems have actual solutions. I haven't seen Gabe in weeks, not since we went over his job talk.

With his sister.

I frown. I don't want to think about his sister.

Whatever. It's not like I can drown faster.

"You're right." I stand up. "But can we be quick?"

We find tacos. I pick at mine for five minutes and try to think about something to talk about that isn't his paper or his job talk. Politics? No, my blood pressure does not need that discussion. Either we'll agree, and we'll get mad together, or we'll disagree and get mad at each other. Sports? I haven't been following sports. As soon as I have a little more time…

"I can't believe you're engaged." It's the first thing that comes to mind.

He snorts. "You make it sound like it's a death sentence. Not all of us are as fiercely committed to our bachelorhood as you are."

I don't think that's a good description for me. I grimace. "Sorry. I didn't mean to sound judgmental."

"I'm a little touchy right now. My parents are giving me shit, too. They keep asking me how I know that Jutta isn't just marrying me for US citizenship. I want to strangle them."

I have no idea how to handle shit like that. I can give him advice on job talks and papers. Family advice is absolutely not my forte. That being said, I'm aware that this is the point in the conversation where I should say something supportive.

I settle on, "That's bullshit."

He shrugs.

"Is Maria giving you shit, too?"

"God, no," Gabe says. "Maria and I have each other's backs. She video chats with Jutta. Has since we got serious."

My first thought—purely dismissive—is this: *Of course Maria is the kind of person who video chats.* It takes me a second to recognize this for what it is: stupid bullshit.

I've been trying to be better since Maria called me out. I apologized to Rachel. I told her I messed up. I didn't make excuses. I didn't tell her that I was judging Maria by a standard in my head, a standard that I let Clio set all those years ago, one that I'm still working on.

I'm trying to hold myself to a different standard now. What would Em think if I told her that I was annoyed that someone video chatted? She'd probably tell me to get over myself. My nose wrinkles. Yeah. So. I'll get over myself.

Gabe must see the face I'm making, because he shakes his head. "Are you allergic to the word *serious?* Getting married is not going to kill me, you know."

"It wasn't that."

Gabe sighs. "Sorry. I'm not trying to be judgy. It's okay that you don't do serious."

"It's not that."

Here's the thing. Gabe and I met at Harvard four years ago. I was dating a postdoc who worked in the lab across from ours. We were together for five months.

We broke up because of academic jobs.

Specifically, I got one in Berkeley. I also was offered a job in Pittsburgh, where Dave had just landed a multiyear contract as lecturer. I didn't even think about the decision, and he wanted me to think about it, and that ended…badly. Really badly.

I suspect that Gabe heard about that decision from both ends. Right now, though, is not the time for me to explain that I wasn't going to rearrange my entire life for someone I'd been with for less than a year. The divergent job searches were not the problem. They were a symptom of the problem. Dave was into me a lot more than I was into him, and it turns out that's not fun for anyone involved.

Gabe and I eat in awkward silence for a little while longer.

"So, serious question," Gabe says. "Feel free to say no. I'm not sure where you are on this right now, but there's this postdoc in bioinformatics I met—"

I do not need my friends to set me up with anyone. I don't even let him finish the sentence. "Nope."

"You don't even want to meet her?"

I'm not sure how to explain. "After Dave," I say carefully, "I'm very wary of any relationship where the other person takes it more seriously than I do."

"Okay, but how will you know—"

"And there's kind of someone," I interject. "She's not local. Nothing's going on. But I like her a lot. I'm not getting into a serious relationship with anyone I like less than her. It wouldn't be fair. Not to me, not to anyone else."

It's funny. I said those words as an excuse. But the moment they're out of my mouth, I realize they are true. I couldn't start a serious relationship with anyone else while I'm still wondering what Em looks like.

I'm not going to stop chatting with her. Or flirting with her. I could date someone else, but how could I ever agree to be exclusive if I was still wondering what Em looks like? It's not that I don't want to be serious. It's that non-serious is the only fair thing under the circumstances. It wouldn't be right.

Good thing I don't know anything about Em, or I'd be so fucked.

Gabe sighs. "I think that's bullshit," he says, "and I think you know that."

"Fuck you," I respond, but I smile so he knows I don't mean it.

"And I think we've hit the end of your free time. So can I make you go on another forced social outing at any point in the near future, or is this going to be too awkward?"

I shake my head. "No. It's cool. I'm busy now, but I like seeing you. You're not forcing me to do anything."

"So." Gabe looks at me "Bioinformatics?"

I shake my head. "Not that. Kick my ass if I ever agree   to   date   anyone   you   know."

10.

December

I obviously hadn't really thought through what was entailed in a massive Cyclone event. "A few hundred people," Blake told me before we drove down, but it seems like more than that. The house we've come to— "Sai's house," Blake says simply as we pull up, "but everyone calls her Saint K."—is massive, and the streets are lined with cars.

I'm not an expert on Cyclone corporate structure, but Sai, whoever she is, either has an enormous salary or...or no, there is no other option. Her house is long, two stories tall, in a California Spanish style. There's a tiled courtyard visible through a gate, an enormous affair with a multi-tiered fountain that's dry in order to pay respect to this year's drought. Signs direct us into the even more enormous backyard—a multi-acre fenced-in affair with terraced levels, xeriscaped gardens, views onto the Bay, a pool house, and a tennis court. The smell of barbecue and smoke fills the air. This place feels more like a park than a piece of private property.

Blake is mobbed the moment he arrives. He laughs, tells a joke to someone neither of us know, and introduces us once, then twice. It doesn't matter. He's soon cut off from us by the press of people.

Tina doesn't try to stay by him. She takes my hand while the attention focuses on him, and together, we slip to the back of the crowd.

The last thing I hear is Blake telling everyone that he has to go help his dad.

"Come on, guys, he's shitting bricks," Blake says. "Do you want to tell him you delayed me?"

"Oh, shit," someone replies. "Let the Eye of Sauron pass over me. I didn't see you. I didn't talk to you."

Whoever says that is joking. I *think*. Maybe. Blake gives Tina a wave over the crowd, mouths some words we can't hear over the throng, and heads over to sparkling glass French doors from the house that open onto the yard. He proceeds to take off his shoes, still talking to the people around him.

"Well, okay." Tina stares after him, then looks over the crowd. "This is going to be fun."

"Yay," I manage glumly. "Fun."

We turn to the backyard.

The house is nestled in foothills. I can't help but calculate the cost of all that land. Double the price for a view of the glittering waters of the bay. Triple it today, for the blue sky and wispy clouds pinked by sunset. It would probably be gauche to look up the estimated value online, and besides, those online estimates would never include the value of the amenities.

There are two grills, one close, one far, both manned by uniformed caterers. People are everywhere— by the blue infinity pool, seated on a stone wall under a wooden arbor...

Tina scoots closer to me. "Crap," she mutters in a low voice. "I am so bad at this shit."

Here's the thing: I don't like being in crowds of people I don't know, mostly because I feel like I'm not in control. I don't mind people; I just don't like surprises.

Tina, on the other hand is a giant introvert. She doesn't like small talk, and this—being abandoned by her boyfriend in a crowd of strangers—has to be her version of hell.

Our eyes meet.

"Poor Tina," I tell her. "It sucks that Blake is just looking for a trophy wife. Now that he knows you're shit at parties, he's probably going to get rid of you forever."

She glares at me.

"See?" I shrug. "Worst-case scenario is that you're just going to be uncomfortable for a couple hours. It's not really that bad."

"You're too reasonable. I need a beer."

"Let's find Anj." I take out my phone and send a text. *Where are you, girl?*

Tina exhales. "Is it bad that even the thought of Anj makes me feel better? Yeah. I can do this."

"It could be worse. You could be *with* Blake right now, talking to his dad."

She grimaces, and at that moment Anj answers the text I sent earlier. *Out by the pool house! Come have fun!*

Fun. Sure.

We weave our way through the crowd, stopping to grab bottles from a cooler. It's a bit of a trek to the pool house. When we arrive, we discover that Anj—unsurprisingly—has amassed a following around her.

Some people, like Tina, are massive introverts—happiest when alone, with the occasional friend to talk to. I'm not that bad. I don't hate large crowds, but I don't like the ones where I don't know anyone.

Anj is, and always has been, unclassifiable. She's perfectly happy disappearing for weeks on end in her attempts to make a chickenosaurus from a poultry embryo; she's equally delighted surrounded by a dozen people.

She's traded her usual flannel shirt for a little black dress, that she has paired with chunky boots. "Hey, Maria," she says with a smile. "And..." She pauses, looking at Tina. "Clara?"

Tina almost, but doesn't quite, roll her eyes. "Tina."

"Right." Anj nods. "Do you guys know everyone here?"

We know nobody. She introduces everyone mostly by profession; everyone else has to supply their own names. There are three programmers, a marketing guy, two adult children of Cyclone parents, and a researcher at Stanford who does cybersecurity work.

Unfortunately, I recognize the last guy, and not as myself. His name is Daniel van Tijn. He emailed me months ago about cowriting a piece together. It feels odd and invasive to know him when he's unaware of our acquaintance.

I shake his hand when Anj introduces us. Our arrival, it turns out, is only a temporary interruption.

He and Anj are having a heated discussion on the question of de-extinction.

"I don't need to know anything about biology or ecosystems," he's saying. "I can already bloody guarantee you it's a bad idea to bring back species."

He's a fifty-five-year-old chaired professor. He reads my blog. I shift uneasily from foot to foot.

"I hate *Jurassic Park.*" Anj frowns. "It ruined everything. I'm not bringing anything back that isn't already here. Prehistoric genes are still buried in current DNA, which is like nature's biggest copy/paste file. It's more like knitting by hand. Nobody has to do it anymore, but the skills are still there."

"You are the definition of a mad scientist," Professor van Tijn responds. "There's a blog you really should read. It's about the possibility of technology gone wrong. It's called MCL from—"

"MCL from the future," Anj finishes with a grin.

I shrink back. Oh. Good. Me. My least favorite topic of conversation. Tina doesn't react beside me. I try not to look out of place. Luckily, I'm not the center of anyone's attention.

Anj doesn't look at me. "And stop threatening me with fiction. Why are lionfish-spearing robots okay, but transgenic sharks so impossible?"

"Oh, for god's sake." Van Tijn throws his hands in the air. "Who said lionfish-spearing robots were okay?"

Anj just folds her arms. "I bet MCL would *love* my transgenic sharks."

It's the Lisa effect. I feel weary just watching. Mention the existence of a genetically modified shark, and all other conversation comes to a screeching halt.

Van Tijn wrinkles his nose. "You actually have a transgenic shark?"

"Only one so far. Just a little GFP shark." Anj is beaming with pride. "Anyone can splice GFP into anything, you know. Do you want to see a video?" She pulls out her phone. "This is Lisa."

Everyone crowds around. Everyone but me. The thought of Lisa reminds me of biting back worry. Of sneaking out the fire escape because our landlord was in the hall. If I had opened the front door, he would have seen Anj's massive aquarium still in place. Lisa's presence in our apartment hung over my head like a glowing, transgenic shark of Damocles.

It's not Lisa's fault I'm a ball of anxiety.

"She is kind of cute," one of the marketing guys says.

"I know. MCL would *love* her. Come on, Maria." She looks at me over the crowd. "Say she's the best shark."

My head empties of all thoughts. My breath seems to stop. *Anj, you idiot.*

She realizes a second later what she's done. Her face goes pale.

It's been a long time since I got hit by an intense wave of irrational fear. The last time was...also caused by Lisa, when our landlord found out and yelled at us. My chest tightens with a constricting, crushing pain. My gorge rises. I reach out; my palms scrape the stone wall, and I steady my buckling knees.

I wait for everybody to look at me. To *say* something.

A second after that—the seconds seem to crawl by like sea snails on smooth glass—I realize that nobody is looking at me. Nobody else heard those sentences as connected. They heard two separate things—MCL would love it; Maria *also* loves my shark.

It's okay. Anj didn't just give me away.

She just got so carried away by her damned shark that she almost did. The pool house starts to spin in lazy circles around me.

It takes my body a few beats to catch up with my brain. To relax. I breathe, and my stomach slowly unclenches. My heart is still racing.

"Maria," Anj says quietly, "my shark is awesome, right?"

She's not asking me about her shark. Except she is.

I exhale slowly. "You know what? I need another beer."

Tina looks at me. "Want me to come with?"

For a second, I hesitate. I need a moment to catch my breath. To steady myself so I can pretend that everything is okay again. I want to be alone. I *need* to be alone. And Tina needs to spend some time with Cyclone people.

"Nah." I hope I manage to sound carefree. "Keep Anj company. I'll be back soon-ish."

Tina bites her lip. "Text me, okay?"

I go off to hide.

11.

I have to park five blocks away to get to my parents' house. As events go, Saints and Dinosaurs stretches the limits of residential neighborhoods. Even with the buses set up to shuttle people in from the Cyclone parking lots, too many people still drive in. Add in caterers, professional waitstaff, and it's officially a zoo up here.

I don't come in through the front door. For one thing, I'm sure there are people I don't know all over the house. For another, I want a chance to take a breath. Set my things down. Instead, I sneak into my parents' home through the garage. I kick off my shoes on the threshold and open the door to the mudroom.

It's not empty.

Instead, the very last person I expect to see is here. Maria Lopez is standing with her back to the door, her head down. She's wearing a green sundress that comes up to her mid-thighs. Speaking of thighs...

Of its own accord, my gaze slides down the long, satiny expanse of her legs. There's a little scar on one knee. Her calves are firmly rounded. Her ankles are...

Shit. What am I doing, looking at her legs? I jerk my eyes to her face just as she straightens.

"Oh, fuck." She plasters herself against the door, a look of horror on her face. "Are you serious? What are you *doing* here?"

I can't quite get the memory of her legs out of my mind. This is the first time I've ever seen her not wearing shoes, and I keep wanting to look down at the metallic gold polish on her toes. Without her heels, she's shorter than me.

She draws herself up as if she's just noticed the exact same thing and wants every inch of height she can get. She glares at me, too, as if this bizarre situation is somehow my fault.

I blow out a breath. "You're Cyclone adjacent," I mutter. "Shit. Of course you would be."

Some days it feels like half the Bay Area is related to, or friends with, someone from Cyclone.

Her arms fold in front of her chest. "My housemate is dating a Cyclone guy. What's your excuse?"

I'm trying not to get baited into another heated exchange with her. I'm counting to five when she snaps her fingers.

"You know what?" she says. "I know why you're such a jerk. You're jealous."

No. She had it right the last time we talked in the rain. I was a jerk because I took all the hurt and guilt from one experience and poured it into permanent blinders. Because I told myself that I had female scientist friends and that made me immune from whatever charge she laid at my feet.

It's embarrassing just to look at her and remember what she told me.

"I'm not jealous," I say slowly.

"No? I bet you always wished you could make decent arm candy. Is that why you're here? I can't imagine that an assistant professorship pays particularly well, not in comparison with *this*." Maria indicates my parents' house. "And there are some pretty impressive Cyclone women."

It's not like I don't deserve this. Not with the shit I've given her. Still, even though I keep telling myself that I need to do better, she knows exactly how to get under my skin.

"Give me some credit," I tell her. "If I wanted to date someone from Cyclone, I wouldn't limit myself to women."

She flushes slightly.

"And I wouldn't do it for the money," I continue, holding up my keyring. "You may have noticed that this is not a public entrance."

She blinks.

"This being Cyclone, whoever you're with likely said it was Sai's house. Maybe they called her Saint Kerawek. But Cyclone has this obsession with the whole first name hierarchy."

She hesitates one second—she probably doesn't know about the first name hierarchy—before nodding.

"So I'll explain. They call her 'Saint' for a number of reasons. First, because Sai is actually religiously observant. Second, because she works miracles. Third, because she intercedes on behalf of Cyclone employees with Adam Reynolds."

"Sure, Professor na Thalang." She folds her arms. "The job suits you. You get to be pedantic all day long. Are we done with this lecture yet?"

We aren't, and it rankles that she's...not entirely wrong about my tendency to go on. "*Finally,* she's called 'saint' because her login name at Cyclone is a combination of her nickname—Sai—and the initials of her last name."

Maria gets it the moment I say those words. She shuts her eyes. "Oh, shit."

"Sai na Thalang is my mother," I tell her. "You'll get no disagreement from me. There are some impressive Cyclone women. My mom is one of them. I'm proud of the fact that she will always outshine me, no matter what I accomplish. I wouldn't have it any other way. So if you're wondering what I'm doing here, I have the keys to this house."

She looks me over with a glint in her eyes. "No," she finally says bitterly. "Of course you belong here. You and your stupid put-on fake accent. Nobody picks up an accent in college. That is such pretentious bullshit."

My temper finally snaps. "Yes, of course. I talk like this because I just *love* it when people constantly ask me how it's possible that I have anything other than a vaguely caricatured accent. Globalism does not exist; my experience is just fake bullshit. But then, you would be the expert on fake bullshit."

I shouldn't have said that last. I know it the instant those words come out of my mouth.

Maria's fists clench and her eyes flash. "Call me fake one more time." She takes a step toward me. "I dare you. I really dare you."

She's not wearing perfume. I can still smell her. She reminds me of something sweet and feminine. There's a little lace over her cleavage, white against her skin.

And that's the moment when my brain intervenes, putting all the clues together.

I saw her face when I walked in, and while the view of her legs might have temporarily short-circuited my rational mind, details trickle back. Lips narrowed to a thin, pale line. Shaky breathing. The fact that she's here, alone in the mudroom, instead of outside with the crowd.

She did not look okay.

She does not sound okay now. Her voice trembles as she speaks, and if I didn't know better, I'd say she was on the verge of tears. For all the crap I've given her, I don't get the impression that Maria Lopez cries easily.

She was upset when I came in. She's worse now.

Shit. Shit. Shit. I wrestle with what to do for about three seconds before my conscience kicks in. It's early December, and I don't walk away from people who are upset.

Even if we will never get along.

Now that I'm looking at her—really looking at her—I can see all the signs I missed. Her chest moves in a shallow rhythm. Her eyes are wide and dark. I step forward, expecting her to slide away from me like we're two negatively charged particles.

She holds her ground.

"I know we don't like each other," I say. "But are you okay?"

"I'm fine," she bites off.

"Do you want me to find your friend? The housemate you mentioned? Or do you need a quieter place to sit where you won't be disturbed? I can get you into the private areas of the house."

She looks away. "You don't have to be nice to me. I'm upset because I broke a nail. That's all."

It's obvious she's lying. It's equally obvious she wants nothing to do with me. I can't blame her.

She raises her chin and glares me down, and for one stupid second, I wish that I hadn't fucked things up between us. That I'd let her talk when I saw her in September. That I'd given her a real apology before now. I wish Em had set me straight before I treated Maria like shit. Instead, we're stuck in a rut of snapping at each other.

"I'm sorry," I finally say. "I shouldn't have said any of that just now. You were right last time. I'm trying not to…" I give my head a shake. "But you really get under my skin."

She just continues to look at me. At first glance, I would have said her eyes were just dark brown. This close, I can see little gold flecks in them. It reminds me of a field trip to mining country I took when I was in high school. I stood in a creek and panned for gold in frigid waters. If I sloshed the water just right, little gold flakes rose to the top of the sand.

Looking into Maria's eyes, I can't help but think that there's gold in them thar hills.

If I didn't have logic, history, and economics to counsel me otherwise, I might throw everything away and go prospecting.

"I get under your skin." She doesn't move her eyes from mine. "Bullshit. You mean it pisses you off that I'm hot. You tell yourself I'm not real because that way, you can pretend this isn't happening."

Thank fuck for logic, history, and economics.

It's the first week of December. I'm aware of the shit I carry around with me. *Painfully* aware. And yes, I'm aware that she's hot.

"You remind me of someone." I take a deep breath. I hate that she has me pegged so well. "You're right. I've mucked this situation up from the beginning. I'm sor—"

She holds up a hand before I can finish. "Please don't apologize. I can't handle it. Hating you is kind of holding me together right now."

I bite back my words. Maria is smart. And she's resilient. She doesn't take my shit. For the first time, I admit the truth: We could have been friends. Gabe obviously thought we'd get along, or he wouldn't have shoved us together in the first place.

We could have been friends and instead, I hurt her. I have an image of the person I want to be, and this is not him.

Logic. History. Economics. I'm never going to be allowed to go prospecting for gold, no matter what untold riches her eyes promise.

"Fine," I say softly. "Then I'll just leave you to fall apart by yourself."

12.

MARIA

$\mathcal{T}$he little laundry room seems smaller and less safe after Jay leaves. I'm not sure how to take his being... Can I call it *nice,* after he accused me of fake bullshit?

No. But it was something approaching nice at a distance, and I didn't like it.

I count to one hundred, giving him ample chance to go far, far away, before I leave the room. The hall spills out onto a vast open-concept living area. The fact that the space looks massive even filled with all these people tells me it's gargantuan. Jay's parents live here. Nowhere is safe.

I sidestep a polite inquiry from someone I've never met. I find my shoes on the patio just outside the backdoor and skirt my way around the crowds in the outside yard. I fall back on my old methods of calming myself. First, I imagine the crowd as a zombie horde, decomposing in the sunlight. I look for safe places, wandering to the side fence. No good. With this many people around, I'd be eaten in three minutes at best.

Second, I take out my phone.

Quick, I write to Actual Physicist. *There's an earthquake right now. What do you do?*

Uh, comes his incredibly articulate response. *Right now? Like *now* now?*

Time, tide, and tectonics wait for no man.

I guess I get in a doorway?

Good answer. Doorways are safe. At least I hope they are wherever he is. I glance behind me. This house is probably okay. It looks like it was built recently enough to be seismically safe.

When I was in middle school and still living with my parents in Southern California, I used to imagine that the Big One—the fabled San Andreas fault quake that, to my great chagrin, still has not destroyed Orange County—would rip apart my classroom. It would make rubble of my parents' house. The destruction of society would have been simpler to navigate than what I faced.

So...why? Actual Physicist asks.

I've stopped wishing that the earth would swallow all my problems. Some safety blankets don't go away, though, and planning the disasters I don't live through has always helped me face the ones I do.

You know, I start to write lightly, *just your everyday average...*

I hit send, looking at that ellipsis, trailing off into the promise of whatever lie I want to tell. A light breeze is cool against my face. I could let my emotions go, pretend that they're washing away with the wind into the foothills. But I don't want to lie to him.

...method of handling some minor anxiety, I finish.

You okay?

I check my internal status. I'm breathing properly. My stomach isn't cramping. My pulse has steadied and slowed.

I'm okay, I type. *Just took me off guard. It's been a couple of years.*

I see the appeal of the world ending, he says. *Just promise that you'll take me with you when it does.*

My pulse starts up again—not in panic this time, but in anticipation.

I can't promise. I type this very slowly. *I don't know where you live. Or what your name is.*

Or what you look like, I don't write. Whether you'd like me if you saw me. I don't know what you'll say when you find out I'm trans. But I know we get along, and I'm tired of holding out.

I stand in place, holding my phone, watching the sun reflect on the surface. Waiting to see him type. As the seconds stretch to minutes, I want to kick myself. Why did I say anything?

Em, he finally writes. *I like you. I like you a lot. I like you so much that I think about meeting you all the time.*

My heart gives a happy thump. Then another. My head knows better. It knows the next word he is going to type so well that it's no surprise when it shows up on my screen.

But.

Of course there's a but. I know there's a but; it's why I've never forced the issue before now.

I like you so much that I don't want this to be serious. I don't want you to text me when you need me, thinking I'll be here. Because one day, I won't be.

I don't want to tell you about me. I don't want to know about you. We can't talk about this anymore, okay?

Shit. I swallow back hurt. Self-inflicted hurt, no less. It's not like he ever lied to me about what he wanted.

Fine, I type.

Okay?

I'm just fine. I knew this was going to happen. I did it to myself. Maybe, even, I did it now because I needed the reminder. Anj will mess up; Actual Physicist will push me away. It's never a good idea to expect anyone will care when I need them to. It never turns out.

I send him a thumbs-up and squish my stupid feelings back into the box where I was carrying them.

$\mathcal{I}$'m still looking at my phone when Anj finds me. She comes to stand next to me by the fence, biting her lip.

"Hey." I try to pitch my voice to normal.

She looks down. "I'm sorry, Maria. I'm so sorry. I slipped."

It wasn't just that. I exhale slowly. I try to imagine telling her the whole truth. *You see, Anj, it bothers me that your shark is more important than I am...*

"It's fine," I say instead. I'm saying that a lot these days. "Don't worry about it."

"Dammit, Maria. Don't tell me things are fine if they aren't. When you sit on shit, it turns into a blowup five months down the line, you moving out, and avoiding me for a year and a half."

I put one hand on my stomach and don't look at her. "I hate arguing. It never changes anything."

She comes and leans against the fence next to me. "I know. I'll shut up and let you talk. No arguing, okay? I promise."

I don't believe her. I look at her. She's standing next to me, one arm propped against the wood of the fence. In the distance, the party goes on, an incessant rumble of merriment.

Yeah. I could tell her. She'd listen. But even if she didn't argue aloud, she'd do it in her head. All love is conditional, and right now I don't want to hear another but. *I like you, but my shark is more important. I like you, but you just weren't a priority in the moment.*

It's fine. I don't need to push it.

"It's not you, Anj," I say, and in at least one way, this is true. "I told you. Sometimes I freak out. It just happens. It's not anyone's fault."

Nobody's but mine, for wanting stupid things.

Anj shifts uncomfortably next to me. "I'm not sure I believe you."

"I saw this guy I know, okay?" It's close to true. "He's a friend of Gabe's, and we don't get along, and he tells me I'm fake, and..."

And I trail off, because it's an effective lie. So effective, that Anj believes me.

"Oh." Anj straightens. "That asshole. What's his name, and where can we hide his body?"

Jay *was* a jerk. He also...almost, for a second wasn't.

I shake my head wearily. "Don't worry about it. He's dead to me, and that's good enough. Want to go find dessert?"

She looks at me a long time and sighs. "Okay."

13.

*E*ven though my parents don't drink, the morning after a party still feels like a hangover. The caterers cleared away the trash, but the house still feels subtly invaded—trampled paths, misplaced items on shelves. The silence seems to ring particularly loudly, as if the echo of a hundred conversations still lingers. Including the one I most want to forget—me telling Em I didn't want to know anything about her. But we're not revisiting that.

I'm in my parents' house, and it doesn't feel like home.

Not that this house ever felt like home to me. My parents had it built after my first year at university. I've only ever been a visitor to this space.

My dad pulls a pan from the oven, and the sweet smell of orange and cinnamon wafts over.

"Just a few minutes more," he says. "If I ice them now, it won't set."

"Fuck the icing," my mom responds. "I'm starving."

People who hear my mom on the phone before they see her usually imagine her as tall and white, even though her legal name is Kerawak na Thalang. She can muster an impeccable English accent when she wants, one that she learned in a posh, century-old British secondary school in Hong Kong. She swears up and down that the King George V school is *not* Hogwarts, even though she was actually sorted into a house—Rowell, not Ravenclaw.

She's tiny and brown, and today, she's wearing a blue shirt—the color of her house. The smile she gives my dad as he bats her questing fingers away from the steaming cinnamon rolls doesn't quite meet her eyes.

I don't think he and Mom could be more different. And yet up until that day in December more than a decade ago, they were always there for each other. Their romance started the day my dad got lost looking for a writing seminar on the Stanford campus and ran into my mother swearing at a vending machine in Thai.

"It was love at first sight," he used to tell anyone who would listen.

"No, it wasn't," my mother always corrected him. "It took me two weeks."

My dad's parents had been gently suggesting that he should find a wife on one of his summer trips back to Thailand.

"They wanted me to choose a nice, well-behaved Thai girl," he would say, looking into my mother's eyes.

"One point five out of four isn't bad," she'd answer. "I was a Thai citizen and I was a girl."

He wrote books; she wrote code. He was from one of the oldest, wealthiest, proudest Thai families; she was ethnically Chinese and hadn't lived in Thailand since she was a child. His parents were soft-spoken and polite; my mom swore up a storm and was far too Westernized for their tastes. Dad was an incurable romantic; Mom was blunt and questioning. He was a Buddhist; she was Muslim.

When I was five, I started kindergarten. After the usual introductions where we talked about what our parents did and where they were from, a red-headed kid at recess informed me solemnly that my parents were going to get divorced. Like his.

"Mom says that's what happens when people are too different," he told me.

It took two weeks of nightmares before my dad asked me what was wrong. He listened quietly when I told him, and patted my head.

"Your friend is wrong," he said. "Your mother and I don't *argue;* we disagree and we discuss. But if you look at us—really look at us—when we disagree you'll see that it's only our minds that are in dispute. Our hearts never change, no matter how different we are."

My dad was right, I came to realize. Nothing could tear them apart. Not religious differences. Not a move to another country. Not my mother's increasing work responsibilities nor her impossible schedule.

No matter how much they disagreed—and they *did* disagree—when they looked at each other, they always smiled. No matter how busy they were, they always had breakfast together. No matter how intense their schedule was, they somehow found a way to take a walk together at night. Even if my dad had to head down to the Cyclone campus near midnight to do it.

Nothing could get between them, I thought. Until I did.

They *look* okay now, if you don't know what to look for.

My dad shakes a finger at my mom. "I will defend my rolls with my honor."

"That's a poor choice of weapon." She pulls a butter knife out of the drawer. "Do you know how much military spending goes to the honor industry?"

"Mmm."

"Approximately nothing—just a few metal doodads and whatnots. A knife, on the other hand—"

She makes a stabbing motion toward the cinnamon rolls, and he grabs her wrist. They start laughing.

The noise seems a little too loud, echoing in a silence that returns in full force when they are quiet again. Their laughter feels like a teacup that has broken into a thousand pieces and been painstakingly pieced together again. It's laughter that recognizes the seams could burst at any time.

And when my parents put the teacup back together again, they didn't use all the pieces. Their laughter doesn't include me.

I don't blame them.

Twelve years ago, my parents split apart. They filed for a divorce the year I left for university. Turns out, the paperwork never went through. They patched things up as best as anyone could. Now they have a new home, new decorations, and a new marriage. Some things can be reforged after they break.

They still broke.

"Stop it, Sai," my dad says. "Are you twelve?"

"I lose a decade of emotional maturity for every ten minutes breakfast is delayed. You *know* this. But you had to show off with your yeast rolls and your fancy proofing."

"You'll wait and you'll like them."

"Oh, come on. What will a little pinch hurt?"

"Fine. Here. You can have a piece early. But just a piece."

I look away from their murmurs.

"Oh, look," Dad says. "We're embarrassing Jay. It's been so long since we managed that."

I turn back to them just in time to see them exchange a triumphant fistbump. I'm not embarrassed. I'm glad that I didn't ruin everything. I'm glad they still argue over cinnamon rolls and other trivialities.

"You're both twelve," I say.

"Yes," my father says, "maybe, but on the other hand, the rolls are cool enough to ice. Crisis averted."

"It's about time," Mom says as Dad turns his attention to the pan. "My stomach is shrinking in on itself. I swear it'll turn into a black hole if I don't eat."

I shake my head. "Fingernails scraping on a chalkboard, that's what you two are. That's not how black holes work."

"How do you know I haven't already produced one? If the event horizon is small enough—"

"Don't encourage him," my father says, putting plates on the table. "We were going to talk to him about his work habits, remember?"

It's ridiculous. I'm twenty-eight. I'm an adult, and one who is responsible for other adults at that.

Still, I hold my breath, hoping that they'll scold me.

"Oh, yes." My mother snaps her fingers and moves her plate to the other side of me, so that I am bracketed by them.

"You guys are going to lecture me about my work habits?" I fold my arms. "You two can hardly talk."

My mother glances down. Her eyes linger—briefly—on my forearms, on the geometric designs that crawl up past my elbow. The ink curls into the back of my hands. Twelve years out, the ink has faded from crisp black to a more muted brown.

Halfway through my final semester in high school, I drove myself to Vegas. Disappeared for three days. Got tattoos that were impossible for my parents to ignore, impossible to cover without long sleeves and gloves that would have been entirely impractical in California.

I came home, heart in my throat, positive that this, *this* would finally trigger their wrath.

They'd just looked at me in exhaustion when I walked in the door. Looked at each other.

"Where have you been?" my father asked.

"Vegas." I'd folded my arms defiantly so they could see the ink.

And I'd waited for the inevitable explosion. *Really, Jay? Is that the best you can do?*

No, I wanted to tell them. *No. I can do better. I should have done better.*

"Well." My father stood up. "I'll tell the police you've come home." And that was all the scolding I received.

That was the moment everything turned around. The moment I went from trying to get them to express their disappointment to trying to prove I deserved to have their expectations back.

I've been waiting twelve years.

And now, now…

"Oh, we wouldn't lecture you," my father says. "We were going to gently suggest a hobby. Tennis once a week. Something like that."

"Nothing so gauche as work-life balance," Mom says with her mouth full. "Just, you know, a *little* life atop all the work. For seasoning."

I smile. It feels like a mask. "Well, I'll just slot that into my copious spare time."

My mother rolls her eyes. "Listen to Mr. Smartypants. I *invented* copious spare time."

Dad cuts his pastry with a knife. "Sai, we agreed to be *respectful* of our child. Remember?"

"Yes, but—"

"I know we have to get used to it, but he's *Professor* Smartypants now."

They both burst out laughing, my mother choking on her food.

"Thanks, guys," I say sarcastically. But it's something. I'll take it, however little it is.

My mom pats my hand. "I just want you to consider that maybe—just maybe—if *I* think you could stand a little time off, you're overdoing it just a smidge, yes? I will *stab* you if you work yourself into a heart attack."

"And then your mother will go to jail," Dad says, "and where will that leave me?"

They ask for so little, and I owe them so much. I pretend to frown at my cinnamon roll. "Very well."

I'm joking. They're joking. We're all joking so hard, and it's just as well. As long as we're joking, we don't have to admit that Chase died twelve years from yesterday.

We don't talk about it. We don't visit his grave. We don't remember him in any way except in the overwhelming silences that swallow our laughter.

One settles on us now. This table is too big for just the three of us. There are too many cinnamon rolls.

I twitch restlessly in my seat. After Chase died, my parents couldn't even stand being around each other. I don't understand how they can bear to be around me.

Except they can, and if they want to spend time with me, I should make it happen. They don't ask for anything else. "I suppose," I say slowly, "I can take a day off next year. One."

"You see?" Mom smiles. "I knew he'd come around."

14.

January

*H*ELP ME, ACTUAL PHYSICIST. YOU'RE MY ONLY HOPE.

I haven't stopped talking to Em even after that night at my parents' house. I feel...terrible. I go back and look at the conversation—at the point where I told her I didn't want to know her—and I want to take it back.

Every time we've talked, I've wanted to say something. I want to tell her that the timing was awful. The anniversary of my brother's death always takes me hard.

But the truth remains: I still don't need to fall for Em any more than I have. And if I had a picture, a voice, a name...

I'm not sure who I'm fooling.

We still talk. We still joke. It's probably just me reading a stiffness into our interactions.

Wait, I say. *What is happening? Where are the plans? Are these the droids I'm looking for?*

Em types back. *Thank god you're there. I need someone to text me in five minutes and tell me there's an emergency.*

Oh? I raise an eyebrow.

This date is terrible, she says. *Neither of my BFFs are responding to my texts. You're the only person I know who won't be doing anything on a Friday night.*

Ouch. I frown at my screen.

It's shitty to be pissed that Em is out on a date. I told her I didn't want anything to happen with her. And even if I hadn't, I don't own her. She can date.

But, the unreasonable part of me grumbles, she doesn't have to tell me about it. Nor does she have to remind me that I'm preparing peer review reports at this time of night.

Pretty please? she asks.

I'm viciously, selfishly glad that her date is going badly.

Fine. It's a good thing tone doesn't translate over the internet. *You will have your "emergency" in five minutes.*

Son of a bitch. Em is dating. I always assumed she did, in fact. Casually. I figured that maybe she went out to a club a few times a month. She's busy, too—it's not like she'd have time for more than the occasional hookup. Nothing more meaningful than that.

I've always assumed she was shy, that those glorious shoes I saw earlier were her one way of defiantly standing out. But I know the truth. Someday, someone is going to break through her diffident exterior and discover that she's smart, funny, fantastic…

I drum my fingers on the table.

That someone isn't going to be me.

I know how things would turn out if we ever exchanged information. They'd turn out badly. I'd end up even more enamored of her than I am. We would talk on the phone. Eventually, we'd agree to meet. Even assuming that half-Chinese/half-Thai guys with confused accents do something for her, I work all the time.

Someday, she would need me, and I...

I shake my head. Nope. It's better this way.

My five minutes have passed. *Hey, Em,* I text, feeling almost malicious. *There's been an emergency Chihuahua invasion in the left reactor. We need you to call in the alligator squad stat.*

I go back to trying to figure out if there is actually any sense to be had in this mangled paper on fault-tolerant quantum computation.

Her reply comes twenty minutes later.

You're the worst. I laughed out loud. Like, sprayed Diet Coke on the table out loud. I had to lie my ass off.

You're welcome, I say. *This is what you get when you text a social recluse on a Friday night.*

No, there's nothing barbed in my response. Not at all.

Aw, A. Did I hurt your feelings?

Yes. A little. *I don't know what you're going on about,* I write stiffly. *Reading papers is a perfectly acceptable activity on a Friday night.*

I need to get laid, is what I need to do. I frown at the ceiling.

Also, I write, *I'm hideously ugly and have a terrible personality. This is why I've devoted my life to science.*

Maybe I want her to ask again. To tell me to send a picture so she can judge for herself.

Not me, comes her reply. *I have a scintillating personality, and I'm drop-dead gorgeous. If we ever met in person, you'd probably burst into flames.*

I've maintained a mental image of Em—sandy-brown hair, too tall, reluctant to maintain eye contact. I know she was bullied in middle school. I've imagined her in glasses, hiding behind a book.

That image of her goes up in smoke now. I am in flames. I am burning up.

I don't think she's teasing me. She says it with an assured confidence that is completely at odds with the image I have in my head.

Yes, she continues, *even if you're not into women. It's not a sexual thing. I'm just that hot.*

You don't need to convince me, I write. My dick is hard. It needs no convincing. *My sexuality has always been people who aren't afraid of differential equations.*

She doesn't respond. I don't blame her. I know I'm being inconsistent. I know it's not fair, least of all to her, for me to jerk her around this way.

There are so many questions she could ask. *What are you waiting for?*

What do you want?

What the hell is your problem?

My phone stays silent. It would be easy if Em were just a girl I didn't know in a club. I imagine her like that—meeting her, not knowing her. She'd be in the back. We'd make eye contact, and I would drift over and start talking.

We'd make jokes. She'd ask me about my accent. I'd ask her about…whatever struck my fancy.

I'd talk her into my bed before I knew I could fall in love with her. I'd take off her clothes, piece by piece, touching her, teasing her into every yes. I'd go down on her until she screamed. I'd get her on top of me, let her ride me, set her own pace, her own angle, until...

I undo my jeans. My hand is on my cock, stroking unconsciously, and I give up. Give in to the fantasy of Em in my bed. Sighing into my ear. Breathing hard, then harder, then setting me on fire as my orgasm comes.

It doesn't make me feel better, just less horny. My mind-fog clears after I come.

Em is not in my bed. I'm not going to run into her in real life. I'm not going to get to know her slowly, find myself entangled before I realize how hard she's caught me.

I'm here. She's...wherever *there* is. I'm entangled now; I just don't want to admit it.

I glance at my phone. I imagine her putting her hand on her hip and shaking her head.

What are you waiting for? She hasn't asked. She hasn't responded to me at all, and I can't blame her.

With my mind now cleared of lust, the answer to that question is obvious. I'm waiting until I believe that Em can have expectations of me.

15.

MARIA

Late February

There are seven of us crammed into a table intended for four, and after three drinks, I really don't care. Anj is on my right; Tina on my left. We're packed thigh-to-thigh, with Erin next to Anj, and Lee, Shan, and Sonia—who I do *not* know, but she's dating Shan—on the other side.

I'm pretty sure it's only been three drinks, which is a sign my tolerance is slipping. It may be Tuesday, but I don't care.

"Is this your twenty-first?" Shan asks.

"Oh, honey." I beam at her over the table. "You're so sweet. I'm twenty-five."

"Quarter century," Anj says brightly, leaning against me.

"Old enough to..." Lee has had a little too much to drink, and zie can't hold zir liquor. "Dammit," zie says. "That oughta be more of a milestone. It sounds like a good one, but you don't get anything at twenty-five."

"Old enough to rent a car!" Tina supplies beside me.

"There we go. You're old enough to rent a car."

"No, no." Anj shakes her head. "You can do that before twenty-five. You just need to get your agent to prescreen your insurance, and contact the corporate..." She trails off. Clears her throat.

For a moment, everyone is looking at her. Anj laughs brightly. "Oh, shit." She runs her hands down her sweater.

"Shut up, Anj," Shan says. "Your rich is showing."

"Dammit. I hate when that happens." But she laughs it off. "Here's to Maria again, then—old enough to rent a car without using her personal staff."

"Here's to my *getting* a personal staff. One day." I brandish my almost-empty cocktail.

"Shit. I'll drink to that."

We do. My drink is citrus and sweet and half-vodka, and it goes down nicely. I feel fuzzier, happier, braver.

I take another slice of pizza. The food here is pretty good—good enough that there's a steady stream of college kids and some actual adults picking up takeout at the front desk.

We're not here for the food, though. The drinks are out of this world. The bartenders have served up things none of us have even heard of—not even Anj—and we're only on our fourth round. Or our third. Maybe our fifth.

Lee grabs the menu. "I want something on fire."

Tina shakes her head. "What, and burn off all the alcohol? That's a waste."

"No, they put extra in—oh, shit, this is Kahlúa and rum and ice cream."

"It's too cold for ice cream," Shan says.

"Not with that much rum it's not."

We look around the room to find our waiter.

But before I catch sight of him, I see someone else. Standing in the takeout line.

It's Jay na Thalang, and his arms are folded. God *damn*, I run into that fucker everywhere. He's talking to the person up front, who is shaking his head apologetically.

I can't hear the conversation, not over my friends, who aren't even the loudest people in the place.

Jay glances at his watch and grimaces.

The man says something to him; Jay shrugs, and retreats to a seat.

Aw, poor baby. They must have lost his takeout order. He's going to have to waste time. I feel an evil grin take over my face. Man, that's gonna burn.

Shan waves her hand and our waiter starts over.

The motion also catches Jay's eye. He looks up, sees me…

I know he recognizes me, because I can see that apprehensive look in his eyes. I mean, not really. I can't *really* see it—he's too far away, and the lighting isn't that good—but his eyes narrow, and I know what he thinks of me.

Yeah. I'm getting drunk with friends on a Tuesday. Fucking sue me for being irresponsible, asshole. Jay judging me is the world doing its regular thing.

Our waiter shows up. "Another round, ladies?"

There's a pause. Lee shifts uncomfortably. Shan bites her lip.

"People," Anj says. "A good collective noun for a group of us is *people*."

"Oh. My bad. People, what can I get you?"

Lee orders zir drinks—*both* the flaming one and the one with ice cream. Anj gets another beer and orders deep-fried cheese curds.

I frown at her. "You haven't had vegetables all evening."

"Sorry, *Mom.*"

"Oh, god, do you call her that, too?" Tina says.

"Duh. Everyone does." Anj frowns at the waiter. "Do you have a fried vegetable on your menu, perchance?"

"Perchance?" Lee laughs. "Who says perchance?"

"Fried zucchini?" The waiter ignores our byplay.

"Ew. Slimy." She makes a face. "Edamame, then. They're green."

"They're *legumes,* not vegetables," I protest.

"They'll do," Anj pronounces. "And I won't have to eat all of them. I can have a single edamame and pawn the rest of them off on you healthy people."

"Is the singular of edamame really edamame? Or is it edamamus?"

"What are you doing? Edamame isn't Latin."

My friends continue this argument about the proper linguistic classification of the word edamame, and the waiter turns to me. "And what'll you have?"

"Another one of these…"—I tap my glass, but I don't remember what the drink was called—"These citrusy fizzy things."

"Got it."

Across the room, Jay shifts in his chair across from the register. My mouth moves before I can use my brain properly.

"Can I send a drink to someone else?" Oh, I *am* drunk.

The waiter just smiles. "Of course."

Anj breaks off her argument with Shan about soybeans. "Wait just a minute. You're sending someone else a drink? Who?"

"Okay, don't look at him all at once. That guy over there, sitting by the cashier."

Of course, they all look over at once. Jay has actually taken out his laptop, and he's staring at the screen. Poor asshole.

"You like him?" Shan frowns. "He's hot."

"I *dislike* him." I fumble in my purse. "Intensely. Who has a pen?"

The waiter watches with amusement.

I grab a napkin and scrawl a message, which Anj insists on narrating over my shoulder. *HEY, THREE SIGMA. LOOK AT YOU, RELAXING, TAKING TIME OFF.*

I write in all-capitals because I'm pretty sure my regular handwriting would be illegible due to aforementioned drunkenness.

DRINK THIS AND MAYBE YOU WON'T IMPLODE FROM HORROR.

"And what drink am I bringing this fine gentleman?"

"Hmm. How pink is the Juliet and Romeo?"

He grins. "*Excessively* pink. And it has the egg white froth, so…"

"That one." I nod decisively.

Of course, after our waiter leaves, I have to deliver the story about how he called me a distraction to my brother and too girly, and then called me fake bullshit. I don't mention him apologizing or asking if I was okay. Dammit, it's my birthday. If I want to bug the shit out of him, I will.

"What a bag of dicks," Shan says.

I hand the waiter a twenty, and he disappears with our order.

We all watch as two minutes later, he approaches Jay, drink in hand.

Jay looks up from his laptop, blinking.

"I hear if a chemist sees his shadow in a bar, we'll have eight more weeks of winter," Shan says. We all laugh.

He looks at the drink. He looks over at me. He reads the napkin. I can't see his facial expressions from here. I hope he's pissed.

He sets his laptop on his seat, and drink in hand, goes to the front where he is given the drink menu.

He doesn't take long. He scrawls something on a napkin, tips the delicate flute back, and downs the pink, frothy concoction all in one go.

Three minutes later, the waiter returns with a thick tumbler for me with an inch of gold liquid and a napkin. *His* handwriting is square and pristine.

Apparently you want things to be simple, so I'll play bad guy. That drink you sent me is what you get when you mix everything together. Nice work, omnivore. But the world's most complex and interesting beverage comes from a single source.

Of course he sent me a single malt.

Share it with your friends, he continues. *Between the seven of you, you might comprehend it.*

"He went there." Lee turns Jay's note over. "He totally went there."

I just smile and turn to the waiter. "What can you make with absinthe? *Lots* of absinthe."

He smiles broadly. "We have a lovely sazerac, but that's really only an absinthe rinse. But you could probably order an off-menu shot on the rocks."

"You know," Tina says, "absinthe doesn't really make you—"

"Hush." I bend over my napkin. "Stop nitpicking."

MODERN SCIENCE HAS PROVEN ABSINTHE TO BE COMPLETELY SAFE, I write. *TOO BAD. IT'LL HAVE TO BE THE THOUGHT THAT COUNTS.*

"*Hell* yeah." Lee grins.

I sip my single malt. At this point, I'm mixing liquors. I'm going to have a hell of a hangover in the morning. I don't care.

Five minutes later, our waiter is back. This time, he sets something gold and bubbly in front of me.

Ginger is an old Asian remedy for increasing mental acuity and reversing memory loss. Unlike your drink, this one is scientifically proven to work. I don't know if it's indicated for whatever you're dealing with, but it can't hurt.

My table reads this in silence. At first.

Tina speaks first. "A, it's a *Chinese* remedy, not a generically *Asian* one, so—"

"Cool your jets," Anj intervenes. "The Chinese were total colonizers. Everyone uses ginger. I bet he's part Chinese anyway. Pretty common in a lot of southeast Asia."

She frowns. "You think?"

"Yeah. The nose…"

I tune out their discussion and focus on the problem at hand. Namely, how to respond.

I finish the gingery cocktail in one long swallow. Then I open my purse and unsnap the container of Mace I keep on my keyring.

I drop this in the glass.

IT HELPED! My handwriting has become progressively less legible over the course of the evening. *I JUST REMEMBERED SOMETHING I NEEDED TO DO. BE A DOLL, AND SPRAY YOURSELF IN THE FACE WITH THIS.*

We have to bribe the waiter with a twenty to deliver this. Jay looks at it, reads the napkin without a flicker of response, sets the glass on a table to one side, and picks up his laptop again.

He works for the next five minutes without looking up, until the kitchen approaches him with a plastic bag filled with containers. He stands, pays, and then turns back to the chair he has occupied for the last twenty minutes. He packs his laptop, then picks up the glass.

He turns.

His eyes meet mine. Then—my heart skips a beat—he starts toward me, step by liquid step. He walks with a grace I can't ignore, not as tipsy as I am.

"Oh, shit," Anj says, taking my arm. "He's coming over."

He doesn't look at my friends. He doesn't look at the waiter. He just takes the glass with my little container of Mace and rattles it in front of me.

"Did you know that pepper spray has a Scoville rating of three or four million heat units?" He asks this question in an amused, conversational tone. "That's ten times hotter than a habanero pepper, but about five times less potent than pure capsaicin."

I search for a brilliant response.

"Uh," I manage.

"The scary thing," he continues, "is that concentrated asinine obtuseness burns twelve times hotter."

My mouth moves. Nothing comes out.

He upends the glass on the table. My pepper spray rattles and falls out. "You don't need that," he says. "Between the two of us, I think we've had enough stupid. I'm done getting burned."

I gulp.

"Have a good evening, Maria. And friends."

He smiles at us, then turns away. As he leaves, I laugh. It's the only thing I know how to do under the circumstances. I can't really complain; I *did* send him drinks telling him I wanted him dead and/or pepper-sprayed. I can't complain that he fought back. After all, I started this round.

"Well played, Jay."

He stops. He almost turns.

A dim memory of a much, much earlier insult comes to mind.

"You know," I say. "The asshole police won't—" Goddamn. Nothing is coming out of my mouth properly. "The asshole police aren't out giving tickets." There was more to that insult. Dammit. How did it go?

Jay blinks. He frowns at me, probably trying to figure out what the words coming from my mouth even mean. Then he sighs. "Serious question. Do the asshole police give out tickets for being an asshole or for not being one?"

My nitpick. He stole my nitpick.

"They ticket *you*," I say with as much drunken solemnity as I can muster. "They are your own personal police."

He does show some emotion then. He smiles involuntarily. And I hate, absolutely hate, the little sparks of whatever it is that flutter through me when he does.

I hate that I lied to my friends about him. I hate that he's not simple. I hate that his eyes dip briefly to my tight shirt, and I hate that I don't hate that he looks.

"Drink some water, Maria," he says dryly. "You're going to need it."

I watch him walk away. He moves easily. Like he doesn't need to turn back and look at me.

"I don't need water," I mutter. "I need more alcohol."

"Coffee." I clutch the five in my hand almost desperately the next morning. "Black. The darkest roast you have. Please."

And *fast*. I don't say that, though, because I've been a barista before, and my splitting hangover is not their problem.

They aren't fast. I stand to the side, clutching my plastic number, wishing my eyelids didn't feel like sandpaper.

My head feels like cotton. My mouth is dry, and the low rustling murmurs of the coffee shop around me seem magnified and echoing. With my eyes shut, the sounds seem louder. More invasive. More...

"We have to stop meeting like this," says a low voice, practically in my ear.

I jump, startled.

Jay is standing right next to me. He has a smile on his face, probably because he knows—down to the drink—how shitty my hangover is at the moment. I squeeze my eyes shut.

"Is there a name for that phenomenon where you keep running into the wrong person?" he asks.

I don't rub my eyes because dammit, I'm not about to smear my eyeliner. "Sounds like a form of confirmation bias," I mutter. "There are probably dozens of people you see on a regular basis. You just don't notice them because you don't know them."

"Oh." His lips twitch into a smile. "You know, you really should drink some water. Coffee is a diuretic."

"Not as much as people think. Your body gets used to it." I think about this. "Mine does, at any rate. No comment on yours."

But my eyes drop accidentally to his chest on those words. That thing where you keep running into someone... It's not fate. It's not a sign. It doesn't mean anything except that I notice him. And I do. He's watching me with a suspicious expression. Like he remembers last night, and...

And, oh my god. I do, too. I bought him *drinks* and sent him *messages,* and pointed as they were, I could have hung a sign around my neck that said: *I NOTICE YOU.* In big, flashing, barely legible capital letters.

A flush of embarrassed heat creeps up my cheeks.

"Besides," I say with a determined brightness, "I had a ginger lemonade this morning, and everyone knows ginger improves mental acuity."

His smile broadens.

"Right now," I say, "I have the mental reflexes of a..."

I trail off. I can suddenly remember Anj and Tina arguing over whether he was part Chinese. I can't tell, but now I'm looking at his nose, his cheekbones, the shape of his lips, as if there is some secret in them.

"Don't leave me hanging. The mental reflexes of what?"

"The mental reflexes of someone who can't think of a good analogy," I say with forced cheer.

He laughs. It's a low, husky laugh, and for one second, I can't tell if he's laughing with me or at me. Then I realize I'm not laughing.

He's holding his drink in a cardboard cup, and I still have a plastic number. Why is he still here?

"Don't you have photons to excite?"

"Photons to excite, populations to invert, and qubits to entangle." He raises his cup in its cardboard sleeve as if in a toast.

But he doesn't leave.

"Okay." I look desperately at the coffee bar behind me. "Let me go before I need to signal a friend to fake-text me an emergency to escape this conversation."

His face goes blank. Utterly blank. For just one second. Then he shakes his head. "I think I hear your phone right now."

"Right. *I'd* have to come up with the emergency, as the one of us who has friends."

He just shrugs. "Bye, Maria. Drink water."

Then, thank god, he leaves.

My coffee still hasn't shown up, but at least I don't have to invent an emergency after all. The last time that happened...

Ha. I smile in bitter memory. That smile lasts about four seconds. Four seconds, while I think of the conversation I had with Actual Physicist. I hate that I'm hung up on him. I need to get over it. I need to go out and find someone and forget, and never mind that I've *tried* that.

Except... In the space of time it took me to think that, an errant tug of memory surfaces. I remember last night, and the drinks, and coming home with Tina, and...

"Oh, no," I moan. "No, I didn't. Please tell me I didn't. Please please please..."

I fumble my way into the chat app. My pleas to erase reality are futile.

Oh, *god*. I *did*.

1:03 AM
Okay you know what, A.? Fuck you.

1:16 AM

Seriously. Fuck you. You wanna pretend we're not really friends.

1:17 AM
That I don't really exist. That I don't have a name or a face.

1:22 AM
But you know what? I have actually been there for you. I have listened to you and supported you and told you about things that matter to me.

1:31 AM
And I am fucking tired of you pretending that this is fake, that we don't know each other.

1:35 AM
I am tired of you flirting with me, then pretending we're nothing.

1:45 AM
And I don't mean that friend zone shit. If all you want is to be friends it's cool.

2:18 AM
You flirt with me and make me feel like the most important person in your life.

2:19 AM
Then you don't even want to know my name. How do you think that makes me feel?

2:42 AM

I believe in respecting boundaries. But your inconsistent boundaries are hurting me.

3:16 AM
For the record, my name is spelled like this:
F-U-C-K
O-F-F

---

*O*h my god. Oh my god. My coffee arrives as I'm staring at my phone; I inhale it in a giant slurp that burns the roof of my mouth.

I check the read receipts. Yep. He saw them at six this morning. Fuck. I hadn't thought that anything could make my hangover worse, but apparently, two hours of drunken, angry texts will do it.

Actual Physicist has not answered. I glance at the time. It's eleven in the morning, and he hasn't answered. The only time he has ever taken that long to answer anything I wrote has been when he was on an intercontinental flight.

Another gulp of searing coffee blisters my throat.

I don't know what to say. How to fix this. I just know I have to say it.

Hey, A., I write. *I'm sorry. I'm so, so sorry.* It looks stupid appended to that chat.

I hit send anyway.

Three seconds later, three dots appear. He's typing. But they go away, and I don't get a response.

I don't get anything at all.

16.

I stumble through the day with the dedication and grace of a Jersey cow performing *Swan Lake*. I nurse a pounding headache that coffee, Advil, and water cannot fix.

I get notes from friends for the two morning classes I missed. I attend my afternoon class on game theory with a grim determination to do something right, and I hope the word salad I blankly transcribe will make sense to non-hungover me in some alternate universe, which preferably will start tomorrow.

I retreat home at the first possible instant.

The sound of water running in the kitchen sink greets me as I unlock the door. It must be Tina; Blake has a class, and besides, the chances of Blake doing dishes without a reminder are about equal to the possibility of an asteroid strike.

I set my bag on the front table, kick off my heels, and move into the open kitchen. The blinds are open, sunlight spilling across granite countertops.

"Hey," I say, turning to the sink. And then I stop.

There's a man standing at the sink, calmly rinsing off a pan. He's older. His hair is a mix of dark and gray and white. He's grayer than his publicity photos. I stare at him first in surprise, then in abject horror. Oh, fuck.

He looks up. His eyes land on me. They narrow briefly, and then he gives me the world's most abbreviated nod. He turns off the water, gives the pan a shake, and sets it on the drying rack.

"You must be Maria." His voice is like gravel.

Once I put a jar of honey in the refrigerator. I remember trying to pour it, holding it upside down and whacking it before realizing it was a futile endeavor. This is what my brain feels like at the moment.

He dries his hands on a towel. "I'm Adam," he says. "Blake's father."

I swallow. "I know."

Adam Reynolds is… He's a legend, so much of one that I still don't know how to get my mind around the fact that my roommate is dating his son. He founded Cyclone Technologies almost thirty years ago and nurtured it from an infant database software company to one of the largest corporations in the world.

He didn't do it by being nice. People usually describe Cyclone as a cult of personality. Adam swears frequently in public, and from all accounts he's worse in private. Blake insists he's a really good guy and not at all an asshole. In private, Tina has informed me that he's not *always* an asshole, which is an amendment that means absolutely nothing. There is, according to Tina, an entire handbook floating around Cyclone about how to manage Adam fucking Reynolds. *The first rule of AFR club is don't talk about AFR club.*

I feel like I've opened the front door to discover a grizzly bear waiting in the hallway. I can't remember if you're supposed to run from bears.

Dammit, Blake. A little notice would have been appreciated.

One of the richest men in the world is doing dishes in my kitchen. You know. No big deal. I have the sudden urge to laugh hysterically.

"Hi." My throat is dry. I tentatively hold my hand out.

He must see that motion, but he doesn't shake my hand. Instead, he turns away, finds a towel, and starts drying the pan that he just cleaned. I'm left with my hand hanging in midair. I swipe it against my jeans.

What are you doing here? What should I do?

"Don't worry," he says dryly. "I don't practice cannibalism during daylight hours."

I choke. "That's...good?"

I should just leave. Yes, it would be rude, but on the other hand, this is Adam Reynolds.

He puts the pan away.

"During daylight hours," he says, "I just do dishes." There's a glint in his eye. He might be joking.

"I see that." I swallow. "Um. Why? Why are you doing dishes?"

He shrugs. "They're Blake's, aren't they?"

"Yes."

He shakes his head sadly. "Literally my kid's only fault. He's a fucking mess. Never picks up after himself."

I draw in a breath. "He's not...that bad."

Adam Reynolds raises an eyebrow in my direction. "I lived with him for twenty-two years of his life. If you're going to lie to me, at least choose a flavor of bullshit that I'm not intimately familiar with. He is exactly that bad."

"Okay," I manage. "Fine."

"Jesus fucking Christ," he says, in what I think might be an attempt on his part to manage a conversational tone. "What the fuck has Tina been telling you about me? Am I that terrible?"

It's not just what Tina says. I mean, practically all of Cyclone is willing to sing his praises. *Yes, he's an asshole, but…* But he's apparently a *compelling* asshole.

He's fine, Tina once told me, *as long as you don't ask him personal questions.*

Truth is, Adam Reynolds is like the popular guy at school times seven hundred. The guy who knows he's got it and doesn't have to try. He's the one who would sit on a virtual throne at lunch, surveying the crowd of kids as if he were a lion overlooking a savannah, trying to find the weakest wildebeest.

I was always the weakest wildebeest. I don't exactly have the best track record with people like Adam.

"Tina's as much of an apologist as Blake," I say.

The corner of his lip twitches up. "There, see? I was pretty fucking sure you had more than a couple monosyllables in you." He pulls out a chair at the island and sits. "So is it just my reputation, or something specific?"

I swallow. "Your reputation is pretty specific."

"Yeah." He's smiling. "It's pretty useful, but I swear on my fucking market cap, I don't usually terrorize children."

"I'm not a child."

He pulls out his phone. "Sure." The word has a mocking edge. He glances at the face of his phone, shrugs, and looks back at me. "Let's have this conversation in twenty years. You're a fucking baby. You just don't know it yet."

There is zero chance that I'll be running into Adam Reynolds in twenty years, but I'm not about to argue with him again. I take out my phone.

He must see something on my face.

"What," he says. "You don't think you'll still be friends with Tina in twenty years?"

I swallow.

"Or do you think that Tina and Blake won't be together then?"

"If we're all babies, why *would* they be together?"

He shrugs. "Blake's twenty-five. That's old enough to know."

"How on earth would *you* know anything about relationships?" Between the hangover and the nerves, the words slip out.

He looks over at me, and for a long moment, I get the feeling that he's considering his next words. His fingers tap on the counter.

It's at this moment—with the hammer-like pain of a headache pulsing through my head—that I realize the truth.

I love Tina.

I *hate* living with Tina and Blake. It's not that they're inconsiderate. It's not that they're coupled off and I'm not. But they're here, doing couply-things, inviting Blake's terrible father over and not warning me about it. None of this is wrong. They *live* here. I just don't *like* it.

I hate not feeling secure in my own space. I hate feeling like I can't complain. It reminds me of living with Anj. It reminds me of...

No. Not going there. All my complaints swell in my chest, a tight bubble of irrational need.

"Good point." Adam Reynolds shakes his head, and I'm reminded of that lion, scenting a wildebeest. "How the fuck would I know dick about interpersonal relationships?"

Great. I've offended him. I gather up my bag and retreat to my room with a whispered excuse.

I hate everything.

J A Y

It's almost eleven at night.

Today has been ridiculous, packed with faculty meetings, a university committee that was never supposed to take up so much time but which will end up being the primary university service component of my tenure application, an unexpected conference call with a colleague...and Em's messages, which I haven't known how to answer.

Your inconsistent boundaries are hurting me. I felt that one. Felt it deep in me.

But tomorrow promises to be equally terrible. The final committee report is due. A faculty candidate is coming through, and I've been drafted as the New Guy/Representative College of Chemistry Minority to be in the group that takes her to lunch. Gabe is giving a seminar up the hill in the evening, so everything I put off today has to be shoved into my nonexistent spare time tomorrow.

And I can't imagine what Em must be feeling. I haven't been able to condense my response into my available time. I'm staring at my screen, trying to figure out what to say. How to say it. What I'm feeling.

Then I see she's writing. A message pops up a moment later.

So the only thing worse than repeated late-night profanity-laced messages would probably be repeated apologies. I'm mortified. I'm sorry. Your friendship is really important to me.

My lip curls, and I manage to condense my complicated, fucked-up feelings into one single word.

Don't, I type.

She doesn't respond. And now that I've broken through that barrier, I can't stop.

Don't apologize. Don't stop having expectations for me.
Don't. Don't. Don't.

She responds with her own tentative single syllable.

A.?

I've read her messages a dozen times in the last day. I know them by heart, every last excoriating word.

And maybe that's why I tell her the thing I didn't realize until it's sliding out of my fingers.

Let me lay this shit out on the table.

I know you're interested in me. You want to know what my name is. What I look like. You want to maybe meet up sometime and see if our real-life chemistry is as good as it is online.

I don't wait for a response.

On my part…

I stare at my phone. Thinking, trying to figure out how to tell her what she means to me. I don't know how to put it in words. And then I do.

Imagine me drawing Maslow's pyramid of needs, I write. *At the base are the fundamental requirements: food, shelter, wifi.*

This gets a response from her. *Ha.*

On the tiers above are things like social acceptance. Basic scientific research. Baklava.

Of course, Em says. *The well-known baklava tier.*

I take a breath, and put it out there. *You do not show up in the drawing.*

While I'm writing my next line, her response comes through. *Gee. Thanks.*

I shut my eyes and hit send. *You are the table the drawing rests on. Em, I'm pretty much in love with you.*

Fuck. That's out there, then. She doesn't say anything, and I can imagine her shock reverberating back through my phone.

I shoved you away pretty hard in December. It was the anniversary of my little brother's death. I should be over it. I'm not.

I don't think I'll ever be over it. She doesn't say anything in response. I only know Em is there and listening because my messages change from delivered to read, one by one.

In high school I was… Popular is the wrong word, but maybe respected? I was in all Honors classes. On the tennis team etc etc. I was a workaholic then, too.

I'm typing more slowly now.

My little brother was a freshman when I was a senior. I knew he wasn't popular. I knew kids teased him. But I thought he'd figure it all out. Kids do. I was busy. When shit was really bad, I let him eat lunch with me and my friends.

I don't want to finish the story, but now I have to.

My parents were busy. My mom is a software engineer, and she had a project on deadline. My dad is an author, and he was also on deadline. And I was busy, dammit, because I'm always busy.

Received, the message status says. Then: read.

I go on.

I didn't know how bad it was. Typing those words hurts, because they sound like an excuse. I don't give myself excuses. I don't deserve excuses. *I should have known. I was at tennis practice the day my brother posted on his LiveJournal that he wouldn't kill himself as long as one person smiled at him on the way home.*

He got one response: "Go ahead. No one cares." By the time I got home, it was too late.

Oh, A., she finally writes. *I'm sorry.*

Yeah. So am I. I should have been there. But it was worse than that.

The girl who wrote it… We were dating. She was sick of Chase eating with us at lunch.

Oh, Em says. *No.*

She didn't think he would do it, I respond. *I'll give her that much. But of all the things my parents ever asked me to do, "Look after your brother" was the big one. And I fucked it up. I'm kind of a mess. I'm freaked out at the idea of people relying on me. I'm freaked out at the idea of them not. I feel like I'm a failure no matter what I do, and I'm afraid of failing you.*

A., she writes. *It's okay.*

It isn't. *I don't want to hurt you,* I tell her. *That was all. I didn't want to hurt you, and I did.*

There's a whole tangle of other emotions. I'm not sure how to explain to her that I want her to expect things of me. That I'm afraid I'll mess it up anyway. I basically said everything with *I'm pretty much in love with you.*

It's late as it is.

Hey, she writes. *So. I have some issues, too. I get it.*

Yeah.

When I was twelve, she says, *my parents kicked me out of the house. It's more complicated than that. I went back for some summers to try therapy with them. It never worked out.*

While I'm trying to digest the scope of that, she continues.

My mom's mother got divorced, and people looked down on them. Or maybe Mom looked down on herself. She didn't want her kids to deal with any kind of stigma. She had everything planned out for us. Then she got me.

I squint at the phone.

And I was not a boy, Em writes. *Even though that's the gender they assigned me at birth.*

It takes a moment for the clue to sink in. For me to understand that she's telling me that she's transgender. To remember months ago, when she sent me that picture of those shoes and told me that she wore them to remind herself that she deserved to feel pretty and feminine.

It all makes sense. I want to gather her up and tell her that she deserves her shoes. That she never deserved what happened to her.

Em's been typing as I try to align my thoughts. *So she'd scold and complain and threaten. I have this thing I do where I just keep quiet, and keep quiet, until I cross some line and suddenly—well, I guess you know now.*

Yeah, I do.

We had a huge fight when I was twelve, Em says. *Mom and Dad and me, and they told me I'd either go to the military boys' school they'd picked out or I'd have to leave.*

Shit, I type. *That sucks.*

My older brother gave me a hundred bucks, she writes, *and I took a bus up to my grandmother's. I had no idea what she would do. I was scared the whole way, but she was my best hope. Even though she was an observant Catholic. When I visited her, she always used to go to mass and take us with her. She prayed to the Virgin Mary for miracles. She had a portrait of Thomas More in her office.*

Shit, I write. *I'm not going to like the way this turns out, am I?*

But she'd always been… Nice, I guess. I arrived on her doorstep at 11 at night and told her everything. I asked her if she thought God could make me into a girl. If that was the kind of miracle he did.

Shit, I write for a third time.

And she said…

I wait. Unable to look away from the phone.

She said, "I think He already did."

I let out a breath I didn't know I'd been holding.

Obviously, she writes, *I have issues with…so much of the Catholic Church. And so does she, really. Religion is a weird mix of weird and ugly and incomprehensible, but it also has in it this beautiful thing that made her love me exactly as I landed on her doorstep. That's why I still go to mass with her on Sundays when I can. It's why when I legally changed my name, I took hers as my middle name. Camilla. So. There you are. I'm complicated. I have issues. I get it.*

I don't have a good response. Not in words. Instead, I send her an emoji string: a heart, a bowl of soup, and heels.

Sorry, I append. *Bad at words.*

No, she types. *I'm pretty sure that's emoji for "hold me."*

Exactly right. She's exactly right.

I sit in place.

I still don't know her name. I still haven't seen so much as a picture. I'm pretty sure that I'm more in love with her than before this conversation started. I don't know how to move forward, but I can't stay in place.

The one thing I'm sure of is that I don't want to hurt her.

My number is 650-555-2761, I write. *I think we're beyond a selfie or two at this point. I want to do this right. I want to hear your voice.*

There's a bit of a pause before she responds. *That's a Bay area code. I'm 415-555-3113.*

That's San Francisco. My pulse is racing. She's right across the Bay. Has been this entire time.

And, she continues, *it's past midnight. I have a hangover, and I need to be up by eight. Call me vain, but when we talk for the first time I want my voice to sound its dulcet best.*

I look through my calendar. Work, work, work, and then Gabe has a seminar in the evening and I've already committed to dinner. *Tomorrow sucks. I have a late afternoon thing and dinner with friends. But I can beg out by eight or so. Pacific time.*

The silence that follows seems fraught.

This is why I was afraid of this, I say. *I'm so fucking busy. We'll get together, and then in a month I'll be like, bye, have to go to Australia for two weeks! I don't want you to hate me.*

A., she says, *I'm busy, too. I was just about to say that if we make it tomorrow at nine Pacific time I can make it.*

Shit. This is happening. This is really happening. I'm scared. My nerves tingle in anticipation. And if her phone number is any guide, she lives just across the Bay.

I'm glad we're still friends, she says. *Who else would I get to emergency-text me, after all?*

I manage a halfhearted smile. *I was just thinking about that earlier today. You know, I think we may be quantum entangled?*

Quantum entangled?

You know. Transmitting information to each other faster than the speed of light.

For me, it's a second way of saying I'm half in love with her already. And maybe she gets it, because she sends back a smile.

Good night, Em, I say.

Good night. Talk to you tomorrow.

Except this time, she really means talk. I set down my phone.

Let me not screw this up.

17.

JAY

I spend the first two hours of my day going over an experiment with Vithika.

"Jay," she finally asks over Skype, "are you okay? You're not paying attention."

I shake my head, "Uh." Shit. "I have a date tonight."

Her eyebrows go up.

"Shut up," I say, even though she didn't say anything.

I spend an hour in my lab talking through experimental design with Gary and Soo Yin. I grab a sandwich in crackling plastic from the campus market for lunch—it's fast, at least, and filling, even if the bread is soggy.

I'm good at working. I'm shit at feeling.

By the time it's four in the afternoon, I'm a complete tangle.

Gabe comes to my rescue.

Yo, he texts half an hour before his seminar. *I was gonna go meet Maria and bring her up here, but I got delayed.*

Gabe. Late again. I shake my head.

Can you bring her up?

I exhale. It's not like I have any option to say no. It won't even be the first time I accompany Maria there. Gabe works at the Lawrence Berkeley National Laboratory, and despite heavy ties to the university, it's a separate entity run by the federal government. Maria couldn't just walk in. LBL employees (like Gabe) or affiliates (like me) can sign visitors in, but otherwise the gates won't open.

Fine, I tell Gabe.

"Well, here we are," I say to Maria a half-hour later when we meet in the courtyard outside my lab. "It's confirmation bias again."

She gives me a level, annoyed look.

"You okay with walking?" I ask.

"Fine," she says tersely.

I sigh.

Maria doesn't like me, and I can hardly blame her. I accept responsibility for the fact that we don't get along, but... Still, we don't get along.

I walked into work today, which means I don't have my car. It's not really my fault that I'm forcing her to walk, but I still feel responsible. Nothing about her outfit looks like it was made for walking.

Her dress comes halfway up her thighs, and the material is a little tight. To make it worse, LBL is up a hill. Calling it a mere "hill" isn't quite fair. The Berkeley Hills are steep, with the road up to the lab at something close to a 20 percent grade. The sun is out, though, and it's a nice day.

"You know that I'm going to have to be responsible for you," I say as we start up the hill.

"Relax, Three Sigma," she says with a roll of her eyes. "I don't run with scissors."

"I'm serious. This is not the kind of site where visitors can wander around and gawk at buildings. It's the kind of site where the wrong person in the wrong place when the synchrotron is running will die of radiation poisoning in seconds. Not that there's any danger of that."

"Aw, you're being a pedant again. Having never visited or talked with my brother, I wouldn't know anything about his workplace."

I accept this sarcasm in silence.

"Although," she continues, "radiation poisoning could solve a lot of my problems. Want to play canary?"

A smile tugs at my lips despite myself. With my blinders off, I have to admit that Maria is something of a trouper. She's wearing a gray sweater dress that clings a little bit too much to her smooth curves. It's tight enough that I can see the round muscles in her ass tense and release as she goes up the road.

I shouldn't be looking. I'm talking to Em tonight. But I'm human.

And Maria and I may be nothing alike, but dammit, I have to respect her. And her ass.

"Don't be shy," she says. "Your death will be for the good of the country."

"I'll tell you what. I'll stick to determining safe spots theoretically and leave the empirical validation to you."

She glances over her shoulder at me. "Running out of breath? I thought you wanted to walk."

I'm not running out of breath. Yes, I'm breathing hard, but it's a hill, and Maria walks quickly. She tilts her head, as if gauging my fitness level. Then she speeds up, which I hadn't thought possible. Her dress sways around her thighs. Shaping her quads. Spilling over her butt.

Maria and I will never get along, but I'm not about to let her leave me behind. I grit my teeth and dig in and move faster. I can't believe that she's doing this in heels.

And that's when my eyes fall to her feet. I'm not much of a shoe person. One heel looks much like another. But Maria is wearing red heels.

Not just *red* heels.

My heart stops. My fists slowly clench. I feel almost dizzy. *Yep,* some undiscovered part of my mind whispers. *Those sure are shoes.* Everything seems to move slowly; I can hear every individual beat of my heart separated by an infinity of silence.

Her shoes are three-inch heels. Red. Chased with a bit of ribbon, decorated with gold butterflies and Swarovski crystals. I know those shoes. I have them practically memorized.

Maria Lopez is wearing Em's fuck-off shoes.

I can't look away from them. They click on the pavement in front of me.

For a moment, I can't even process what this means. Why is *Maria* wearing Em's shoes? Do they know each other?

No. My mind may be moving slowly, but I know the truth. Words I can't even say in my mind.

Maria can't be Em. That makes...

No, I correct myself. It doesn't make no sense. It makes a *lot* of sense.

The floodgates of recognition open. Maria is the right age. Em is, and always has been, a... Well, a nerd for lack of a better word. Maria knew enough statistics to know what *three sigma* meant. She knew enough physics to understand her brother's job talk. And she gave me hell for assuming she couldn't do these things based on how she looked.

Maria has a brother and a grandmother. Maria told me off; when I texted Em minutes later, she snapped at me and said she wasn't in the mood to comfort me.

The clues land with a nauseating churn in my stomach. Maria was drunk, and Em had a hangover. Em is transgender, and Maria is...tall.

Maria is Em. Em is Maria. Shit.

I look up at her. Her hair is loose, and the breeze picks up. Wind catches little wisps of her perfectly styled hair, letting it swirl in perfection over her shoulder.

Maria is Em.

A second fact slots into place. There is no way I can tell her what I've just discovered. Em would never forgive me if she knew who I was, and I don't want to lose Em. I *can't* lose Em.

But what am I supposed to do? My accent will give me away the moment we talk on the phone. Which we are supposed to do in four hours. I could invent an emergency, put her off—but I've been shoving her away all this time. She'll never forgive me if I do it again.

My mind jumps from lie to stupid lie, each worse than the last.

I can't tell Em who I am. I can't. I listen to the click of her shoes. Watch the swish of her hips. Fuck. Fuck. *Fuck*. It's even worse than I thought. Maria is wearing her fuck-off shoes tonight, and I know exactly why. They're for me.

I could look up the exact conversation we had about them, except I don't have to because I have it memorized. I know what they mean. *You wish you could get with this.*

A third fact follows in logical progression. I will ruin everything if I tell her. I suddenly understand exactly why Maria snapped at me about her brother in the beginning. Why she told me I would never understand.

Of course she did. Of course she would. I know, I *know*, what he means to her now. *He bought me a bus ticket.*

Maria is Em. She has always been Em, and I never saw her. I couldn't see past the bullshit I'd made up about her to see her in the first place, and that means that I can't tell her. I knew I was in the wrong last November. Now I understand *exactly* how wrong I was. I thought, before, that we could have been friends.

Now? Now I accept how pale that realization is compared to reality. If we hadn't managed to hate each other first, Em would have been it for me. I failed to see her on every conceivable level. How do I admit that?

I'm going to lose her. We're stuck in some kind of strange attractor, drifting impossibly far apart every time we get close. I don't see any way out.

The road bends. Up ahead, the security gate lies.

Fact four rises out of my circling mental state. I can't *not* tell her. Not telling her would be a lie of the most epic proportions. If she ever found out...

Would she have to find out?

No, whispers some stupid part of my brain. *No, she doesn't. And if she ever does, you could play dumb. Say you didn't realize it either.*

I stop walking. It takes her a few steps to notice that she can't hear me behind her. She stops. She's breathing heavily; there's a faint sheen to her forehead, and she gives me a delighted smile.

"Can't take the pace? Don't worry. We can wait until you've recovered." Her voice is saccharine.

"You know," I say stupidly, "I've just realized that…"

Oh, fuck how even to end that sentence?

"That actually," I hear myself say foolishly, "we get along really well."

She frowns at me. She tilts her head. "Are you having a stroke?"

"No," I say. "I mean it. Yes, we argue all the time. But…um…sometimes, arguing…"

She rolls her eyes. "Jay, I know you've been staring at my ass for fifteen minutes, but you know you can't finish that sentence in any way that makes sense. I know the difference between arguing for fun and arguing because someone doesn't respect me. Just take me to my brother's seminar, okay?"

That hurts. It hurts because it's true. I can't tell her. I *can't*. We continue on. I sign her in as a visitor. We continue on up toward Gabe's office.

I've made up my mind not to say anything. I haven't figured anything else out; I just know I can't tell her. I need time to untangle everything. A week, maybe, and I'll know how to handle this. A month…

Except last night, my conscience whispers, *you didn't want to hurt her.*

I stop again. The wind brings with it a wild, sweet smell. From up here, we can see the Bay spread before us, a glittering expanse crossed by bridges. The San Francisco skyline is hazy just beyond. The grounds nearby are covered with half-wild dry grass and browning bushes.

It's a beautiful place, and when Maria turns to look at me, her hands going to her hips, I'm aware for the first time of how beautiful she is.

I've always known that she was hot. It's not like I could turn off my unconscious appraisal. But it was a heat I rejected. Maria Lopez was always someone else's version of hot. Those heels. Those long legs. Those slight curves. The dark wings of eyeliner framing her eyes; the plummy shade of her lips. The brown of her skin almost glows in the evening sunlight.

"What?" she demands.

Here's the thing: Some problems are only hard because you're in the wrong basis set. If I start with the assumption that I don't want to hurt her, this is easy. Really easy.

Fuck *if she ever found out.* Fuck *I might lose her.* This is easy. It's actually the easiest thing in the world.

I have to tell her. I have to lose her, no matter how much it hurts. Because Em doesn't deserve my lying to her.

There is no good way to start. I have no plan. So the first thing that comes out of my mouth is… "I've committed a classic mistake."

"What?" She crosses her arms and turns to face me, her voice a little more querulous.

I shake my head. "It's such a sophomore-level physics error I'm pissed at myself."

"Are you okay?" She takes a step toward me.

I meet her eyes. They're warm and golden-brown, and now that I'm this close, I can see that her skin isn't flawless. There's a smattering of freckles spreading from her nose to her cheeks. Foundation doesn't quite cover them. I don't know why I've never noticed them before.

"We're not quantum entangled," I tell her. "Never attribute quantum properties to macroscopic objects. There's always a classical explanation. Always."

She glances at her watch, then heaves a sigh. "Fine. I know scientists. We have about five minutes. Do you need to write down whatever it is you've just figured out, or can it wait until we get into the seminar room?"

I am painfully aware that I'm mishandling this, but I have no experience admitting to my worst enemy that I've been secretly in love with her alter ego. So I say the next idiot thing that pops into my head. "Your middle name is Camilla. Of course it is."

She looks at me suspiciously. "How did you know that?"

"Because your initials are MCL."

She stills all of a sudden, stiffening into a statue. The wind catches her hair and tosses it over her shoulder. A part of my mind makes a note: This is what Maria looks like when she's scared. For this moment, she's probably as scared as I am. It feels like forever that we stare into each other's eyes.

"Yes," she finally says. "My initials are MCL. Are you trying to tell me something?"

"Em." My voice drops. "I'm trying to say that actually, we get along really well."

She makes a choked sound in her throat. "No."

My gaze flicks down her legs. Those fucking shoes. I could kiss her for those shoes.

Her eyes follow mine. She sees her shoes. I can hear her intake of breath.

"No," she says again. Her hands shake at her sides; she presses them together.

Funny. You can put someone in a box and not know them at all. *I'm proud of being a girl,* Maria told me at that dinner with her brother months ago. *It's not an insult.*

I wasn't wrong about her. I just was so far from right that I've managed to punch myself in the stomach. Everything I've said to her, every dismissive thought I've had, plays back in my head. I wasn't *mistaken* about who she was. I was just an ass. Such a complete ass.

"I'm sorry," I say. I feel sick.

"*I'm* sorry." Her voice is shaking. She looks around wildly, her gaze latching on to the building where her brother is supposed to give his talk. Her attention shifts down the road, toward the molecular foundry along the ridge of the hill. "I'm sorry, but I can't do this right now."

I don't know what to say. How to say it. What to do. But she turns and starts walking away from her brother's office, and… Fuck.

I follow after her. "Maria. I can't let you walk away from me."

She turns back. "That's such bullshit. Give me one good reason."

I'm more than half in love with her. She's become one of the most important people in my life. Right now, I want to tell her it will be all right.

I'm pretty sure it won't be all right.

"It's not bullshit." I sigh. "I signed you into a government lab. I'm responsible for you. I'm not allowed to let you wander off."

She looks at me in silent entreaty. She looks down at her hands. Then she shakes her head and starts laughing.

"Oh my god," she says. "We are so fucked."

MARIA

We are so fucked. I'm upset, and I don't have the space to be upset.

I walk into the room where my brother is giving the seminar. I smile at him. Give him a hug. Say "yes" to some question that he puts to me. I have no idea what he actually says, but *yes* appears to be the appropriate answer, because he smiles back and goes to the lectern at the front.

I slip into a seat.

Jay follows me into the room. I don't want to look at him. I don't want to think about him. I don't want to see him out of the corner of my eye. I don't want the image of him to start merging with A.

Jay doesn't sit near me. I hate that he knows I need space. I'm also glad he knows it. I don't look at him as Gabe is introduced. I refuse to acknowledge his existence as the lights dim and the room takes on the eerie glow of projected slides.

I finally look in his direction after ten minutes. He's watching Gabe's slides, dropping a few notes on a pad of paper. In the darkened room, he fades into the background until nothing is left but the glitter of his eyes.

He looks my way. Our eyes meet.

Nobody should look good by the harsh light of reflected PowerPoint, but Jay may be the exception. The blue-tinged light sharpens his features, exaggerating them, making his eyes seem deeper, his nose just a little more cruel.

I look away. My stomach churns. I plaster my hand to my thighs, as if I'm holding myself in place. I wait, carefully, for my heart to slow. For my pulse to stop racing. Then I look back.

My emotions are tattered shreds—impossible to make out, flapping in a brisk wind that only I can feel. I wish I'd never met Jay. That he didn't know my brother. That I got to call him tonight. We could exchange names and photos and flirt outrageously. We could meet for coffee.

I wish I could have told Tina about him piece by piece. The dark expressive slash of his eyebrows. Those lips. His fucking accent, back when I hadn't had four months to associate it with condescending bullshit. His features are clouded by ugly memories.

Concentrated asinine obtuseness burns twelve times hotter. Does it ever.

He looks at me again. Our eyes hold.

He doesn't hide the fact he's looking at me. I wonder if he's remembering what I said to him.

I don't want to think about my part in our ongoing war, even though I'm absolutely certain I've had one.

Em, I'm pretty much in love with you.

I flinch away from him.

Over the space of the next half-hour, as I listen to my brother make goofy jokes about laser plasma accelerators and semiconductors, I manage to think myself sick.

Jay knows about my blog. He knows about high school. He knows about my grandmother, soup…

Fuck. I'm on the verge of tears, and I don't want to cry in the same room with him. He might comfort me. I might *let* him.

My brother finishes his talk. The lights come on. Jay asks a question—he obviously hasn't had his entire world rearranged, if he can think of questions—and I sit in place, trying to smile and be supportive.

Calculating the moment I can escape.

Alas. I go to say my good-byes to Gabe as he's packing up his laptop. He's talking to a white-haired man excitedly about beam requests and something something something—I can normally translate his science, but I can't concentrate tonight. Gabe turns to me before I can vanish.

"Sorry, Maria," he says. "Another ten minutes, and we'll head to the restaurant. Jay, where are we going again?"

Jay looks over at me. Our eyes hold a third time. I can't imagine swallowing a bite of food. Fuck. Apparently, when I agreed to hang out with Gabe after his seminar, I agreed to have dinner with Jay.

I can't right now. I just can't. I exhale. "Actually, I'm not feeling well. I was thinking of just going home."

"Are you sure?" Gabe's too distracted to catch my distress. Or maybe he thinks I'm really just not feeling well.

I nod. "I'm sure."

"Well, thanks for coming. We'll catch up soon, okay?"

I escape as swiftly as I can, sliding through the door, out into the hall.

My heels echo on the tile, and now that I'm looking down, I realize this is the worst part. My shoes were supposed to be my safety. My emotional armor. And what did they do? They gave me away.

My phone buzzes as I'm standing in front of the elevator.

Slowly, I pull it out.

It's from *him*. Actual Physicist. A.

Who am I trying to fool? It's from Jay.

He's sent me three emoji: Heart. Soup. Shoes.

God, it hurts. I look up to see him stepping out of the door. He looks at me. He doesn't say anything.

He doesn't come near me. He just stands outside the door and...looks.

"I know," I call down the hall. "You signed me into a government lab. You can't let me wander around."

He doesn't say anything.

I look down at my phone. This was, we agreed, emoji for "hold me."

Virtual hugs are better than physical ones. They don't impinge on my space. I don't have to accept them. I can imagine them in a bubble, isolated in the cold vacuum of my heart.

He's watching me from down the hall. He is, and he isn't, A.

A. and Jay were both driven. But A. made jokes at his own expense, while Jay was serious. A. was vulnerable, and Jay…

Shit. I look at him standing in the hallway, watching me.

I can't pretend they're different people. They aren't. And if A. was vulnerable…

Slowly, I turn and walk back to him. Each step feels like my feet are dragging through mud. He doesn't take his eyes off me. He doesn't say anything. He just watches.

"I'm guessing you like me about as much as I liked you," I say.

"Which you?" he asks. Then he exhales. "No. I'm pretty sure I like Em more than she likes me." He looks away. "I'm also sure the same holds true for Maria." He wipes a hand over his face.

I swallow and look away. I don't want to feel empathy for him. In a way, the fact that I'm thinking of *him* feels like the biggest betrayal of all. He made me like him. Even now, I'm already dissecting the things he said. The things he did. I'm beginning to understand.

I don't want to understand why he hurt me. I just want to remember that he did.

I exhale. "You're probably as upset as I am."

He shakes his head. "I was pretty terrible to you. But Em, I didn't want to hurt you and I did. I feel like such shit right now."

I look over at him. He told me once that he was laser-like, and right now, I can feel the force of his concentrated, unwavering attention. I feel naked.

I am both unreasonably glad that he feels like shit and sorry, because I don't want him to feel bad.

"Can I give Actual Physicist a hug without giving Jay one?"

"I'm pretty sure we're the same person."

"Shut up," I tell him. "Fuck. I need a week." I bite my lip. "I can't even tell Gabe what's wrong because he doesn't know about my blog."

"He doesn't know about your blog? I thought you two were tight."

I make a face. "We are. It's just… Never mind." I look over at him. In these shoes, I'm just a little taller than he is. He's close enough that I can make out his eyelashes as individual lines. I can see a little dark spot on his cheek. If we'd never met, we'd be talking on the phone tonight. I'm so mad that I lost that chance, and *mad* is the easiest emotion to grapple with at the moment. Anger is simple. It has an object, a reason.

If I'm angry, I won't have to sort out anything else.

But I look into his eyes one last time, and I can't even give myself the gift of simple emotion.

Last night he told me about his brother. I told him about my parents.

"Fine." My voice sounds flat and low. "I think I need you to hold me anyway."

And he does. His arms come around me, not hard, but gentle, gathering me to him. And I'm hugging him back with all the feelings I haven't acknowledged— interest, affection, and a feeling of sad, hollow loss.

My arms sneak around his waist. I lean my cheek into his neck and breathe in the scent of him. I can't classify it. It just smells like…him.

I'm aware of his every breath. Of the feel of his shirt against my fingers. The feel of muscles beneath fabric. The rise of his chest, the whisper of wind as he exhales.

"This doesn't mean anything," I tell him.

It means everything.

He squeezes me just a little, and I'm afraid I'm going to start crying.

He lets me go, and the hallway feels suddenly cold. He reaches out and slides a strand of my hair behind my ear. His fingers leave a trail of confusion on my skin.

Then he turns around and goes back into the room. I can hear him talking to my brother. "She really doesn't feel well," I hear him say. "Do you have a car here? I don't."

I don't hear my brother's response.

"Well, you should probably take her home if you can."

It's a nice thing to do. It's thoughtful. I hate that he's nice and thoughtful. I hate that he can *be* nice and thoughtful. I know this side of him far too well, and if Jay had let me see this earlier...

But he didn't, and now it's too late.

When he walks by me, I don't make eye contact.

I don't dare. If I look at him again, I might not let him leave.

18.

I call her at nine.

She answers. "Hi." It's all she says.

"Are you okay?" I'm pacing in my living room, trying to figure out what to say.

"No." She exhales. "Are you?"

"No."

We settle into a silence.

When your relationship is all text, there's a lot of silence. But silence on an actual voice call is audible and real in a way that an absence of typing is not.

I don't see the read receipts telling me that she's there, that she's listening.

"I fucked up," I say. This is an understatement. I feel like the captain of a ship, surveying a gash in the side, wondering where that iceberg came from and why there are so few lifeboats.

"Me, too." Her voice is low.

I wish this feeling were new. That I didn't know what it was like to break things so badly that I can't blame someone for giving up on me. I don't know how to say "trust me."

But I want to know how. I want to know it desperately.

"I need time," I tell her.

"Me, too."

"Em?" I realize I've called her by her other name a second after I do it. I don't take it back. "Everything I said last night still stands."

She exhales.

"Come by anytime you need…" I trail off, not knowing what to offer. A hug. Some soup. Me. I don't finish the sentence.

"Okay," she says. "Okay."

The room is cold, and the air conditioner is running even though it's February and below sixty outside. It's been two days since I talked to Em, and I'm still at a loss.

Some people are reminded of their childhood by leaf piles or the smell of pancakes. For me, it's the feel of artificially cold air on my neck, the clinical smell of ozone and the scent of antistatic wipes. It's the persistent hum of server rooms, of a raised floor that clacks beneath my feet. I encounter pockets of heat from machines that do their best to overcome the industrial-strength climate control.

This space brings back old memories. Sitting in a conference room and doing homework. Occupying emptied cubicles at night with some of the other kids. Challenging each other to network duels.

It's been years since I came here, but Eric out front still recognizes me and waves me through.

My mother is talking to a group of people in the corner of the room. She is holding a mug of coffee in a metallic gold travel cup, gesturing to a whiteboard. Flecks of marker dust dot her cuffs. She is completely in her element, arguing with someone about a black box pentest on enterprise level server systems.

Cyclone has a tendency to grab people and never spit them out. My mom started at Cyclone six months after I was born, never intending to stay past the moment Cyclone went public and her stock options turned into real money. She's talking to Kenji Miyahara, who I've known since we were both teenagers, back when *we* did penetration tests after school for fun and Cyclone shares.

Now he plays red team/blue team hacker games for a living and bosses around people twice his age.

For a moment, I think about leaving without disturbing her. I'm not even sure why I'm here, or what I'll say to her.

Kenji is half-Japanese, half-black. He's shaved his head since the last time I saw him. He towers over my mother. She still manages to dominate the room, gesturing, brushing back her hijab when it catches on her shoulder.

Kenji sees me first. He turns. "Hey!" He starts toward me. "Script kiddie!" It's an insult we used to use—a *dorky* insult, because when you're a kid whose parents work at one of the largest computer companies in the world, coding prowess is the only measurement of worth you tolerate.

I raise my chin in his direction. "Give me twenty years and and all your boxen will belong to me."

"Have fun with that," he says sarcastically. "I'll stick to computers I can back up without destroying the results."

"Asshole." In the Cyclone style, I say this with affection. I shake his hand as he offers it.

He punches me in the shoulder with his free hand. "Saint K., I didn't know we were getting a visit from the prodigal son."

"Oh, I'm prodigal, am I?"

"Doing all that science and then putting it in the public domain? Whew." Kenji grins. "That requires a hell of a lot of forgiveness."

"Spoken by the man who has never had to deal with a university patent office."

My mom comes up beside me. "I am unspeakably embarrassed." Her hands go to her hips. "Jay, did you show up unannounced to engage in this sorry excuse for shit-talking? I taught you better than that."

"Of course not," I say. "I want to talk to you. I'll wait until you're done."

Her eyes narrow, and she tilts her head to one side. I feel like she's looking through me, past the half smile on my face.

I keep it in place, but I'm not fooling her. It's the middle of the day. The middle of the week.

"You want to talk to *me*. And you can *wait.*" There's a subtle emphasis on those words, as if she can't quite believe what she's hearing.

I stuff my hands in my pockets. "Yeah."

She dusts off her hands. She's wearing jeans and a white shirt—now marked with red and blue flecks that almost match her flowery hijab—and she doesn't even

come to my shoulder when she hugs me. She smells like
the shampoo she's used since before I was born. Some
part of me has classified this smell as Mom. It brings
with it a wave of nostalgia. Of comfort. Of safety.

It makes me think of grilled cheese sandwiches
made on a hot plate in the corner of this office and
tomato soup nuked in a microwave. My version of
comfort food.

"Shit just got real," says Kenji.

Mom pulls back and frowns at the calendar on her
watch. "I'll just tell Aaron I'm going to lunch. We're
done here, anyway. I can rearrange my afternoon."

"I don't want to bother you. I know you're busy."

She gives me a look. "If we waited until I wasn't
busy, we would never talk to each other."

Over the last five years, I've been busy, too. A lot. I
look over at her and swallow.

"We can go down to the Cyclone cafeteria, if you
want," she says, "or we can splurge and head to Nikki's."

Nikki's is a soup and sandwich shop that's two
blocks from the Cyclone campus. It's not expensive;
when she talks about splurging, she's referring to the
time it'll take.

She doesn't wait for my answer.

"Never mind. If you came all the way down here,
Nikki's it is."

We don't talk about much on our way there. Mom
drives, and I try not to distract her. It's not that she's a
bad driver; it's exactly the opposite. She's great, and she
knows it, which is why she swears at everyone who is a
worse driver than her—in other words, everyone.

"Why, why," she rants, "why is your turn signal on? Merge if you want to change lanes. If you don't, fuck off!"

The other drivers, thankfully, can't hear her.

She's given a table in back when we arrive. Mom comes here often, and they know who she is.

I consider the menu when we're seated. Sandwiches. Breakfast all day. But I think of Em, and order minestrone.

"So," my mother says after the waitress leaves. "Why are you here?"

"I need some advice."

Her eyes get subtly wider. I have not asked her for advice since…no, I didn't even ask her about my choice of university.

"Advice about what?"

"I think," I say carefully, "that I'm a little like you."

One eyebrow raises. "In what way?"

My soup arrives, as does a salad for her that comes laden with garbanzo beans.

"When it comes to work."

"In some ways, yes. In others, probably not. Why?"

"So." I swallow. "I work hard. I don't have time for much of anything except my job. I take what I do very seriously. There's no point doing something if you can't be the best, right?"

My mother stabs her salad. A garbanzo bean skitters away from her fork and flies across the table. She picks up the errant bean idly and slips it into her napkin. "That is not an entirely complimentary description of either of us."

"Sorry." I shake my head.

"It's also not wrong. It has taken me many, many years to get to the point where I can let things go. The joy and the agony of being a perfectionist in a changing world is that you will never succeed in being without fault, but you also never run out of chances."

I nod.

"But I don't think you came here to talk about Cyclone's product release cycle." She gestures with her fork. "What are you really asking?"

Until this moment, I wasn't sure. But I think about Maria's face. About Em. About wanting to take back six months of my life, starting with a single moment of inattention, and not knowing how. I think about Chase, and about how much that inattention can sometimes cost.

"How do you fix something that's completely broken?" I ask.

She freezes. She looks down at her salad. "Um." She sets her fork down. "Okay. That's a pretty massive question."

It's twelve years massive.

"What do you do," I say, "when you fuck up so badly that nobody can ever expect anything of you again?"

"You're talking about your father and me," she says. "And Chase."

"No." My heart is pounding. "Yes. Maybe a little." I want to know how to pick up all the broken pieces and put them together again. I want to think it's possible.

I want to think it's not too late to patch together what I had with my parents, even if it is too late for Em.

I want my mother to tell me what I did wrong. I want her to give me something to fix.

All this time I've been working. Waiting to finally meet her standards. I pushed away the idea that I could be enough, now, as I am.

But at this point—one PhD, twenty-three peer-reviewed journal articles, and seven serious grants into my life, it's obvious this is not working. Will thirty publications be enough? Fifty? A chaired professorship?

I want to know. I want to know how I can be enough for her, because this method isn't working. It's not working for anyone.

She flinches away from me. "It's a good question." She flattens her hands on the table. "I've thought about it for years. I think it comes down to…I was arrogant."

I look at her. I blink. I don't know why she's talking about herself.

"I was on top of the world. Everything was going so well in my life. I knew something was off with Chase, but Wat had issues when he was younger, and he came round—so I just let it slide."

I open my mouth. I close it. I don't understand.

"I should have asked Wat for advice. Or spent more time with Chase. Or…" Her voice cracks. She stares at the wallpaper for a long moment, before she clears her throat. "Or anything. Sometimes, when you're wounded, you lash out. Your father and I said some things to each other that were unforgivable."

I'm not sure I understand what she's saying. "But you did," I say eventually. "You *did* forgive each other."

"Well, that's the thing. Sometimes when you're hurt, you can't get past yourself. *I* hurt. *I* was wounded. What *he* said to *me* cannot be forgiven. Give it a little time, though, and the *I* starts to disappear. You let go of your guilt. You acknowledge the shame at having hurt someone. Love doesn't mean you never screw up. It means you don't hold on to the unforgivable."

I consider this.

She sniffs and turns her head to the wall. "I hate showing emotion in public. Give me a moment."

I do. I wait until the glimmer is gone from her eyes. Until her breath evens out and she picks up her fork again.

"What do I have to do?" I ask.

Her gaze darts to mine over the table. Her eyes widen in surprise. "What do you have to do for what?"

"What do I have to do," I say, through a throat that seems too thick, "for you to forgive me?"

She stares at me as if I've grown extra arms.

The words start coming out. "You always told me Chase was my responsibility. That I needed to take care of him. I knew better than you that something was wrong."

"No," she says. "No, no, no."

"Clio was the one who pushed him over the edge. And afterward, no matter what I did, I knew I'd disappointed you guys. You stopped pushing. You stopped asking, even. I disappeared for three days and you didn't even ground me."

She puts her fork down. Then she stands up and slides next to me in the booth.

"No," she says. "No, no, no, no, no." Her arm slides around me. "Not that. Never that. I can't speak for your father. On my part, I stopped pushing because you were the only thing in my life that *didn't* hurt. How could I punish you for grieving when I was at fault?"

I slide my arm around her. "You weren't."

We don't say anything for a while. There's nothing to say. No words to communicate. My chest feels heavy and light all at once. She squeezes me and I squeeze her back.

"Huh," she finally says. "We *are* a lot alike."

"How so?"

"Both a little too good at guilt."

I think of Em again. "Maybe," I say. "Or maybe we're both just bad at giving up."

When I get back to my office, I don't check my email. I avoid the chat app on my phone. I slide my unread papers into my bag and ignore the committee report I have to read sometime in the next three days.

Instead, I lock my door. Students are walking out in the courtyard. Someone's taking a break and feeding who knows what sort of junk food to a squirrel.

My father's books still sit in a row on the shelf. I take the first one down, hold it in my hands.

I sit down and spread the book open to the first pages.

The dedication is simple: *For my boy,* my dad wrote.

That's me. He always called me that when I was little—"my boy." Chase was always "my kid."

I've never been able to read it. I've always been afraid in a bone-deep way of what I would find. It's a story about a man losing his child. Maybe I would end up the villain. Maybe I wouldn't find myself at all, viciously erased from the most traumatic incident of my own life. Maybe—and this is what I've never been able to admit until now—I was afraid that he would forgive me, when I've never been able to forgive myself.

I start reading.

My father always told me that he never based his books on real life, except when he did. I see that in play now. He writes in a simple, literary style—the kind that gets warm reviews in trade magazines.

This book isn't about him. It isn't about me. It's just about losing someone you love. And it's about *not* losing everything at the same time.

It's not about me at all. It's about a man who loses his daughter in a white-water rafting accident, then his job to depression, his house to foreclosure. He manages to avoid making it sound like a bad country music song by investing it with a growing sense of humor and hope.

Sometimes, losing what you think of as "everything" makes you learn to love what you still have. It's a messy, serious, complicated book, and I'm left with the feeling that if I knew a single thing about literary analysis, I'd get a lot more from it.

I get enough.

Dad never bases his books on real life. Except when he does.

By the time I'm done, it's dark outside. I wake up my computer, shake my head at the sixty-three emails in my inbox. They can wait. I turn on my phone.

Em hasn't tried to chat with me. She hasn't called.

I ignore all the other notifications and dial.

My father picks up the phone.

"Hi," I say.

"Hi, Jay."

The silence stretches. I'm sure he's talked to Mom. I'm sure that he's wondering what to say, how to make things better.

There's no *better*. It's messy and it's complicated. There's only forward.

"Do you have time for lunch sometime this week?" I finally ask.

"Always,"   he   says.   "Always."

19.

I know something is wrong the next morning when I step into my lab and see Soo Yin and Gary, my two newest graduate students, look over at me in pure terror. They freeze like rabbits where they're huddled over a notebook on the lab couch. They're first-years, and this is the first semester where they're doing research instead of teaching. Which, no, does not mean that they do actual new science. Not yet. It means that they learn fundamentals.

The fundamentals start from "learn how the tunable laser works," and work up to "duplicate this controlled-NOT gate using cooled, trapped beryllium atoms."

It doesn't matter that I feel sick to my stomach. That I may have lost someone who was really important to me. Life doesn't stop.

I've thrown my new grad students in the deep end of the pool—preparation, of course, for throwing them in the ocean—and I have to make sure they aren't drowning.

"Uh," says Gary as I look over at them. "Hi, Jay. I—uh—we have, uh, a homework set due in stat mech and it's pretty complex, so, uh—"

"So you have a half-hour to talk about how the experiment went," I say, pulling up a chair. I straddle it backward.

"Um." Soo Yin looks at Gary. Gary looks at Soo Yin. "So… Um, maybe if we talk tomorrow…?"

"Then you'll be able to stay up all night to redo the experiment and pretend you did it right the first time?"

Soo Yin exhales and looks away.

"People." I fold my arms. "Don't lie to me. You're really bad at it. This is like walking into a kitchen with a puppy and finding trash all over the floor. 'Who, me?' doesn't work."

"We're…um, not exactly sure what we did wrong. But we'll figure it out." Gary is as earnest as my hypothetical puppy.

"Sure. Of course you will." I gesture to the whiteboard. "Because we're going to do a post mortem right now."

Soo Yin winces.

"Step one: stop feeling self-conscious about things not working. You want a PhD? Well, guess what. You're going to be issued a wall, with instructions to beat your head against it for a few years. If you're lucky, the wall will crack, and you'll write about the structural integrity of walls. If you're unlucky, your head will break, and you'll write about the structural integrity of heads. Either way, we have to talk about failure. If you can't get over your ego and just talk about what you did and what happened, this will take four times as long. You failed. Get used to it. Some of the biggest scientific breakthroughs came about because someone failed and figured out why. Don't worry about failing. Worry about failing wrongly."

Soo Yin nods, and slowly, they start explaining how they set up the ion trap. I listen. I nod. I tell them to stop and check when they hesitate.

I need a post mortem for myself. I need to figure out precisely how I fucked up so badly with Em—and fuck up I did.

I get up at one point to circle something on the whiteboard. I knew I was wrong even before now. But how did I end up *so* wrong?

As I listen to Soo Yin and Gary, I start making a list of mental reasons. I was mistaken; that's all. Everyone makes mistakes, right? And it's not like she was nice to me in response. It's not *all* my fault. It was a series of snide remarks and shitty blunders on both sides, and we fucked up in equal measure.

That characterization doesn't sit well. I break it down over dinner—alone—later that night. I assumed Maria didn't know math because she was hot and dressed well. Worse—I assumed she was a judgy bitch because of the same. Was she perfect? No. But I started it, I continued it, and I made only a halfhearted effort to apologize. This situation may not be *all* my fault, but I'm lying if I pretend it's less than about ninety-five percent.

This realization takes a few days to sink in, for me to really understand it. I wasn't just *wrong* or *mistaken*. I apparently have the notion, rooted deep in my subconscious, that women who look nice aren't *real*.

I know I'm coming close to the truth because it makes me squirmy. Even after I realized Em had a point, I had to fight to remember it.

If she has time to spend on her clothes...
Of course she video chats...
If she didn't want to be judged on her appearance...

I'm four scientific generations into quantum mechanics. Even Einstein found quantum physics too strange for his tastes. He couldn't get his head around basic tenets of the discipline that he called "spooky action at a distance" or "God playing dice." I'm two scientific generations removed from Eric Llewellyn, who thinks "groovy, dude" is what people my age say.

Even Einstein messed up. He knew how the world worked, and when it didn't fit his view, he dug his heels in. He became the ninety-year-old who couldn't figure out the remote on the VCR.

The lesson I drew from this when I was young was that even brilliant minds can stall out if they let their brain get stuck on the way they think the universe works instead of examining the actual evidence. "Bad data; reject" is how scientists miss the existence of quarks.

The actual evidence is that if I can't wrap my mind around my own failure, I'm fucked as a scientist. If I can't wrap my mind around this, I don't know what I'll say if Em—if *Maria*—ever decides she wants to talk to me again.

That thought, on day four after discovering that Em is Maria, is what jars me loose from my moorings.

All this time, I've been trying to figure out how to explain myself to Maria. How to come up with an explanation for my actions that won't be too incriminating. I've been trying to figure out how to save myself. To avoid just a little bit of blame.

But come *on*.

She came home. There was trash everywhere. And I was the puppy sitting in front of her, panting eagerly. Em's not fucking *stupid*. She *knows* what the explanation is.

The explanation is that she was right in front of me the whole time and I didn't see her. "I don't think women are stupid per se; I reserve that judgment only for the women that engage in overt displays of socially constructed femininity" is an inherently wrong belief. It wasn't a onetime mistake or an accident that I applied it to her.

It was a fundamental flaw.

All this time, I've been wondering if she'll be able to get over what I did.

Wrong question. What I need to know is this: Will I?

---

*O*n my way home that night, I drop into a shop. Behind the cones of incense and the specialty cards, there's a display of handmade paper—delicate pieces with texture and fibers you can feel, sold by the sheet for almost as much money as an entire ream would cost from an office superstore.

I pick out three sheets of light brown paper and a matching envelope.

I go home.

I don't message. I don't email. I don't call. All of those feel invasive. They have read receipts and time stamps. None of them feel right at the moment.

No; there's only one thing that seems to fit.
I write Em a letter.

M A R I A

*T*here are some times when soup is not enough. For those times, I have my grandmother. After nursing complicated, broken feelings for days on end, disappearing for the weekend seems like a better and better idea.

Just getting on the BART makes me feel better, like I'm going someplace where the revelations of the last week can't touch me. A train ride and a bus transfer later, and I'm walking up to her apartment.

When I tell people that Nana is a Catholic Latina, they tend to take a certain view of her. They imagine her speaking only Spanish, answering to abuela, wearing a cross around her neck and spending her weekends at mass praying her Rosary. They also imagine her as an infinite source of tamales.

The truth is…not like that. Yes to the cross. Yes to mass on the weekends, and yes to the Rosary. But my dad's mother was always abuela instead, and as to everything else? My grandparents got a divorce when she was in her twenties, and that was long enough ago that it still had a whiff of scandal.

Nana had been a stay-at-home mother up until that moment. She finished an undergraduate degree after the divorce was final and went to law school. Now she works for the City Attorney of San Francisco, and when I say she works, she *works*.

Standing in the hallway outside, I get a whiff that brings me back to my high school years—a hint of the powdery stuff that she sprinkles on her carpets to make them smell rainforest fresh, or whatever manufactured scent this is.

I don't knock. She doesn't expect me to, and if she's working, she won't appreciate the interruption. I get out my keys, and the door opens to reveal a maze of white cardboard evidence boxes.

"Nana?"

No answer, but her heels are right by the door, so she's here. I follow the trail she's left behind—nylon stockings, colorful silk scarf, pieces of mail—until I find her on the couch. She's still wearing the business casual outfit she wore to the office. She has a legal pad and a voice recorder—she's old enough that she hasn't adapted to the ubiquity of computers—and a white cardboard box in front of her. I could chart my high-school years by the case names on the boxes.

She doesn't notice me entering. She doesn't see me sorting the mail, tossing the junk, setting aside the power bill that she won't put on Autopay because she doesn't trust bank computers. She's skimming, making notes, and occasionally speaking into her recorder. The only way that she's let technology change her is that she now uses a tiny MP3 recorder to take dictation. She only switched to that because she stopped being able to buy cassette tapes in the grocery store.

I know better than to interrupt her when she's busy. Instead, I go to the fridge and open it.

Moldy cheese. A withered apple. A round plastic tub that proclaims that it can't believe it's not butter. A carton of eggs. I open the latter; a single brown egg sits forlornly inside. I peek in the plastic tub, because I do not believe it's butter. I am correct. It holds two pieces of gross, dry pizza.

In other words, Nana has a case that is going to trial, and she hasn't paid attention to anything around her for weeks.

She taps her recorder again. "Affidavit of David Caftan, white. File thirty-seven, box six. Pertinent facts: Contacted Infinity Housing on May 11, 2015, regarding the apartment listed in the paper. Was told the apartment was available, and Infinity made an appointment to show him the place." She will be at this forever.

I slip back out the door and head down the street. If this case goes like her cases usually do, she's going to live on apples and cheese, eaten hastily only when she remembers to look up from her work. I've tried to get her to take breaks for meals, but she even forgets about microwavable dinners.

It's been a little less than four years since I left for college, but in that short space of time, Nana's neighborhood has changed. The painted, ever-changing mural that used to face her building has been torn down and replaced with a glass-walled organic ice cream shop. The bodega down the street has turned into an upscale market.

When I enter, the cashier's eyes follow me carefully. Some blond scruffy guy wearing a hoodie advertising some app I've never heard of frowns at me as I consider the varied cheese selection, as if I'm the one out of place in the neighborhood where I went to high school.

The apples are all organic, and the bread bears the logo of some fancy bakery. I shake my head and get them anyway. I add a few things for dinner tonight, and we're set.

I return to my grandmother's apartment, put the groceries away, set the table, and, on further contemplation, start cleaning the bathroom.

When the light starts to fade, I turn on the light in the living room. She still doesn't seem to notice that I've arrived.

Nana's ability to concentrate is incredible. There's a reason she's one of the best trial attorneys in her office. She can shut out everything except her work for weeks on end. The sofa has a permanent indentation where she sits and works. She's one of the leading experts on fair housing law. From what I've been reading in the papers, she's about to bring one of the city's largest landlords to trial.

She puts the folder she's working on back in the box, reaches for the next, realizes she's come to the end of the box, and finally looks up.

"Oh." She stretches and blinks, as if the bright light of reality is blinding. "Maria. What time is it?"

"Seven thirty-six."

"You've been here an hour already?"

More like an hour and a half at this point.

"One day," I tell her, "someone is going to break into your apartment and steal everything. You'll be home, but you won't even notice they're here."

She smiles. "As long as they don't take my notes, I really don't care. And on the bright side, I won't get shot confronting them."

"I got dinner."

She frowns and peers in the direction of the kitchen over the edge of her reading glasses. "That looks nice. Did I have chicken in the house?"

"Don't take this the wrong way, but I didn't trust anything in the fridge. It was sketchy as hell."

"You didn't have to do that."

I don't say anything to that. The truth is, she took me in when I most needed her. Being useful is the least I can do after that.

"You went shopping." She stands up, her eyes narrowing. "Maria, you're a college student. You shouldn't be buying me groceries. That is exactly backward."

"It's nothing."

It is, really. The truth is, at this point, the ads and affiliate payments from my blog generate a little over a thousand dollars every month. Add in the fact that Blake Reynolds owns the house where I live and refuses to accept rent. I don't make enough to repay student loans or manage all the other adult bills I might otherwise have to deal with. But I still feel rich as hell.

She glares at me. "How much did you spend?"

"Thirty dollars."

"I'll pay you back." She glances around the living room. I hadn't gotten to the living room yet. It's littered with paper, boxes of evidence, a suit jacket, three blouses still in plastic dry cleaning, a take-out bag from a local Chinese restaurant, used wooden chopsticks...

"I'll pay you back," she amends, "when I find my purse."

"You mean you'll pay me back when pigs fly."

She sticks her tongue out at me, glances at the next box of evidence, and then stands.

"Oooh." She sets her hand on her stomach.

"Are you okay?"

She winces. "Fine. I just think I was sitting too long."

My grandmother is usually an excellent conversationalist. She's one of those people who can talk intelligently about everything. She can ask insightful, interesting questions about anything anyone can throw at her. She's bright, funny, and intelligent...except when she's about to go to trial. Then, her brain gets so crammed with the record from whatever case she's working on that there's no space for anything else. She sits at the table, in front of the plate I've made for her, and stares blankly at the setting as if she's forgotten what a fork is for.

"So. When does trial start?"

"Tuesday." She's still distracted. "I'm going to have nine days of witnesses." Her hand goes again to her abdomen. I translate this into layperson terms. With interruptions and bar conferences, with presentations from the other side, opening and closing arguments, drafting instructions to the jury... I can expect Nana to be completely out of commission for almost a month.

"Expecting anything good to come out at trial?"

"I don't expect. I know." She taps her fork against her plate. "And yes, it will all come out about as I expect.

There are always a few surprises, but it's not television. I can't tell you anything else about it."

I understand that. She's scrupulous about her ethical duties. She'll tell me all about cases after they've happened and everything becomes public; before trial, though, she just stares straight ahead like she's a zombie.

"You should eat," I point out.

She jumps and blinks, and then carefully takes a bite of the chicken that I have so carefully obtained from the market.

"I was thinking," she says slowly.

"Yes?"

"You're graduating in…" Doing math overtaxes her current brain capacity.

"Four months," I supply.

"Four months." She nods. "I can arrange things, I think. Take a vacation. I have…a lot of vacation days saved up. We should do something to celebrate."

I'm not sure if we're celebrating my graduation or my impending descent into the drudgery of full-time work.

"What do you want to do?"

She shrugs. "I don't know. Go somewhere?" She picks up a roll and rips a piece off. "Somewhere that has never heard of section 3604. You know. I'll do a brain dump or something."

"That's most of the world outside a courtroom."

"Then let's not go to a courtroom," she says. "You decide."

I look over at her. She appears to be serious. "Antarctica."

"Sure."

"It'll be winter there that time of year," I point out.

"Mittens," she says distractedly.

"Norway," I counter. "Everyone there is white. They don't have to worry about racial discrimination in housing rentals."

She smiles hopefully at nothing across the room. "Perfect. Although at the rate things are going, San Francisco will turn into entirely on-demand short-term housing in three years anyway. Just in time for me to retire."

I sigh and set a reminder on my phone to ask her whether she actually means this vacation talk when she's finished with her trial. She's probably serious about the vacation; she definitely would not want me to decide it all on my own. She is a woman of decided opinions. Or rather, she *will* have decided opinions. In a few weeks, when the trial is over.

I look over at her. She's eaten half her roll, a few bites of chicken, and no salad. She's already looking yearningly at the next box back in the room.

"I'll go get your box if you finish what's on your plate," I tell her.

Nana blinks and looks over at me. "Oh." She considers this. Her eyes slip back to the box, and then she shakes her head. "No, no. I'm being a bad grandmother. I should ask you what's going on in your life. Have you decided on a job yet after graduation? Are you seeing anyone?" She frowns. "I don't think I know the answer to any of these questions."

I take her hand. "You could never be a bad grandmother," I say. "Never, ever."

I'm not sure she hears this, and I'm glad. I don't want to talk about the person I'm not seeing. I don't want to *think* about him this weekend. Not once. She's looking back at her box.

"Eat your salad," I say. "I'm going to go get…what, you're on box seven?"

"Mmm." She touches her stomach again. "I'm not really that hungry, you know?"

"You are," I tell her. From experience, she is hungry—she just doesn't notice it. She'll notice it at midnight if she doesn't eat now.

I bring her the next box and her legal pad. I set her recorder next to her.

"Go ahead," I tell her. "Work. It's okay. I don't mind. I have things to do."

She picks out a file and starts reading. "You know," she says, "you really should have higher expectations."

I'm honestly not sure if she's talking to me or the file.

She presses record. "File one, box seven. Deposition of Frank M. Church, building manager for East Heights…"

She's not talking to me.

Some people might think that being ignored by my grandmother for weeks on end is cruel. Truth is, it's not that she's ignoring me; if I really needed her, she would be there for me. I know from experience. And it never lasts. In high school, I would spend a few weeks cleaning and making dinner, and then I'd come home from school one day and find her asleep in her spot. She'd sleep for a day and a half, and when she woke up, she'd take me out and make up for every last hour that she'd missed.

You can't pick and choose the people you love. The woman who throws herself into her Fair Housing trials is the same woman who has worked in the City Attorney's office in San Francisco for the last twenty-five years. Her office drove the lawsuit that invalidated California's ban on same-sex marriage under the state constitution back in 2008.

There was a reason she took me in without a question when I showed up on her doorstep. She didn't need an explanation. She'd already asked all her questions at work, had already made up her mind as to the answer.

And so when her work needs her, I'm willing to share. Because I know she'll wake up and remember that I'm here eventually, and when she does, it's always worth the wait.

20.

I don't want to talk to Jay. It takes me five days—the weekend I spend getting ignored by Nana, feeling my heart leap every time my phone buzzes—to realize that I don't want to *not* talk to him, either.

But since our late-night phone conversation after Gabe's seminar, he hasn't initiated a chat online. He hasn't emailed. He hasn't commented once on my blog, not even when I made a science error on purpose to draw him out. He's left the ball firmly in my court.

I tell Tina. She listens to the whole story quietly.

"What should I do?" I ask her. I'm not sure what I want her to say. Maybe I want her to tell me to get over myself. Maybe I want her to tell me that I'm better off without him.

She just frowns. "I suck at giving advice. What do you want to do?"

I look upward. "If I knew the answer to that, I wouldn't have to ask you, would I?"

I check the website for his group once, then a second time. He adds a new paper to his publications list on the fourth day after I found out who he was.

Because I am a dork, I read it.

His group picture, with him in a lab coat, arms folded, looking severely at the camera—doesn't change. I know this, because I check. Often. The only reason I spend more time on Facebook than his stupid website is because he's Facebook friends with Gabe.

He doesn't post anything on Facebook at all—at least nothing that is visible to me.

I make sure that all my posts are visible to friends of friends, and tell everyone how much fun I'm having. Since I also have two midterms in the days that follow, this is a complete lie, but I don't care. I make sure to have a long, rambling discussion with my brother in the comments of one of Gabe's photos. Mentally, I dare Jay to like my posts. I double-dog dare him with whipped cream and a cherry on top.

He doesn't.

I call Anj and spill everything that happened. Well, I kind of spill. I exaggerate. I make Jay out to be not just a jerk, but the giantest jerk on the face of the planet.

"Ooh, awkward," she says, when I get to the final reveal. "But in his defense, you *are* kind of a girly-girl."

I roll my eyes. "Thanks."

"I'm totally kidding. But seriously, Maria. People make mistakes. Either you get over it or you don't."

I try again. "He hasn't even tried to talk to me."

Anj continues with her unfair and impartial reasonableness. "You said you needed time. How dare he respect your boundaries." She doesn't even make it a question.

I frown at my phone. "Can't a girl vilify a man without getting rational pushback?"

"Is that what you were looking for?" She sighs. "You should have just said so. He sounds like the worst. The absolute worst. I hope he dies in a fire."

"Thank you," I say. "That's much better."

It doesn't feel better. If Jay were nothing but an asshole, this would be easy. I can ride out catastrophes. I've managed far worse.

It's the possibility of so much more that scares me. I know how well we can get along. I know we could make each other laugh. I know he…likes me, and that's the strongest word I'm willing to let myself think, no matter what he told me the other night.

Most relationships are an unknown when they start. With Jay, I know exactly how good it could be. I also know precisely how bad it might get.

Exactly one week after I learn that A. and Jay are the same person, I break down and look up the location of his office.

His office is in a building kitty-corner from his lab. The wooden door with his name on it is ajar when I poke my head out of the stairwell. I creep up to it and wait, cautious as a cat, expecting to hear him talking to someone.

I hear nothing but the click of a keyboard.

I raise my hand to knock, but my courage fails me. I lean against the wall.

I imagine opening the door more than a crack and poking my head in. He would look at me. I'm not sure if he would smile or frown and shake his head. I don't know what he would say. I'm not sure what I would say back. I want to be at my cleverest, but the truth is, I'm not sure how to use words out loud with him. We've only ever used spoken words to claw at each other.

I'm afraid that any face-to-face conversation will be nothing but barbs.

I'm afraid that if I take too long to come by…

I don't finish that sentence.

I may be doing this the coward's way, but at least I'm doing it. I take out my phone and send him a message. *Do you have a moment?*

I can hear the ding of his phone from his office. I wonder if he has a special tone for me. I don't have time to wonder anything else, because a moment later, my phone chirps in response. *I was afraid you weren't ever going to write to me.*

I bite my lip. *I needed time. Not forever.*

You don't exactly like me, he responds.

You don't exactly like me, either.

There's a longer pause. I can imagine him tapping away in response. *I like you,* comes his reply. *I like you exactly and precisely.*

My stomach roils. I've known that he likes me since… Since he sent me emoji in the hallway. Since he backed away when I told him I needed time. Since he told me he was basically in love with me, a sentence I still refuse to process.

My phone chirps again.

Also, if you're going to message me from the hallway outside my office, he writes, *either silence your phone or come in. It's distracting.*

I look up. He's standing in his office door looking at me. He's wearing jeans and a plain black shirt. He's watching me with an intensity that I can sense from here.

My skin prickles. Slowly, I straighten from where I'm slumped against the wall, brushing my skirt back into place.

His gaze falters to my hand as I smooth fabric down my thigh.

I don't say anything. I just walk toward him, step by unsteady step.

His gaze drops to my shoes—ivory kitten heels with powder-blue glass beads making a little swirling pattern—and comes back to my face.

I stop a foot from him.

We still haven't said a word to each other—not out loud—and I don't want to break that trend. Messaging is easier.

He steps aside, giving me room to enter his office.

I sit in the single plastic seat across from his chair as gracefully as I can under the circumstances.

He leaves his door open and slides into the high-backed executive chair on the other side.

His office is not what I expected from an overworked academic. My brother's desks—both his desks, at home and in his office—are piled high with stapled papers, notes on graph paper in pencil, seven-month-old utility bills, old sandwich wrappers…

Jay's desk has a grand total of three pieces of paper on it. Three.

His shelves are full. There are textbooks, books on computing, a series of monographs on lasers. There's an art piece on the wall. A sculpture on his desk.

No plants.

I'm avoiding looking at him. I make myself turn and look back at Jay.

He's watching me, waiting to see what I say. Maybe wondering if I will even use words.

Oral communication is overrated. *Better?* I send.

He glances down at his phone and his mouth quirks in a smile. *Better.*

He is...not hideously ugly. The opposite. His jaw is determined; his eyes are piercing. And when he smiles, all that purposeful certainty softens into something that feels like a welcome.

He smiles now, and I silently forgive him for not liking my comments on Facebook.

What happens now? I type.

He looks upward, then shrugs. *Something between us never talking again and us making out in my office right now. I have a strong preference between those two.*

I can't help it; I laugh. It's the medium. The fact that when our screens are between us, this is who we are to each other. We've been flirting for far too long, and it's become too second nature to us to stop.

Is the last one even an option? Aren't there rules against professor-student relationships?

He exhales and writes for a longer time. My phone buzzes again. *For obvious reasons, I looked up the code of conduct to figure out where we stood. You're a senior. You're not in my department. I do not have, and do not reasonably expect to have, academic responsibility for you. Unless you're planning on going to grad school here in chemistry and/or physics and you never told me?*

I shake my head.

Then it's not an issue. Also. I love your laugh.

I look over at him. I want to forget everything. I also want to enshrine it in my memory. I shake my head and write. *You are such a liar.*

He raises an eyebrow. *I've done a lot of shit wrong. But that was the truth. I love your laugh.*

Not about that. My gaze drops to the curve of his bicep, visible beneath his T-shirt, and then slides up. I take a deep breath. *You said you were hideously ugly.*

His lips twitch into a smile. *Beauty standards are complete shit. Also, I wanted to lower expectations.*

Fine. But get out of this one, I write. *Actual Physicist? You're in chemistry, not physics.*

He snorts and shakes his head as he types. *Remind me to send you an explanation of the weird division between chemistry and physics in the UK versus the States. It's not a one-to-one mapping.* He considers a moment, before typing again. *Besides, I told you I had a terrible personality. It's not my fault you didn't believe me.*

I consider this. *You do have a terrible personality.*

I know. I merited the fuck-off shoes.

I look down.

So does he.

I'm incredibly conscious of my shoes right now. I hadn't been thinking of him—much—when I put them on. The glass beads sparkle in the fluorescent light of his office.

These, I write, *are shoes I wear for courage. Which is why I'm messaging you from five feet away, instead of safely in my house.*

I'm sorry, he writes back. *I'm sorry. To say this was a fuck up is an understatement.*

I look at him. *I did start some of it. Some of the time. I seem to recall sending you drinks that one time.*

He suppresses a smile. *Some. But not most. My ego is fine. We don't need to pretend this started with anything but my treating you with utter disrespect.*

I look forward, and then type the scariest thing I have ever typed. *I keep asking myself if we can just start over and pretend none of this happened.*

He exhales. *No. We can't. I knew at LBL that if I said anything, it was over.*

I desperately want the alternate reality he posits. *You're such a dumbass. Why didn't you keep quiet? I give you retroactive permission to not tell me.*

He shrugs. *You would have found out anyway.* He pauses, frowns at his answer on the screen, and types again. *It would have hurt you if I kept quiet, and I couldn't hurt you any more than I had.*

I look up. He's watching me with an intensity that I don't want to understand.

It's too much. I can't—I just *can't*—take more of this. More and I'll have to think beyond the confines of my phone, to put him in a place in my life. I'm not ready to figure out where he fits.

I stand up.

He does, too. He looks at me across his desk, and I think about him saying we could make out. This is no longer a hypothetical possibility. It's *real*. I don't know what to do with this kind of real.

I need a little more time, I write.

He looks over at me, then types one last time. *I have something I've been holding for you. Can I give it to you?*

I consider this. *I like presents.*

It's not a present.

He opens a drawer on his desk and removes an envelope. The paper is almost translucent, stamped with tiny brown fibers. There's one word on the front, handwritten in a dark black: *Maria.*

I remember his handwriting from those damned napkins. I swallow. He holds it out to me

I reach out carefully. So carefully. I make sure I don't touch his fingers when I take it. I look over into his eyes.

We haven't said a word to each other the entire time.

I don't leave, though. We stay in place for several minutes, looking at each other. I don't know what he sees. I can't imagine what he's thinking. All I know is that this is Jay, and he hurt me.

I want to not hurt. I want, not with the power of lust, but with a deep-down desire, a quiet intensity. I want us to be friends. I want him to hold me. I want to lean my head against his chest and have the scent of him wash away my memories.

I know if I ask him to do it, he'll try.

I don't say the words.

"Thanks," I finally say instead. My voice feels rusty. My chest almost hurts. "I'll see you." Our eyes can't seem to break away from each other. "Good-bye, Jay."

He gives me a half smile. "See you around, Maria."

I'm aware of the letter tucked in my bag all the way home. Text should be text; I've exchanged hours and hours of messages with Jay. But somehow pixels on a lit screen, notifications that flash one second, are responded to the next, and scroll off into nothingness, pushed away by the next exchange of messages, are different than a physical letter. There's no timestamp telling me when he wrote it. For all I know, he's had it sitting in his drawer for days.

I can't respond immediately. He can't tell when—or if—I read it. It won't be backed up to any cloud service.

I wait until I'm home and can retreat to my room. I don't even pretend that I'm going to put it off any longer.

I tear the envelope open.

Dear Maria, he has written. *I am so sorry.*

I feel a pang in my chest. So am I.

I fucked up. I can't count the ways that I fucked up, but I will try.

1. I jumped to conclusions. I'm not going to excuse or explain myself; that's not the point of this letter.

I exhale slowly. He doesn't have to excuse or explain himself. The truth is, he already has. I put together the pieces slowly over the last week. He told me—the Maria me—that I reminded him of someone. He told me—the Em me—that he'd had a girlfriend who said something terrible to his brother. It's not hard to see what happened.

Even the fact that he was attracted to me probably messed with him. He doesn't trust his own judgment.

And yeah, he was still an ass. But having someone be an ass in a vacuum is a really different thing than understanding why someone was an ass.

2. You got under my skin early, and I treated you like crap because of it.

No excuses. I realized I'd come to an erroneous conclusion about you, and I hate being wrong. It was entirely obvious that I was wrong, and so I took it out on you. That was also fucked up.

In a way, I'm glad I waited to go talk to him. The day after he told me, I wouldn't have been able to hear this.

Yes, he did provoke me. But he also tried to apologize. And while I can't pretend that we were equally at fault, I can recognize that for the last couple of months, I've been the one pushing most of the hostility. He was the one making jokes about confirmation bias.

3. I don't know how to go forward. I don't know if there is a forward. But you are important to me.

I don't know what to do with that. It's the simple truth. You are important to me.

You're important enough that even if there is no when, if there is no what, and there is no longer a me in your life, I'm going to do better.

Yours,

Jay

I'm not sure what to do with this letter. Maybe I was hoping that he'd have some magic insight, something that changed everything. Maybe I was hoping that he'd give me an excuse. Some way that I could forget what happened.

I put my head in my hands.

Maybe *I* want an excuse.

And maybe, maybe what that tells me is that he's important to me, too. It tells me that there is a when, there is a what, and I want him to be in my life.

And that scares me most of all.

JAY

$\mathcal{T}$he day after I give Em the letter, I bury myself in everything I can find.

This is why I find myself hovering over my poor graduate students. I provide four separate (yet equally valid) solutions for one of the problems I give them. One uses Feynman diagrams, even though they haven't covered Feynman diagrams in any of their classes.

Work expands to cover all bruises. I wonder if Em's read my letter. What she thinks. I don't let myself wonder too long. Looking at my phone leaves me with a hollow, empty feeling, so I don't look.

I'm still in my office at nine at night. Everyone reasonable has left; the hall is dark outside my door. I'm not tired enough to go home yet. If I'm tired enough, I won't dream about her.

Dreams suck. In my dream last night, we sat in a dark room. We talked—or rather, she talked. She asked me questions I couldn't answer. Couldn't, not wouldn't—in my dream, I felt like I was gagged. I tried to find words, but my throat wouldn't work. My mouth struggled against cotton. Nothing I wanted to say came out.

So today I work, because working is as close as I can come to answering her. I'm trying not to think about Maria, and I'm failing miserably.

I think of her as I draw a quantum circuit. I sketch in a controlled-NOT gate and try not to remember two months ago, when I was drawing gates and exchanging rapid-fire messages. I imagine her every time my email pings, every time my phone buzzes with a notification.

I hear the squeak of one of the metal fire doors down the hall, and I have to tell myself that it's not her. There have been people in the hall all day, and they haven't been her.

The automatic lights turn on, banishing the darkness with cold, clinical fluorescence. I hear footsteps and the sharp click of heels against tile. I shut my eyes and look upward. The image in my head is...not one I think I will ever be able to dispel.

Anyone could be here wearing heels. Karen, one of my colleagues, could be stopping by her office after going out to dinner.

The association between heels and Em is permanently, distractingly embedded in my brain.

The footsteps stop near my door.

I shut my eyes.

It won't be Em. It *isn't* Em. It can't be Em. The building is locked and she doesn't have access. But whoever it is doesn't move. I wait a minute. Then two. Then I give in. I shut my laptop and go to the door.

It *is* Maria. Even illuminated in the dim fluorescent lights of the hall, she's striking. Tonight she's wearing a skirt that comes just past her knees, and—of course—

heels. Shorter heels, this time—an inch of shiny blue, and then the long expanse of her legs.

Her legs are so fucking perfect. I can almost feel them against the palm of my hand. I can imagine them wrapped around me, with her perched on the edge of my desk...

She sees me standing there, and at that exact moment, the energy-saving, motion-sensing lights give up. There's a click, and we're plunged into darkness. The only light in the hall trickles from behind me.

It's too much like my dreams. I speak, just to make sure that I can.

"Maria." My voice sounds as dark as the hall.

She doesn't move, and so the lights don't turn on.

"Hi." Her voice sounds like velvet. "You're still here. Rachel let me in. I told her Gabe needed me to give you something. I hope that's okay."

"It's okay."

I can only see her silhouette, the dark shadow of her. Those legs. That slight lift to her chin.

"Rachel said you talked to her. About what happened that night in November. That you...were sorry, and were working on things."

Repeating that I'm trying is unnecessary. It's beyond the point now.

"Em," I say instead. "It's good to..."

See her? I can't, not really. Hear from her? She's said basically nothing. But it's still good to be around her.

She exhales. "I need to know. Is this it? If I say no, we're done, do we just...not even talk to each other again?"

"Yeah," I say. "That's pretty much how it works. If you don't want to talk to me again, then yes, we don't talk to each other again."

"Were we even friends?"

"Don't take this the wrong way, but I'm not up for a metaphysical discussion on the nature of friendship. If you can't figure out that we were friends on your own, we probably weren't."

She takes a step toward me, something I sense—the click of her heels, the breath of disturbed air in the hall—more than I see.

"Jay being an asshole," she says, "that, I can forgive. But *you.*" She says that word as if she's still trying to reconcile me with…*me.* "*You,* you knew me. And you kept pushing me away. No names, no numbers. You wouldn't even admit we were flirting with each other."

I exhale. "I know. I'm busy, and that tends to fuck up relationships. I'm not perfect. I'm still working things out."

She takes another step toward me, and now I can resolve a hint of her features in the darkness. Dark pits where her eyes must be. The curve of her nose. The play of shadow across brown skin.

"You shoved me away." Her voice shakes. "How do I know you won't again?"

"I don't know." My hands clench at my sides. "I'm still getting to the point where I can forgive myself. How am I supposed to tell you how to do it?"

It's harder to talk now that I can see her. Now that she's close enough that the back of my mind is calculating the diffusion of room-temperature air. I'm wondering how many of the molecules she breathes are reaching my lungs.

The chances of any one molecule crossing that gap are miniscule. But there are a lot of molecules.

"Aren't we a pair." She shakes her head. Her hair moves slightly, and I feel a slight breath of air—Em's molecules—wafting over me. "All this brain power, and we can't close these last inches between us."

"We can figure it out." I sound more certain than I am.

Underlying my back-of-the-envelope calculations— now with added nonequilibrium perturbations for the velocity of our breath—is a simple truth: I want her. I want her a lot. I want to run my hands through the silk of her hair. I want to pull her close. I want to take her home with me and...

"Stop pushing me away, you idiot." She takes another step in.

I can see her eyes now, brown pools glinting in the dim light from my office behind us. I can see her lips, sweet and slightly open. I can see the way she's looking at me.

"Stop thinking. Just hold me."

I reach out and set my fingers on her cheek. She's warm, so warm to the touch, and she doesn't pull away. She looks up.

My fingers slide down her jaw. Her hand comes up, touches mine. But she doesn't push me away. She pulls me closer, and I drift in.

Talk is hard. Talk requires a theoretical basis for understanding the phenomenon at issue, and this is one aspect of reality that I simply do not comprehend.

The theory of how we work together may be insoluble, but empirical study is possible. Inevitable, even. Her touch on my hand. A smell that makes me think of cupcakes—sweet and vanilla—as I bend my head to hers. Her inhale, then that sweet, slow exhale as we close the distance between our mouths.

Talk is hard; kissing is easy. It's the easiest thing in the world to kiss her. To feel a hum of satisfaction in the back of my throat, to step even closer, to wrap my free hand around her waist and pull her in. It's the easiest thing to brush my lips against hers, once, and then twice.

I'm not sure if I'm coaxing her or if she's coaxing me. We're equally wary. Equally wanting. She opens to me the way I open to her—slowly, impossibly, undeniably.

Kissing Em is easy.

It's been too long. The last time I made out with anyone was five months ago. At a bar. With a woman whose name I've since forgotten. It was what other people might call "meaningless" sex.

It wasn't meaningless. Touch is never meaningless. It's a need I can't completely jettison, no matter how much I wish I could—the desire to touch and be touched. No matter how hard I try, it's a base animalistic requirement, one that's wired as deep as thirst or hunger, and I'm famished.

I kiss my way down her neck, pulling her close. She's almost trembling.

"Em," I whisper. "Maria."

"Jay."

We say each other's names like they're universal constants, things that are unchanging no matter what distance we traverse.

Our tongues are tangling, now, saying all the things that our brains can't figure out. We shift; somehow, my back ends up against the wall, and Maria settles against me. Her legs brush mine. I'm beyond hard, and my body wants something that is impossible, because there is no way I'm taking her home tonight.

"I hate you," she says.

"I know."

"I wish you weren't you."

"I know."

"I really, really like you."

"I know." I kiss her again, because words aren't helping.

We kiss like this is the first time and the last time, all wound up in one. And maybe it is. Maybe this is the way I'll end up saying good-bye to Em. Maybe this is it. There will be no conversation, no resolution, no farewell. Just this kiss, burning into us forever until everything we could have been to each other turns to ashes.

I angle her chin up and pull her against me.

Somehow, that slight movement, after all this time is what sets the motion sensors off. Ugly yellow-tinged light floods the hall.

She pulls back an inch, and we look into each other's faces. "I missed you," she says.

Most of the breath we share is nitrogen. It's inert in human beings—we breathe it in only to expel it. She's right. I pushed her away. I can pull her close. I don't know how to convince her to trust me. To *expect* that I won't mess up, when we both have every reason to believe I will.

But I won't figure it out if I don't start. "Have dinner with me tomorrow," I say instead.

"Okay."

It's as easy as that. Her phone chimes, and she glances down at her watch. That's the point when I notice that she's wearing a Cyclone Vortex. Of course she is. Everyone has a Vortex these days. Mom would be so proud.

"I'm sorry," she says. "My ride is leaving in five minutes and I don't want to walk home in the dark."

"Your ride?"

She makes a face. "This is so weird. I…long story short, my housemate is my BFF."

"That's not weird."

She bites her lip and looks away. "We live about a mile from campus. I share the house with Tina and her boyfriend. I can walk or take the bus, but he has a car. So if we're leaving at the same time, it's easiest to carpool."

"Where are you meeting them?"

"The parking structure a block from Soda Hall."

"I'll walk you, if you want."

She looks at me. "Yes."

She doesn't say anything to this. I thumb through some papers in a drawer from my desk, get a messenger bag, and then shrug on a jacket. She watches me carefully.

"What the hell are we doing?" I ask as I join her in the hallway.

"I have no idea."

"Good. We're in this together."

"Here." Her hand slides into mine.

We don't talk. We hold hands. I could say it doesn't mean anything, but I prefer not to practice self-deception. I'm holding her hand because I want to hold her. Because I care about her. Because I've spent years not letting myself have expectations and dammit, I want to expect her.

We arrive in the area she's designated, and I take a look around. "Your ride isn't here yet."

"They'll be… Oh, there they are." She drops my hand. "Tell me when will work for you tomorrow."

"Seven?"

"Okay."

The two figures I see across the way approach.

"Hey, Maria," says a female voice.

Then…

"Oh my god," says the man with her. "Jay?"

I freeze in place. That voice brings back too many memories. Afternoons at Cyclone, because my parents were busy and the only way Mom could make sure we were doing our homework was to have us there. My brother, wandering down the halls of Cyclone, hiding in one of the computer labs.

All our old red team/blue team games. That's the point when I remember that Maria's housemate—the one who lives with her—is dating a Cyclone guy. She didn't mention that he was *that* Cyclone guy.

I exhale and turn. "Blake?"

He gives me a genuine smile. "Jay. What are you doing here?"

"Discovering how tiny the world is. Em, I didn't realize that *Blake* was your housemate."

"Technically, Tina is my housemate," Maria says. "Blake is... Um."

"By the transitive property of housematery," I reply, "I'm pretty sure that makes Blake Reynolds your housemate, too."

"There is no transitive property of relationships."

"Not generally, no, but housematery is a special case."

Our eyes meet. Maria smiles first—a shy, sweet smile, then a larger one, until we're grinning at each other.

"Look how sweet that is," Maria's housemate says. "They're flirting with math."

I can see the slight hesitation in Maria's smile, and I remember that we've been down this road before. Last time she mentioned flirting with math, I pretended it wasn't happening.

There's only one way to get her to believe I won't push her away. I have to not do it. Over and over again, until she believes in me.

"In my defense," I say, "math is pretty hot. And I only have so many tools."

Her smile broadens. Our hands twine, briefly, warmth on warmth.

I've got one chance to make this work. Whatever I do, I'm not letting it go.

21.

MARIA

$\mathcal{E}$ating in the restaurant where I had dinner with Jay and Gabe last September is giving me the strangest sense of déjà vu.

The waitstaff even conducted us to the same table—a square thing, still sporting the same unlit candle, the same plastic flower arrangement. Instead of sitting across from Jay, though, I sit kitty-corner from him.

Our shoes brush under the tablecloth. Our hands could touch.

Jay orders the same thing that he did in September—spaghetti with marinara sauce. I order the same ravioli.

He waits until the waiter disappears with our orders before turning to me.

Last time we were here, he offered to make me a deal. He leans in, and I almost expect him to say those exact words. *I'll make you a deal.*

He doesn't, though. He just looks at me. I can feel his gaze like a physical caress. It feels like he's trying to memorize me, which is silly, because he knows me.

A fragment of a chant flits through my head. *He knows me; he knows me not.* I could dismember every plastic flower in here looking for an answer to that question. All that would give me was fake green stems strewn with thorns. All too appropriate; he can still hurt me.

That's true of anyone—friend, family, lover—at any point. But for Jay, it's not a hypothetical. I know he can hurt me because he *has*.

Looking at him almost stings. I'm used to seeing my own failures in his eyes.

"So, Mr. Laser." I wield the humor in my voice like a shield. "What's a focused guy like you doing in a place like this?"

He looks down at his hand on the table, fingers lightly tapping next to his silverware. Then he looks back at me. The corner of his lips curve in a smile.

"What's it look like?" he says. "I'm focusing."

Oh. Everything I have flutters—my breath, my body, even my experience of sensation.

"On something that isn't science?" Teasing is easy. "I'm shocked."

"Turns out," he says, "I'm tunable between four hundred and fifty nanometers and you."

He picks up his glass of water and takes a sip.

"My," I say primly. "What a large wavelength you have."

He chokes, coughing on his water. Then he looks back at me, and that small smile blazes into a bonfire. He coughs again, wipes his mouth with his napkin, and glances upward. "Look what I almost missed out on by being an idiot."

"Who are you talking to?"

"Mental note," he says. "To the universe. Just in case I forget. Which I do not plan to do." He puts the napkin down and sets his hands on the table, palms up.

He's wearing a blue button-down shirt over jeans. No tie. The first two buttons at his neck are undone. I think for him this is dressing up. Just beyond his cuffs, I can see the lines of dark ink on his skin, a spill of dull black from his wrist to his palm.

It's an invitation. For a moment, I hesitate.

But I didn't come here to hesitate. I already care about him. He can already hurt me. I'm putting myself out here like this out of pure, unadulterated selfishness. If I'm going to get hurt, I'm taking every last drop of pleasure I can wring from the experience first.

So I reach out, set my fingertips on the edge of the geometric pattern, and ask. "What is this?"

"My little brother used to draw these really intricate designs in his school notebooks at lunch." For the first time during dinner, his eyes shift off-center.

He told me about his little brother just over a week ago. I know him, and I don't.

"So it's a memorial."

"Something like that." His voice is low. "And someday, I'll tell you everything about my baby brother. But...maybe not today."

No. I swallow. I put a second finger on his palm. "Fine by me."

We don't say anything for another few seconds.

"I didn't mean to make things awkward," he says. "Although, I suppose that is our specialty."

"Your specialty." I smile at him. "Not mine."

"Mmm. I won't ask for examples."

His palm is warm against my forefinger. And somehow, it's simple to slide my fingers down his palm to his wrist and then trace them back.

"Actually," I say, looking at him, dropping my voice and doing my best to imitate his accent, "have you noticed that we get along really well?"

He laughs. "Don't remind me. That was...not me at my best."

My fingers slide back to his wrist; his fingers curve up to tickle my palm, sending a shiver of anticipation up my arm. Our hands interlock.

"Oh?"

"Oh." He half-smiles and looks at me. "Or I'll remind you that two can play at that game."

"Oh?"

"In fact," he says, "let's talk about my accent."

I look at him.

"My pretentious, holier-than-thou, godforsaken British accent." He tilts his head at me. "Did I miss an adjective?"

"Oooh." I try to pull away, but he closes his hand around my wrist.

"I see how it is. It's all fun and games until I start teasing you." His forefinger is gentle, stroking my arm, and somehow, being able to smile about what we've said to each other... It doesn't make it better. It just makes it more manageable.

"Fake," I tell him. "Don't forget that I called it fake."

He looks at me. "Admit it. You love my accent."

Heat builds in my inner core. "Maybe. I mean, sure. Everyone does. So explain. I know you went to Cambridge, but that's rather late in life to develop an accent and have it stick."

"It's not from Cambridge." His finger traces my wrist. "It's simple, really. My mom went to a fancy-pants British school in Hong Kong when she was growing up. So *she* has something of an accent."

"Okay."

"Then when I was five, my mother was given charge of Cyclone's European software localization team, headquartered in London. So I went to a fancy-pants British school, too."

"Oh. I didn't know that."

"I lived in London until I was eleven, when Mom was put in charge of the entire programming and applications division. We came back here. By that time, my accent was firmly in place. I tried to lose it in high school, with mixed success."

"Oh," I say faintly. "I see. It's all very simple."

"Precisely." He smiles. "It sounds put-on at this point because it's a bit of posh London, a sprinkle of Silicon Valley, two summers in Thailand with my dad, a visit to India where my uncle lives, a month in Hong Kong—the usual." He shrugs.

The usual. "I've left California exactly twice," I admit. "Once was to go to Gabe's hooding at Harvard. The other was for an interview a few weeks ago, where I learned I hate New York City. My parents are from California. My grandparents are from California. My great-great-great-great grandparents, at least the ones we know about, are from Mexico, but only in the sense that they're from the part of California that used to be Mexico."

"Now *that* is complicated." His fingers tickle my palm, gently first and then with increasing pressure. "All those people, all coming from one place? What are the odds of that? Were they descended from the original Spanish settlers in California?"

I shake my head. "Who can actually trace their family back that far?"

"Uh." He grimaces. "Me? On my dad's side, at least, we're descended from one of the long-lost branches that's related to former Thai royalty."

I blink at him. "Does that mean you're in line for the throne?"

"Now you see why I never give out my name online. That's not remotely how the succession works. Only in a novel does the nineteenth cousin of a long-ago king, fifteen times removed, who renounced Thai citizenship at eighteen—"

"Wait, how were you a Thai citizen?"

"My mom was born in Thailand, although she's ethnically Chinese."

"Right," I say. "I should have known. The simplest possible answer."

"It only looks complicated from the outside. This is what normal looks like in my family. I haven't really delved into half of it. I should also mention that while my mother is Muslim, my father is Buddhist."

"And you?"

He shrugs. "I'm flexible."

I blow out my breath. "So what I'm hearing is that your mother is Cyclone royalty and your father is *actual* royalty. I'm a peasant by comparison."

One of his eyebrows goes up. But before he can say anything, the food comes.

I look at our hands, entwined on the table, my left hand locked with his right. We're different. We're so different, but our hands fit together. And they will, as long as we don't have to eat.

"Em," he says in a low voice, "it really is simple. I'm going to let go of your hand now because I have to eat. But I'm taking it again when I am done, and I'm not letting go until you tell me I have to."

I want to believe it is that simple. That every complicated thing in our past can be wiped away with dinner and the look he gives me. I want to believe that this is a start.

I look into his eyes. He hurt me before, inch by inch, piece by piece. He didn't see me. He pushed me away.

But I didn't come here to nurse my hurt. I came here to be brave. I came here to admit what I want, and to take it. There's no place for my fear except deeper inside me.

And so I push my worries into a little ball and let go of his hand.

---

*J*ay helps me into my coat when we're leaving, which—let's face it—is basically an opportunity for him to put his hands all over me, and for me to discover that he is utterly confused by the concept of a structured coat with a belt.

I helpfully pop the lapels back into place, untwist the fabric strip of a belt, and let him pretend that he can actually tie it in something like a bow.

He takes my hand just outside the restaurant. If this weren't the middle of winter, I'd be up for walking aimlessly. But my breath freezes with every exhalation, and three inches of my thighs—between my coat and my boots—are bare to the wind.

What would be a meander turns into a forced march. I'm not sure where we're going, or what we're doing. I'm shifting from foot to foot on a street corner, waiting for a light to change, when he finally speaks.

"What is the opposite of rose-colored glasses?"

I blink and look at him. The red from the signal paints his hair in stripes of burgundy. It gives his eyes a deep, heavyset feel.

"You mean glasses of pessimism? Ones that make anything look worse? Why do you want to know?"

His hand is warm in mine even though it's cold out. He looks at me. "Just trying to figure out what I was wearing before. Somehow, I knew you for months before I noticed you were the most beautiful woman in the world."

I turn to him. The line should be cheesy. But he delivers it in a tone of confusion, as if he's just coming to the realization. As if he didn't know he believed it until he spoke out loud.

I laugh in response. It sounds fake. "Wow," I say instead. "That was smooth. Nice setup. Great execution."

His nose wrinkles and he looks away.

My emotions are like a knife in my stomach. They're confused by the waft of pheromones, the tight, tingling physical awareness between my legs, and the sparkle of nerve endings coming to life in his presence.

My mental state feels like the afterimage of a hundred little jabs burned on my eyelids, assailing me every time I shut my eyes.

The light changes, and we start across the street. Our hands clench together tightly. He squeezes my fingers as if I might disappear.

I want him. I want him to make me laugh. I want him to interrupt me in the middle of my day with a funny message. I want to not flinch when he tells me I'm beautiful. I want to trust him.

The thick branches of an oak tree hang over the sidewalk. It casts us into darkness when we pass under it.

I tug him to a halt.

His eyes catch the reflection of a passing car: bright one second, dark the next.

"What is it?"

I take my hand from his. "You have something on your chin." His jaw is smooth and defined under my fingers.

"Oh." He stands still under my exploration. His sigh warms my thumb.

"Here." I reach up. I bracket his face with my hands.

"*Oh,*" he says. His voice drops a half-octave.

Before I lose my nerve, I lean in. His breath is warm. I hesitate—one tiny second—and he wraps his arm around me, fingers pressing into the small of my back, and kisses me.

My eyes flutter shut. Those searing afterimages—
memories of what we've done to each other, every time
we've hurt each other—skip across my vision.

I kiss them away. Nibble by nibble. Exhalation by
exhalation. The tentative touch of our tongues is a burst
of forgetfulness. We kiss with the lingering sweetness of
the dessert we skipped at the restaurant.

"It's not the rose-colored glasses," I say when he
pulls away slightly. "It's the light source."

"Trust you to pick an analogy I can understand."

I know Jay the way I know shadows cast on a wall.
Move the light, and the shadows change. I've seen him in
sunlight and in the harsh glare of traffic signals. Now, we
kiss in time to the intermittent headlights of passing
cars—a long, slow melding of mouth and body, breaking
away, and starting all over again.

We pass heat back and forth between us. His chest
is a hard plane beneath my hand. I can feel his erection
coming to life against my hips.

I pull away an inch. "So why do we always kiss in
the dark?"

His eyes bore into mine. "I have lights at my
house."

This time, when I laugh, it doesn't feel forced at all.
"Wow," I say. "That *was* smooth."

He just removes his hand from the small of my back
and holds it out, palm up. "Are you coming?"

Hurt or no, memory or no, I know myself. Jay has
been my friend for ages, and despite what has happened,
I know the truth. I want him. I want *this*. Nothing else I
feel changes that.

I take his hand. "How far away are you?"

"Four blocks."

Now that we've embraced once, we don't want to stop. We don't just hold hands; our fingers explore. Our bodies brush, hip to hip.

Our eyes meet when we cross the street, and I feel myself flush from my face down to my thighs. That wash of heat lingers halfway down the block.

"Are you okay to walk in those heels?" he asks. "I should have asked before."

These heels are short—a mere inch, which on knee-high black leather boots is nothing.

"I'm fine."

"So what do these shoes mean?"

The meaning of these shoes is pretty standard. I just smile and shake my head. "Guess."

"You wore them for good luck on an exam."

My smile broadens. "Nope."

We cross a street, and he looks down, as if he's genuinely puzzled.

"Huh." His thumb strokes mine. "I don't want to be so self-centered that I imagine they're intended for me."

I return the caress of his thumb. The cracks in the sidewalk sprout bits of grass, golden-orange in the streetlight. "Be self-centered," I say. "I wore them for you."

His gaze jerks down again, lingering. His breath stutters a moment.

"They're 'let this not be a horribly awkward date' shoes," he guesses.

My laughter gurgles out. "No."

"They're generalized first date shoes," he guesses.

I laugh again. "*Generalized* first date shoes? How do you generalize first dates? Is this even a first date?"

His gaze sweeps me from head to toe in a lengthy, searing glance. "It's a first date, unless you're counting the time I drove you down from LBL and we snapped at each other."

"What about the time you walked me up to LBL and we yelled at each other?" I point out.

"There was a somewhat provocative rendezvous in my parents' mudroom."

"I bought you drinks and sent you insults." My cheeks flame. "I want a rematch. I was half-drunk at the time."

"Well." His fingers run up my arm. "That's what you get for not being prepared to engage in mortal combat at the drop of a napkin. You can't defend against a takeover of the realm like that."

Our eyes meet. And I laugh. Laughter loosens that tight tenseness inside me. Being able to laugh about everything that came before gives me hope. Tingling, aching, breath-holding hope.

"Let's just put brackets around all those," Jay says, "and call them date zero. One spectacularly terrible date. And we're here."

We've stopped in front of a house. I'm not sure what I was expecting. An apartment, maybe. If I'd really thought about it, I would have envisioned his parents' palatial estate in the hills ten miles from the heart of Silicon Valley. Instead, Jay's house is small and cozy, painted wood beams in multiple colors framing the windows. A yellow light by the door is on.

He leads me up the steps to a wooden front porch, and drops my hand long enough to unlock the door. "Here we are. Home sweet home."

It's the kind of older craftsman home that nobody makes any longer. The carving on the door, the wood beams bracketing the windows, suggest careful attention to detail. The porch is swept and leafless.

Jay sets his shoes on a shelf and opens the door.

"Should I take my boots off?" I ask.

He ushers me in and flips the inside light on. I get a glimpse of golden wood floors, walls in cream and light green.

"That depends." When his voice deepens, his accent seems more prominent.

"On how long I'm staying?"

Slowly he shakes his head. "On whether you'd prefer me to take them off instead."

My nerves coalesce in my stomach into a heated boil. I can't look away from him. "Well." My voice starts a little hoarse. "That would be the entire point of wearing these."

He looks down. I'm aware of the pressure of my boots against my skin—a palpable presence, soft and warm and safe. He's about to strip that away.

He undoes my coat, button by button. His hands linger on the belt. "You never did tell me what the shoes meant."

"You never did guess."

"They're take-me-off shoes." His hands slide the belt ring out, then glide lightly up my sides. I've never been so aware of my own body. Of the heat of his.

I shake my head. "Close. Not quite."

He slides the coat off me. I'm not sure what I was expecting—maybe for him to toss it to one side and kiss me. Instead he opens a closet and puts it on a hanger. He hangs up his own jacket before he turns back to me.

"You put things away."

There's no mail on the side table. No cups strewn about the living room.

He shrugs and gestures me to a chair. "Sit."

I do.

He kneels in front of me. His hands skim up my boots. I can feel the soft leather give slightly against that gentle pressure. He looks up into my eyes, and warmth washes over me.

He finds the zipper at my left knee and slowly, slowly pulls it down.

"In common parlance," he says, "one would call these fuck-me boots." His fingers touch the sensitive flesh at my knees, and an electric current arcs through me. He hasn't taken his eyes off me. "The thought occurred to me…possibly the moment I laid eyes on you at the restaurant." His finger travels down my leg, down the silky black stocking I am wearing, to my ankle. He shakes the boot loose. "But here's the thing—if they *are* fuck-me boots, I want you to say it."

I can scarcely speak. "They are fuck-me boots."

He exhales. Finds the zipper of the other boot. "I would hate to be presumptuous. After all, you would have wanted to make up your mind sometime after you put your boots on."

"No." He unzips my other boot, and my voice skitters up a few notes as cool air hits my thigh. "Not at all."

"No, you haven't made up your mind?"

I shake my head. "No. I intended to do my best to fuck you when I put on the shoes." It was the only simple truth in this whole mess. This will likely come crashing down. But since it's inevitable, I might as well enjoy myself. And him.

Slowly, he peels back the leather. "Maria." His fingers slide down my leg. His eyes meet mine. "Do you think I'm the sort to put out on a first date?" There's a glint of humor in his expression. His thumb brushes my knee, telling me that he is exactly that sort.

I reach out and run my hand down his jaw. His eyes flutter shut when I brush my thumb along his lips. "Jay," I whisper, "I have always known—deep down—that I could bring you to your knees. It was just a matter of wanting to do it."

He's on them now. He doesn't protest. His hands come to the tops of my thighs. "Fair enough. I've always known what I would do if I ended up here." His voice is like rich, dark chocolate. "Anything off-limits here?"

I exhale and let go. "Touch everything." He slides my legs apart. Leans down. That first touch of his mouth against my kneecap... My eyes shut, and I give in to the sensation. His palms burn hot against my thighs. His mouth slowly kisses up my inner thigh. His fingers crawl up my hips and hook in my underwear.

"Tell me you love it," he growls.

My voice is trembling as I speak. "I like it."

He lifts his head to look into my eyes. "Careful. I enjoy a challenge."

I run my hands through his hair. "I know."

He exhales in a rush and pulls my panties down. But instead of tossing them to the side, he deliberately shakes them out. Folds them. Sets them next to my boots.

When he returns his full attention to me, I want to shiver. He always did tell me he was focused, and having him look at me like that...

My throat feels dry. My fingers curve against his scalp.

"Watch out." He slides his hands up from my knees. His thumbs press into my inner thighs. "I don't think you've ever seen me when I have something to prove."

I'm pretty sure Jay has always had something to prove. I shake my head. "So prove it."

He gives me an intense, breath-stopping half smile. Then he bows his head and leans forward.

The first kiss against my inner thigh is tender. Then he pushes my skirt up and leans in, and the next kiss—a few inches up—is searing. My legs fall open. I tilt my head back.

He shifts, spreading my legs farther apart, hiking my skirt to my waist, and kisses me right between the legs—right on my clit.

The moan I make seems to reverberate in my chest. My toes. He glances up and his tongue flicks out, touching the bundle of nerves that makes up what is now my clit. It's light, but sensation scatters through me.

The lights seem brighter. Hotter.

"Do you love it?" he growls.

"More." My hands tangle in his hair, and he brings his mouth back to me. Licking. Caressing. Fingers spreading me open, petal by petal, tongue caressing my center.

I've held back everything I can, trying to close my heart like a fist. But I unfurl for him now.

If he was trying to prove that I was vulnerable—that after everything we've gone through, I'd open for him, soft and trembling—he's done it. I can't hold anything back. I let everything go, kiss by kiss, caress by caress. I let him know my secrets. Let him discover what makes me tremble.

"I love it," I moan.

He looks up long enough to meet my eyes with a knowing, triumphant smile.

I let him into me, one lick at a time, until my heart is beating in time with the rhythm he develops. Until it feels like he's holding on to my soul. I let him in, and finally—I let go.

He holds me as I let out a little noise. Searing pleasure rushes through me on a wash of warmth. It overtakes me completely, wiping all thought from my mind. Then, it ebbs slowly away.

When I can finally focus again, he's watching me. His eyes seem almost black.

My hands are tangled in his hair.

I smooth the strands back in place. I clear my throat, just to be sure my voice will work again.

Then I speak. "Are you done?"

"Not hardly."

"Good." I swallow. "Take me to bed."

He does. I don't really have a chance to see the house. It's a blur of cream walls and exposed wood beams. His bed is low and long, white linen and turquoise pillowcases.

That's all I notice before he catches me up and kisses me, pressing his body against mine. My eyes flutter shut. Our bodies fit together so perfectly when we're standing. I can feel the hard length of his cock against me.

"Hey." His voice is dark. "Maria. I want you so much."

I let my hands fall to the button of his jeans. His hands encompass mine. We undo the snap together. He shifts the fabric over his hips as I undo the zipper.

I trace the length of his erection through the fabric of his boxers. His breath hisses out.

"Em. I'm so fucking horny."

I take off his shirt. His chest is a light brown. The light gives it a hint of gold.

"How do I take off your dress?"

I turn around. "One zipper."

His hands are warm on the nape of my neck. Cool air whispers against my spine as he unzips me.

I'm aware of the echo of my last orgasm, fading but still resonant. His fingers brush my hips. My shoulders. He undoes my bra.

I let my clothing slip to the ground and turn around.

That intensity in his eyes is dialed up. His gaze sweeps over me. I felt vulnerable before; now my breath is a hot miasma in my chest.

"Em." His voice caresses me. "You're..."

My eyes meet his.

"You're utterly lovely."

He pulls me to him and kisses me.

It shouldn't be this easy to give up everything. To let myself relax against him.

It is.

It's easy when he pulls me into bed. When he cradles me with his arms, making me feel safe. When he kisses my throat. My jawbone. The underside of my breast. I catch fire again when he kisses my nipple.

"Anywhere you don't want me to touch?" I ask in return.

He shakes his head and kisses me again.

It feels so safe in his bed. So safe kissing him. Learning his responses touch by touch. Shifting his boxers down his lean frame, learning the way he clenches his jaw when something feels good.

He pulls away for a minute—to dart into a bathroom and come back with a condom and lube.

I roll the latex down his length. Let him push two slick fingers inside me.

I guide him inside me. "Shh." I hold up a hand. "You're big. Let me adjust."

He kisses me. I lied. He's perfect. It's not my body that needs to adjust. It's my heart. I'm not sure how it is that he's fitting, but he is.

I love the feel of him inside me. Of him taking me. Of me opening for him. For the minutes when our bodies join, I love that I can almost let go of my lingering fears. I sink into the feel of his mouth on mine, his body on mine. I give myself over to the slide as we join, and the friction as he pulls out. He adjusts his hips so that he grazes my clit at the end of every stroke. I give myself over to the feel of him, the feel of us.

When he comes, I feel it.

I open my eyes first. His hair is damp, slicked back against his forehead. He lets out a shuddering breath. Then he opens his eyes.

I knew I couldn't keep myself safe from him before. I knew I was going to care about him. That I was going to get hurt.

I was fine with it.

But right now, looking up into his eyes, having tasted perfection, I'm aware of just how much he can hurt me.

And   I   almost   don't   care.

22.

JAY

"*Y*our bathroom is like a spa. Except that it doesn't have any plants."

I blink, and look around me with new eyes. To me, it's just a *bathroom*. The one I use all the time. From Maria's point of view, though...

Warm sandstone contrasts with an inlay of polished river rock. The sink is poured dark concrete, and glass shelves hold fluffy towels in white and green.

There's a console by the entry that controls radiant heating in the floor, and another one low on the wall for the bidet.

"Alas," I say. "I kill plants."

"Your housekeeper could water them."

I look at her. "I don't have a housekeeper."

Maria looks around. She's appropriated a T-shirt of mine, and it hangs just at her hips. "Oh dear. That makes this worse."

I struggle to explain. "Um, well. When I bought the house, it was kind of falling apart. So I hired an architect—"

She laughs. "No, not that. I mean, you don't even have a razor out on the counter."

I rub my chin. "Courtesy of the world's slowest-growing facial hair. It's not quite nonexistent, but…"

"Replace razor with comb. It's a general comment." She looks back at me. "I'm beginning to suspect you're a neat freak."

"Ah, that. Guilty as charged."

She looks away. "This is never going to work. I'm going to leave hair all over your bathroom. You'll resent my toothbrush and all my hair things. I'll try to put them away, but it'll end up a massive cluttered drawer of tangled cords. We'll start arguing about my toothpaste. We'll hate each other in months."

I feel one of my eyebrows rise. "Or," I say slowly, "we'll accept that we're different people and we'll figure out an acceptable equilibrium."

She wrinkles her nose at me. "Sure, if you have to be all reasonable about it."

She's been a little withdrawn since we got out of bed. I look at her. She produces one of her aforementioned hair thingies and pulls her hair into a ponytail, and from there does something that turns it into a bun.

"I'm taking a shower," I tell her. "And I'm going to bed. You're welcome to join me for either activity."

I step under the faucet. The soap stings my eyes. I'm washing Em away—her skin on mine, her sweat on me—and I don't know what she's thinking.

Not until I hear the door to the shower open. I turn my face up to the spray. Her palm lands on my hip.

"Speaking of reasonable equilibria." Her voice is low and sexy in my ear. "I'm not good at this."

I turn to her and blink water from my eyes. She's shed her temporarily donned shirt, and she's totally naked. Her breasts are small and rounded, her nipples erect in the spray of the shower. She's let her hair down, and it's collecting droplets.

"Not good at showering? I'd never have noticed."

She gives me a mock glare. "Not good at...afterward. I'm always expecting things to end. I know I shouldn't, but..." She sighs. "I started my blog partly as a way to make fun of myself. I figured if I was going to catastrophize everything, I might as well have fun doing it."

Her parents kicked her out of the house when she was twelve. I would never have guessed that to look at her. Maria is smart, self-assured, confident. I would never have known her shoes were armor, not until she took them off.

I'd catastrophize everything if I were her, too. Little beads of water trickle down her face.

"Are you getting cold?"

She nods.

"Come stand under the showerhead."

She takes a tentative step toward me. Then another. She lifts her face into the steaming fall of water.

Liquid cascades down her shoulders, flattening her hair, darkening it to an almost black. She takes the soap, and works up a lather.

It takes her five minutes and a washcloth to get the last of her mascara off. Without her makeup she looks...young. Vulnerable, even. Although that might be the look in her eyes.

Somehow, her letting me see her like this seems like a measure of trust, maybe even more so than actually having sex.

"Are you making a list of things you need to leave on my counter?"

She looks up at me.

"Because you're allowed." I brush her wet hair off her shoulders. I don't let go. We lean into each other, forehead to forehead.

"After one date?"

"It's been two years, Em. We had a long date zero."

Her eyes shiver shut. Our lips brush when she lifts her chin. I inhale the scent of soap. I taste warm drops of water. I'm not sure when Em became as necessary to me as air. Our mouths meld under the heated stream of water. My hands slide down the side of her body, rib by rib, hip, thigh.

She's not cold, but she gasps under my touch.

I let her lips go only to kiss my way down her neck. She pulls me closer. Our naked bodies tangle and slide under the water—breast to chest, belly to belly, hip to hip.

I wouldn't have thought it possible so soon, but I rise to the occasion—getting hard slowly, surely. Kiss after kiss, skin against skin.

I haven't recovered so fast since I was a teenager.

I lift my head. I wonder if she sees in my eyes what I see in hers—the burn of hope, the unspoken wants.

The water washes away all the extra trappings, and we kiss again. And again. And again, my hands tangling in her hair, pulling her close. The air is humid and warm and her skin is hot. She kisses me as if it's the last time.

As if breath is unnecessary, as if all other wishes have failed and these are our final moments together.

"Hey, Em."

She looks up at me, liquid glittering on her face. Not tears, I don't think—but the fact that I can't be sure twists inside of me.

She's not worried about making a mess in my home. She's worried I'll leave one in her life. I've been the catastrophe in this relationship, and we both know it.

I fucked this up. I hurt her. And once again, all I know how to do at this point is...everything. Do everything right, and hope that if I do it long enough, someday she'll expect more of me.

"Wait." She pulls away from me a moment. A wave of cool air hits me as she opens the shower door.

I hear her rustling around in the cabinets, but her form's a blur of hair and skin through the steamed glass.

She comes back with a condom.

"You see?" I smile at her. "And here you were thinking there was no good reason to keep the medicine cabinet alphabetized."

She bursts into laughter. Every smile I win from her, every heartfelt expression of mirth, feels like a victory.

"It was not!"

"Maybe not." I want to do everything right. But her hands are on my cock, gliding in sure, sweet strokes. Touching the underside lightly, then more heavily, the water lubricating everything.

This time when her eyes meet mine, she smiles.

I return the favor. It would be stupid to say she's wet, because she's dripping water. But she must have found the lube in the bathroom, too, because she's slick inside and out. Her eyes shiver shut as I run my thumb over her clit.

"Oh, god," she whispers. "There."

"One second."

I give thanks to genetics that she's tall. That the angle works so perfectly for us, with me pressing her into the tile, pushing up into her, her leg curling around my thigh.

There's just room for my hand between us. She lets out a little noise.

If I do this right, maybe one day she'll expect this of me. I push the growing sensation of pleasure away. Refuse to let my desire pull me into mindlessness. I find the angle where I can tease her. Her chest expands against mine.

"Em. Sweetheart."

She makes a ragged noise. Her hands clench hard on my hips. "Don't stop. Please don't stop."

I don't. Not until she's shaking in my embrace. Not until I feel my own orgasm coming. It's like lightning seen at a distance—a flash of light, signaling the inevitable, and then a low rumble that shakes my entire world.

I return to reality. To the feel of water hitting my back. To my knees, scarcely holding my weight up, and Maria around me, looking into my eyes.

I touch my fingers to her cheek. Something about statistics and path-dependence flits through my mind. I am so lucky to be me, here, with her.

And because I want this to work, I tell her exactly what I'm feeling.

"Months ago," I say, "you told me I was enough. I didn't want to keep hold of it. I didn't let myself believe it. But I kept wishing it would be true."

My fingers trace her jaw.

"What I want," I tell her. "What I really, really wish for at this moment, is that I will be your enough."

I want her to say it now. *You are enough.* I want it more than anything.

Instead, her eyes round. Her lips part. I think my heart breaks just a little in the two seconds that pass.

Then she touches my face. "I want that, too."

MARIA

$\mathcal{I}$t's seven in the morning when I slip into my house to change.

Tina is, unfortunately, awake. She's sitting at the breakfast table with a mug of coffee, reading the news on her phone. She looks up when I come in.

Our eyes meet, and I feel myself inexplicably flush. There is no such thing as a walk of shame, not unless you buy into moral disapproval from a half-century ago, and neither of us do. It's not even the fact that she knows. I texted her that I was staying last night. I don't know what this stupid emotion is.

Tina holds up a hand. "Way to *go!*"

I raise my own hand almost reluctantly. My fingers meet hers halfheartedly. We manage something more like a somewhat-elevated four than a high five.

She looks at me, then at her coffee. "So, that turned out. I guess?"

"I guess." I know myself too well. I'm quick to care, quick to forgive, and slow to let go after everything's burned to the ground. It's a dangerous combination.

"I need to change and get ready."

She nods. "I'll make more coffee."

I bury my feelings in routine. I don't have to think about anything except picking shoes. Choosing a blouse. I make choices deliberately, perfectly, as if they had as much weight in my life as…Jay.

It's eight thirty by the time I'm ready, and that means there's not a lot of time to talk before we have to get to campus for our first class.

Tina knows precisely how long it usually takes me, but she doesn't call me out on my foot-dragging. Instead, she hands me coffee in a thermos. I know before I take the first sip that she's adulterated it with condensed milk and cinnamon—coffee the way I make it for her when she's feeling like crap.

I'm not feeling like crap, but I take another sip as we set off for campus at a walk.

"You okay?"

I nod.

"Come on. Spill. Was it good, bad, terrible?"

"It was great." That's the simple truth.

I think about Jay last night, about the way he looked at me, the way he held me.

"And it's serious," I say instead. "Even if it doesn't last. Let's be honest—I like him. And…there's this weird forced vulnerability between us because we have this history. But give us enough time in real life, and we probably won't get along. We *didn't,* after all."

"Okay, but does he like you? Is he treating you well? Are you okay?"

"Yes," I say. "Yes. And...I don't want to talk about that. I don't know."

She frowns and looks at me.

"It's like a roller coaster," I tell her. "It's going to end, and you're going to feel like you're falling, so you might as well throw your hands in the air and scream the whole way down. There's no point talking about it now."

We're nearing the edge of campus. I can see the dark green tiles of the computer science building where Tina's first class is.

Tina has no thermos of coffee to occupy her hands, and so instead, I see them fluttering at her side. But she knows there are some times she can't push me. I've put my foot down; the conversation is over.

"Fine," she eventually says. "New topic of conversation. Have you given any thought to where you're going to live next year?"

"I still don't know where I'm going to have a job."

She rolls her eyes. "Come on, Maria. We both know the chances that you'll move away from your grandmother are basically nil."

"True." Especially since I haven't heard from the one New York firm where I interviewed.

"Especially if Gabe gets that job at San Jose State."

Last I heard, he'd gone down for an interview with the provost, one of two candidates. I'm crossing everything for him.

"True." I sigh. I don't want to think about my job search. I don't want to think about this semester ending and going on to the one boring job I have on tap. I haven't even decided how to let my blog go. Deciding where I'm going to live on my tiny salary is low on my priority list.

"And I'm either going to UCSF or I'm taking this position at bioLogica." She makes a face. "But I'm in San Francisco either way. Have you thought about getting a place together?"

I look over at her again to see if she's joking.

She isn't. I had hoped to avoid this conversation. I love Tina. I like Blake. I agreed to share a house with them because I assumed Blake would leave.

But this whole we-might-break-up thing? I'm not buying it for another year. Third-wheeling it makes sense when one of those wheels is unsteady. It completely sucks when everything's great.

"Tina, do you really want that?"

She shrugs. "I mean, Blake's probably skipping out on school after this year and moving back with his dad."

I look at her skeptically.

"He'll be around when he can. And when I have time."

It's one thing to share a six-bedroom, four-thousand-square-foot house with Blake and his occasional visiting father. I calculate the meager starting salary I have been offered. I subtract student loan payments. Prescription copays, *if* I'm lucky enough to have insurance that covers my HRT. What's left is enough, if I'm lucky, for a birdhouse in a bad part of town.

Sharing my prospective birdhouse with Tina and her incredibly messy boyfriend? That sounds pretty awful.

"This is kinda premature," I say. "You don't know where you're going to be. I don't know where I'm going to be. I did apply for that job in New York."

"I thought you weren't excited about the New York job."

"And you know me," I bull on. "It's not like I could conduct a housing search without a spreadsheet. How can I make a spreadsheet when we have no parameters?"

"Fine," Tina says. "We'll talk about it later."

I nod. With any luck, before later comes, Tina will come to her senses.

Two weeks later

What are you doing? It's two in the afternoon when Jay's message comes through, and I can't keep from smiling and pouncing on my phone.

Never mind that until he left on this most recent trip across country, we spent nearly twelve days together. Never mind that we met for lunch—and dinner—and that I've rarely gone home in that time. He's in Boston at the moment. It's been twenty-seven hours since I last saw him, and stupidly, I miss him.

Some part of me is aware that throwing myself headlong into this relationship is not a good idea. The other part of me wishes he were here.

How was your talk? I ask.

Oh, you know, he says. *Couldn't get the projector to work. I eschewed PowerPoint and did all the equations by hand, old-school style. I should do this all the time. But I'll be home tomorrow.*

I grin.

And you didn't answer my question. What have you been doing in my absence?

I bite my lip. *Are you in private?*

Yes.

I waggle one eyebrow, even though he can't see it. *Because this is the kind of risqué sexy talk you don't want to risk others reading over your shoulder.*

Is that so? he writes. *Good thing I went back to my hotel before dinner.*

I let him have it. *I am making a spreadsheet to evaluate job offers, which are now officially plural.*

There is a pause. I can imagine him laughing.

Ooh, he writes. *Congratulations on the plural. But also—spreadsheet. You need a spreadsheet to evaluate two job offers?*

Honestly. It's like he doesn't even know me. I write quickly. *You have it completely backward. I *want* a spreadsheet to evaluate my two job offers.*

In some ways, it feels like old times. Bantering about…well, I can't call the entirety of my economic future precisely nothing, can I? Still.

Oh dear, he says. *Clearly I've been decision-making incorrectly all my life.*

Clearly you have, I respond sternly, settling into my pillows. *How else would you account for the cost (and opportunity-cost) of commuter time, various benefit levels, likelihood of advancement, etc?*

His answer is on point. *Um. With my brain?*

Just as I'm about to respond, my phone rings. I glance at the number—unknown caller—and almost don't pick up. But because I'm interviewing for jobs, I can't afford to miss calls.

"Hello, Ms. Lopez?" The woman on the other end sounds vaguely familiar. "It's Emily Lucas from Harding and Wilkins."

I inhale and look at my spreadsheet. Harding and Wilkins is a consulting firm in New York. I had an interview there a month ago, and had assumed that the passage of this many weeks was equivalent to a no.

"Everyone loved you," she says. "I'm sorry it's taken so long to respond. We'll be sending you a formal offer letter, but until then…"

I scarcely hear her. My fingers move of their own accord. *Harding and Wilkins*, I type in my spreadsheet in a cell to the far left.

She's rattling off numbers now. It's good that I have my spreadsheet open; there's no way I'd believe them if I weren't writing them down as she said them. I type a number three times larger than the next closest amount in the offered salary bar.

Yes, it's New York. Yes, money will go fast. But I upgrade my potential housing from *birdhouse* to *studio*. It's not like the Bay Area's cheap.

I'm in shock. "Thank you," I say. "This is my dream job." This is true, for some very limited values of dream.

"We're looking forward to having you."

I don't accept. Instead, I fret internally while she talks, folding my pillow in two. I try to reduce the details she gives me to an equation. I fail. I have two main problems, and I don't know how to fit them on my spreadsheet.

One: I wish I were excited about anything other than the salary. The hours will be long, and while *eventually* I'll advance enough to get some interesting work, it will take years of slogging to get there.

It's my dream job. Or at least it will be somewhat close, if I work at it long enough.

But the salary. On that salary, I could afford an actual vegetable to put in my ramen, and based on my graduating friends' experience, I know how ridiculously rare this outcome is.

The rest of the conversation passes in a daze.

When we're finished, I set my phone down and stare blankly ahead.

I would pinch myself, but I'm not even sure I'd feel it. I should be screaming for joy. Instead…

My phone flashes, and I realize that Jay's been messaging me through the entire call. *Um. Okay. It doesn't have to be dinner. Or the day after is fine, if that works better.*

Two: It's in New York. My grandmother is here. My friends are here. My brother might be here. New York is cold and dirty. The Mexican food is subtly wrong. The pizza is so wrong, it barely even qualifies as pizza in my mind. Expressing either of those thoughts to a New Yorker would likely get me shanked, and I don't want to die.

I nod at this bit of morbid fantasy. This irrationally premature obituary is easier for me to acknowledge than the other thought that flits through my mind. That is this: Jay is here.

After twelve days together, I'm aware it would be stupid to make a decision this massive on the basis of Jay.

If I told him, I know what he'd say. *It's your dream job. Take it.* Or maybe: *It's your life. It's your decision.* He wouldn't push me.

Still, I don't want to tell him.

I pick up my phone. *No, you dork. I got a phone call.*

I scroll back through the messages I missed. I think about telling him about the job. We've known each other forever and he knows so much about me. Just...not everything. In one sense, this is the most intimate relationship I've had. I've told him things I haven't told anyone. I let him close before I knew who he was.

It's also the most lonely. He's only realized my name for a handful of weeks, and all the things we would otherwise know about each other—favorite colors, food preferences—got skipped over. He knows everything and nothing, all at once.

I find his original message. *So do you want to come over for dinner tomorrow when I'm back? I was planning on making food native to my peoples.*

In the end, I smile helplessly. Decisions can wait; he'll be back tomorrow.

Which people? Thai? Chinese? American?

His response is so swift that I know he set me up. *None of the above. I am, of course, referring to beans on toast.*

I grin as I'm typing. *Oh, well. In that case... Sure.*

23.

JAY

"What are you doing?"

I look up from the little plastic tent I have set up on the counter. Maria has let herself into my house—as I told her to do. She's standing on the other side of my kitchen island, watching me with a puzzled expression.

The house smells faintly of woodsmoke. Which it should since I'm juggling a handheld smoker trailing clouds of burning applewood chips. The fan whirs, doing its best to draw up the smoke.

"Hush," I say. "I'm nearly done smoking the beans."

"You're smoking beans?"

"Yes." I set down the smoker and juggle the beans out of the bag and into a container. I sprinkle bread crumbs on top.

She sets her bag down. "You promised me beans on toast. Isn't that normally like canned baked beans on bread? And less like…?" She gestures.

I haven't seen her in days. Of course I broke out one of my dad's more impressive cassoulet recipes for her.

"Deconstructed toast," I say, gesturing to the breadcrumbs. "Deconstructed beans. Be quiet. I'm trying to impress you."

One hand goes to her hip. "Which is why you told me you were making me beans on toast."

"Lowering expectations is a fundamental part of making a good impression."

She just shakes her head.

"And it was either impress you with my cooking skills or, you know, lasers. I have a limited repertoire."

"Ha. I can think of other things you can do."

I turn off the smoker and put my cassoulet in the oven.

"Then come here and let me do them," I say.

She stalks around the counter. Comes up to me.

I wrap my arms around her and kiss her.

Two weeks should be nothing in a relationship. But every day I was gone, I felt her absence in my bed like a palpable thing.

The kiss ends, but I don't want to let go. "Did you have a good time with your grandmother?"

She shakes her head and lets out a little gurgling laugh. "She's still at trial. I went over and made her eat food, and she made a few protesting noises. I'm not sure she even noticed I was there."

"Poor Em. Everyone ignores you. I was out of town. Your grandmother was at trial."

She shrugs. "I'm used to it. I don't mind."

"Want a glass of water while we're waiting?"

She comes with me to the refrigerator and watches as I pour water from a filter pitcher. Her eyes narrow, and she reaches into the fridge and removes a plastic container of cream cheese.

She opens it. It is, unsurprisingly, cream cheese.

She nods. "I thought so," she remarks in a grim tone.

"It's almost like you're psychic," I comment. "Or—alternate explanation—you can read."

She shakes her head, as if I've said something amusing, and takes the glass of water.

I wait until we're sitting down on the couch. "Speaking of your grandmother," I say slowly, "I want you to meet my parents."

Her eyes widen. She doesn't pull away from me—not really—but she leans forward to set her water glass on the table, and when she comes back, somehow, we're not touching anymore.

"Maybe we should hold off on that." Her voice is flat. She presses the palms of her hands against my thighs.

"If you want." I already told them about her. "But they would like you."

She gives an involuntary shake of her head. "You don't know that."

"I do, actually. My parents have a pretty firm no-bullshit clause for significant others. It comes from their own relationship."

This doesn't calm her down. She shakes her head again and looks away. Her breathing is rapid, too rapid. Her lips look pale.

"Em. Are you all right?"

"Fine." She grinds the word out in the exact tone that suggests she is anything but fine.

I set my hand on hers. "Maria?"

"It's fine."

I don't say anything. But maybe she can read the disbelief in my expression. She looks up at me and exhales.

"It's not fine," she finally says. But she leans into me when she says it.

"Bad experience with someone's parents not liking you?"

She stares at her hands. "Jay," she says slowly, "*my* parents don't like me."

Oh. I don't speak out loud. Truth is, I met her parents once. They came out to visit Gabe at Harvard, and took a bunch of his friends out to dinner. They seemed nice. I don't say this.

"It's complicated." Maria's hands tangle with mine. "They kicked me out when I was twelve, and sometimes I wish that was all it was. But it doesn't work that way. There are no clean breaks."

I pull her closer. Her skin is cool against mine.

"There were summers when we tried to work things out. And sessions with therapists. Every time my mom would call and say she wanted to try, I'd get my hopes up. I'd start daydreaming. And then we'd try, and I...listened to my mother explain how hard it was for her, how all she wanted was for her children to have the safe place she never had as a child, and how it was my fault it hadn't happened. I had my list of things that I wanted. It wasn't long. But I never got to present it. She thought that if I just understood how my existence hurt her, I would change."

"Oh. Em."

She brushes off this sympathy. "And it's fine. It's fine now. But every time we'd try to work things out, I'd start believing, and…" She smashes her hands together, squelching those hopes. "So I have issues with things like this. I had this period in high school where I had massive anxiety attacks. My grandmother would come home late from work and I would work myself into a state thinking that she left me."

The closer I hold her, the more I can feel the little tremors in her shoulders.

"And here's the thing that made it better," Maria said. "Part of it was seeing someone. Getting a prescription. Having people tell me that what I was going through was a normal reaction to trauma. But have you ever read *From the Mixed-Up Files of Mrs. Basil E. Frankweiler?*"

I shake my head. "Sorry."

"Well, you should. It's about a couple of kids who run away from home and live in the Metropolitan Museum of Art. In any event, I decided that if my grandmother ever threw me out, I'd hide out in the library. I had a plan. I hid boxes of granola bars behind the encyclopedias and everything. Every time I started freaking out, I'd tell myself it was okay because I had somewhere to go."

I'm playing with her hair as she talks. She's not shaking anymore.

"I'm a lot better," she says. "I don't have an active prescription right now. But weird things still freak me out. It took me years to believe Nana when she said she loved me. I used to wonder if she was trying to lull me into a false sense of security."

She shrugs. I'm still not sure what to say.

"People talk about unconditional love," she says quietly. "But all love is conditional. I'm just a little neurotic until I figure out the conditions. And until I do, I need to take things slow. Have a place to hide. Just in case. So can we hold off on meeting your parents?"

I think my heart is breaking for her. I think of my father's book. Of his dedication. Of my mom, taking me out to lunch in the middle of her day. I spent years wondering how to make up my mistakes to my parents. I'm slowly beginning to understand that I don't have to. All love is not conditional. It sucked when I thought it was. I hate that she lives in a world where she still has reason to believe it.

"You're not neurotic," I say. "My parents adored me, and when my brother died, I disappeared and drove to Vegas to get these." I hold out my arms so she can see my tattoos. "I wanted to piss them off. I wanted them to get mad at me and blame me. They didn't."

She gives me a wan smile. "Did you keep on trying?"

"Of course. I had applied to Cambridge for university on a whim. I told them I was going. I think I really wanted them to say, 'No, that's too far, you can't do it.' But they didn't. So, seven and a half years later, I had a PhD."

She begins laughing.

"What?"

"You may be the first person in the entire world who rebelled against his parents by getting a PhD in physics from Cambridge."

"I doubt it." I lean in. "You're not neurotic. You've built emotional muscles that most people never need to use. You're not standard, but I adore every nonstandard inch of you."

She looks up at me.

"Does that freak you out?"

She nods. "A little."

"Then find a place to hide and remember it until you start believing me," I say. "And it's okay. My parents can wait."

She exhales. Then, slowly, she shifts her weight and kisses me.

MARIA

J'm not sure if I'm kissing Jay because I want to, or because I couldn't bear to hear him talk any more. Truth is no matter what I say, there is part of me that still doesn't understand how we're here—how Jay is the person I'm slowly beginning to trust. Trust scares me.

I know how to care for other people. I know that far too well. It's hard to let them care for me in return.

We feel like mismatched puzzle pieces—no matter how we kiss, I'm not sure we can ever come close enough.

But we can try. He stands up and wraps his arm around my waist, pulling me close.

I want to forget my own memories.

His fingers drag down the side of my cheek and a flare of desire wakes in me. It's bright, so bright that it almost drowns out the core of doubt that won't let go. The catch of my breath, the slow slide of his mouth against mine—they aren't enough to replace all my fears, but they're enough to pretend.

Maybe I'll forget. Maybe I can hide in our kiss.

Maybe he wants me to forget as much as I do, because our mouths meld. His hands slide down my waist. His fingers hook in the band of my skirt.

"Hey, Em." His voice is low. I open my eyes. He's looking at me, his face inches from mine. His irises are brown and gold against a ring of black. He rubs his nose against mine, and as he does, his hand presses into the small of my back.

"Hi, Jay." My voice is fluttering. My chest beats with an uncertain rhythm. I feel like my lungs are hollow, waiting to be filled by his kiss.

He kisses me again, this time harder. More. My mouth opens, and I taste him—smoke and salt and a hint of sweetness. Just a kiss, but I can feel the tension between us. The desire, caged and held back, the hesitation.

I don't know if it's his or mine.

I don't know what the future will hold. But the wavering beat of my heart is timed to the rhythm of his breath, and it's scary and comforting all at the same time.

"Did you ever read *A Wrinkle in Time?*" I ask.

"No." His face is close to mine. His fingers slide along my waist.

"You haven't read anything. It was my favorite book in fourth grade. It was the center of my existence, and all because of the tesseract."

"A four-dimensional cube?" He nods. "I love extra-dimensional geometry."

"No. That was a jumping-off point. It was used as a sort of five-dimensional wormhole travel."

Jay pulls away and frowns over my shoulder. "You know, mathematically—"

"Don't you dare nitpick the math." I mock-glare at him, and he looks back at me. "This is not about the math. It was fifth-dimensional travel, and you could *think* the right way and land on the other side of the galaxy. With a tesseract, I could escape anything. In our normal three dimensions, there are walls and doors and the vastness of space between you and your heart's desire."

"Ah." He doesn't pull me closer—not physically—but he shifts, and it *feels* like he's closer. More intimate. More aware.

"In our typical three dimensions, we start out with the basics. You see what someone looks like first. Then you get a name, what they do for a living." I don't look at him. "Sex often comes at the point when it's still safe, when you've only swapped funny stories about your childhood, and not any of the real vulnerabilities."

He exhales against my skin.

"You and I—we've tesseracted all the way past our most vulnerable moments," I say. "We did this all backward—vulnerability first, names last. And now we're all tangled together and there's no good way out. I don't have any real hiding places."

He exhales. "Then I won't hide. I've never wanted anyone the way I do you."

"Oh." His face is smooth beneath my touch—jawbone, chin, lips. I feel heavy and light at the same time. He can't really mean it. Not the way it sounds. "Oh," I swallow. "Say those words again."

"I've never wanted anyone the way I want you," he repeats steadily. "Inside and out. Morning and night. Yesterday and tomorrow, in four dimensions, or five." He squints. "Which is scientifically silly. Can I just specify every extra rolled-up dimension predicted by string theory?"

"Oh." It seems a ridiculous thing to say in response to those words, but everything else I feel seems to be caught in my rib cage. "Oh." I don't know what to say to any of that. It's too much. I don't want it.

And very selfishly, I never want to give any of it up.

"Oh." My hand is on his face. My thumb is on his lips. He turns and presses a kiss into my palm, and it sears me.

"Well." My voice sounds foreign and strange to me. "I'm pretty sure I feel the same way."

Something heated flares in his eyes—a bright blossom of desire. I feel naked. Vulnerable.

He takes hold of my hand—just my hand, but there's a hunger in the grip of forefinger and thumb around my wrist.

"Come along then," he says. He leads me to his bedroom, and this time, when he turns to me, there isn't the slightest hint of uncertainty.

He sits on the bed and pulls me on top of him.

There's a slight callus on the pads of his left hand, and I have no idea how he got them—writing papers likely wouldn't do it. I don't ask.

I take off his shirt, baring a lovely expanse of brown skin, lightly muscled biceps...

I run my fingers down his chest, down the line of his ribcage. Down his abdominal muscles.

"Oh, hell." His hands tighten on my hips.

I undo the snap of his jeans. I know what he looks like already, but I still feel a sense of electric anticipation as I slide them off.

I can see the bar of his cock through his underwear—heavy and large and waiting for me. It takes me a moment—just a moment—to reach for the elastic band of his boxers.

To slide the blue fabric down his hips. My throat feels dry when I touch him for the first time—that firmness, the hiss of his breath. The look in his eyes.

I've never wanted anyone the way I want you.

I can't think about that. I lean down and kiss him. Kissing him naked, on a bed, is an entirely different thing than kissing when fully clothed. I want him—every last inch of his skin, every taut curve of his muscle. Every ounce of desire I see reflected in his eyes. My nerves feel on fire. His fingers undo the buttons of my blouse, lifting it over my head.

"You're beautiful."

I make a noise.

"No," he says. "That's not the right word. 'Striking' was what I thought the first time I saw you. There's something utterly compelling about you. I can't look away. And that's what it feels like at a distance."

"And up close?"

"You're made of the stuff that binds the universe together."

"Thanks, Actual Physicist." I exhale. "Isn't everyone?"

He shrugs. "Sure. But I only notice it with you."

He kisses me again, and this kiss is different still. He traces a path down my throat. He leaves little searing kisses on my collarbone. His palm cups my breast, and my nipple responds in a blaze of sensation.

He breathes in as I exhale. We shouldn't fit so well together. I'm feeling utterly shattered as he unsnaps my bra. Presses his mouth to me. His tongue is warm, and I'm so damned sensitive, and every part of me yearns for him. My hand finds his hip. The joint, then his inner thigh.

He undoes my skirt. My panties are a pale pink, almost translucent.

"Hey, Em."

I look at him. My hands are feeling just a little shaky.

"Hey, Em," he says again. "You know me."

And I do.

I know the way he slides his hands down my hips. The way he nudges my legs apart, catching one finger in the material of my panties. I know the way he caresses me, light at first, then leaning down, touching me with tongue and fingers, gentle and sweet and filthy all at once, letting all the feeling, all the desire build in me. I know the way he touches me, fingers dipping inside me with lubrication.

When he lifts his head, his eyes look like molten bronze. "Hey there."

I can't think at all when he slides inside me. Not one word, just the feel of him.

"Jay."

"Maria." He moves, ever so slightly. He shifts his position. And, oh god, it's ruining me for anything or anyone else. There's something utterly adorable about him. Maybe because he isn't holding anything back.

Maybe because his body fits mine, stretching me. Maybe because he's looking at me with an expression I understand.

Maybe because I have nowhere to hide, and I don't know when that happened or what to do about it. It's almost too sweet, the feel of his hands on my hips.

I can feel my orgasm coming—slowly, surely building with every stroke, taking over me. It washes through me with a shattering force.

"Em." His forehead touches mine. "Em. Sweetheart."

I'm not sure what to do with endearments. I kiss him instead. It's easier when he starts moving again. When he's so clearly in pursuit of his own pleasure. When he lets out a little groan, his muscles tense and spasm.

The kiss afterward is too much—too much intimacy, too much implied affection. I'm not sure what to do with my feelings, as awkward and ungainly in this room as a baby giraffe struggling to stand.

He comes back to bed after he cleans up. He slips one arm around me.

"Em," he says.

I turn to look at him. How can I not?

"You know I really like you."

I nod. "I…" It's hard to say the words. "I really like you, too."

"I know I fucked up with you. But—"

I set my hand over his mouth.

"No buts. Not now. Not like this."

"Right." He smiles.

I have too many *buts* inside me. Too many *howevers* and *what-ifs*. I don't want them spoken. All love is conditional. Even this.

"No buts," he says. "I really like you." His fingers find a little wisp of my hair. He rubs it lightly, as if the texture is an object of fascination.

"I feel like something is wrong," I say.

"I know." He whispers this against my skin. "If you're used to everything being wrong, rightness feels out of place."

"No." I sit up. "I mean—when did you put your beans in the oven?"

His eyes widen. He turns to me. "Shit," he says. "Shit, shit, shit."

And then he's jumping up and reaching for his pants, and we're both laughing.

J A Y

T haven't seen Gabriel Lopez in over a month—not since the seminar he gave at LBL, the one I scarcely heard because I'd just discovered Maria was Em.

Now I'm sitting across from him at four in the afternoon in a wooden booth, a pair of celebratory beers in front of us.

"San Jose State," I say. "That is so freaking awesome!"

And it is. It feels like I've spent my last years making friends just in time to say good-bye.

Gabe raises his glass. "Hey, I'm here to stay. It *is* awesome."

"So Jutta is moving out here. Does she need a job? Is she looking for industry or academics? And do you need a hand?"

"The latter." Gabe gives me a smile. "We would love it if you could call one of your magic contacts and see if anyone needs a computational mathematician."

"Done." Gabe hasn't said much about his fiancée, but I've heard from Maria, who Skypes her regularly. She seems cool, from what little Maria's conveyed.

"And I'm near family." Gabe glances at me. "Not exactly near my parents, which is…probably for the best. But my grandmother is here, and Maria is probably staying in the Bay Area after graduation—"

I frown at him. "What are you talking about?"

He waves a lazy hand in my direction. "Eh, fuck off. I know you don't like her, but she's my sister, and I don't want to hear your crap."

My beer suddenly feels heavy. I set it down with a thunk. "What do you mean, *I don't like her?*"

"Unless you suddenly changed your mind overnight—"

I don't think before I respond. "I'm dating her."

Gabe snorts. "Ha!" He swallows beer. "Good one."

I stare at him in amazement.

He stares back at me, the truth slowly dawning. "Oh. You're…really not joking."

I don't respond. I'm going through my mental calendar. It's early April now, meaning that it's been five weeks since I last saw him. Four weeks since Maria and I had dinner and I took her home. I've seen Maria literally every day, barring the two I wasn't in town.

During that month, I'm sure she's talked to Gabe a dozen times. Exchanged texts with him practically *daily*. She Skyped his fiancée from my house.

I just assumed that he knew. How could he not? She's the cornerstone of my day. And she and Gabe are good friends. Not meeting my parents is one thing. How could she *not* have told him we were together?

"You're not joking," Gabe repeats.

I shake my head. "I'm not joking."

"When did this start?"

Years ago. "Weeks ago," I say. "Four weeks ago."

Gabe looks at his beer glass. His upper lip wrinkles, and he frowns at the coaster. "Maria will kick my ass if I go all big brother on you," he finally says.

"Yeah. Well. She'd have to *talk* to you about me first."

He doesn't seem to register my muttered complaint. He sets his hand on the table—just a little bit too hard. "And Maria can take care of herself. She's not a little girl anymore. She doesn't take shit, and—" He blows out a breath, and gives up on pretending not to interfere. "Dammit, Jay. You do not have the best track record."

"Thanks." I don't quite keep the sarcasm out of my voice.

"You work all the fucking time."

"I'm sure she hasn't noticed, since she's remarkably unobservant."

"And you told me to kick your ass if you ever dated anyone I knew. I know Maria is capable of pushing back on your bullshit, but she's more vulnerable than she lets on, and—"

"You know what?" I'm not going to listen to this anymore. "We can make a list of all my faults—and trust me, Maria is more than aware of their existence—but how many times have you talked to your sister in the last month?"

"I don't know. A dozen? Two?"

That's about what I figured.

"Don't give me shit about my track record," I tell him. "If she didn't tell *you*, how seriously do you think she's taking this? Do you really think I have the capacity to hurt her?"

He considers this. "Huh. Probably not."

"We're not going to make this weird by having me talk exactly about how much and in what ways I like your sister," I say. "So let's talk about what kind of first-year research support you're getting."

He exhales. His face darkens. "Fine."

It's   fine.   Everything's   fine.

24.

MARIA

"*H*ey." It's cool and dark when I meet Jay outside his office. I can't see his expression. At first, I don't think anything is weird when he doesn't kiss me—I am completely on board with his "no PDA near the college of chemistry" rule.

"How was your study group?" he asks.

"I know as much as I'm going to know." I shrug.

Maybe he sees through my nonchalance.

"Of course you do." He doesn't take my hand, though, not as we pass through a darkened mass of trees. The nearest light is an emergency call box. It tinges his face in an eerie blue light. "It's easy for you, isn't it?"

Easy isn't the right word. I frown. "No. That's not it. Game theory was hard the first time I encountered it. And the second. It's just that I've always been interested in a lot of stuff, so this isn't really fair. I'm seeing things the tenth time when my classmates are encountering it for the first. It's not *easy*. I'm just lucky."

He snorts.

"It's like the guy who got a five in AP chemistry," I say, "and takes Chem 1A anyway. Of course he's going to get a good grade."

"Sure," Jay says.

"Or it's like Blake. When he was five, he'd build a space station at Cyclone and the engineers would help him calculate the rotational G-forces to determine the appropriate scale."

"That sounds like 'it's easy' to me."

He still hasn't taken my hand. I stop and turn to him. "Is something wrong?"

He exhales slowly. "Look. I don't want to be weird about this. But I had beers with Gabe today."

My heart gives a little thump, and a little prickle of anxious energy surges through me.

"And you have a test first thing tomorrow morning, and—"

"It's okay. We can talk."

"I don't know if I should apologize for spilling the beans about us or be pissed that you didn't tell him we're together."

I glance over at him. "Sounds like you've already decided."

"It's okay," he mutters, putting his hands in his pockets. "I mean, we haven't talked about where we are, not really, and it's not like I can get mad. I just thought…you talk to him all the time. If I was important to you, you would tell him."

He doesn't actually need my permission to get mad, and despite his words, I suspect he didn't wait for it.

"It wasn't like that."

He stops walking and turns to me. In the darkness, I can't see his eyes. I can barely see *him*. Still, he faces me, and I can feel the intensity of his regard.

I shrink away.

"I didn't tell him because I assumed we were going to break up in a few months," I say quietly. "You guys are friends. I didn't want to make things awkward for you."

He folds his arms. "Why would you think we were going to break up, though?"

"Why wouldn't we? I lose people I care about all the time."

For a moment, he just looks at me. I can hear the sound of his breath—a little too loud for a slow walk. I don't make a list for him. I don't have to.

He knows it already.

Here's the thing. It's been more than twelve years since I got on a bus headed to San Francisco. I've spent half my life understanding, over and over, that my parents only wanted to love the me they'd made up in their minds, not the me I was.

They've been mostly good years. I have family that loves me: a brother and a grandmother. I have friends who are closer than my parents ever could be. I have job options. I'm a month from a degree, and...

And somehow, all I can think of right now is arguing with my mother. Trying to tell her what I wanted. Having it dismissed as selfish.

I exhale. My stomach is cramping. My parents aren't here. I'm okay, but there's some shit I'm going to carry forever. *This will not last* is engraved on my heart.

"Oh," Jay says in a low voice. "It's a hiding place. That's what you want. I get it. It's okay."

It shouldn't be okay. It *can't* be okay. But his arms come around me.

"It's okay," he says again. "I should have known."

"Shut up," I say, because my eyes are stinging. "It's not okay. It's *stupid*. It was a long time ago."

I don't know how to process kind words and caresses. I remember what it's like to get the hope knocked out of me. I can only pretend to tell myself that this time it will be different. Different is not how the world works. Caring too much gets me hurt, and I definitely care too much.

The more rational I can make things sound, the better. Lay it out with game theory; build a model of disease transmission. Put the end of the world in numbers, and estimate the risk. If I can do that, maybe one day I'll get rid of the fear that I'll lose everything.

Childhood scars are not susceptible to computer models. They don't go away, no matter how small the risk.

The more I care about someone, the more I worry.

He takes my face in his hands. "Hey."

"I'm fine." I'm trembling. "It's stupid."

He touches my nose. "It's not stupid. You're not stupid."

"It was so long ago. And it *wasn't* everyone. I should be over this by now."

"Hey." His voice is gentle. "It's okay. What helps?"

I breathe. I think. "Here's the thing about the apocalypse. It's always about bad things that haven't happened to me yet. And it's weird. Thinking about good things happening to me freaks me out. Thinking about terrible things? It makes me feel better." I feel naked admitting that.

"So, earthquakes?"

I shut my eyes. "I drafted a post about supercolliders and temporal rifts today. Want me to tell you about it?"

He doesn't laugh at me, and I was kind of expecting that he would. He takes my hand. "Well." His voice drops a few notes. "There's that. Let's see if there's anything else that works, too."

JAY

"*I* thought 'anything else that works' was a euphemism," Maria says, one hand on her hip.

So, fine. There may be a reason why she would think it was a euphemism. We're in my bedroom. We held hands the entire walk home, and by the end, "holding hands" meant "touching each other all over."

We've been making out for the last fifteen minutes, enough that every nerve of mine is on point. Ready for more.

That's why I asked to see her post on temporal rifts.

"What?" I ask. "You thought it was a more polite version of 'nice shoes, wanna fuck?'"

She glances at me. There's no heat in her expression, though; she's barely holding back a grin. She points to her bare toes. "No shoes."

I shrug. "Hey. That does it for me."

"Well, then, in that case—"

"Nope." I fold my arms. "You promised me mayhem and a temporal rift. Give me details. Temporal rift to where?"

"When, more like. And the answer is the cretaceous period."

"Ah." I waggle an eyebrow at her. "Ye olde velociraptor invasion. Excellent."

"I don't think you can call it 'ye olde velociraptor invasion' if there's never been one before."

Here's the thing about Maria—I can tell I shook her up earlier. And she's right. When she's feeling shaky, it helps her to talk about something as silly as a ridiculous way to end the world. I wonder idly if I could plot her mood over the last years by her blogposts. I suspect I could.

"*Ye olde* refers to the source of the velociraptor," I explain. "Old velociraptors come from the cretaceous. Gosh-darned newfangled velociraptors"—I give this phase as close to a Southern twang as I can manage, which is not very close—"are the ones created by humans out of bioengineered hubris."

She sits back on the bed. Her mouth quirks as she considers this distinction that I just now made up. "Well. That's a surprisingly reasonable explanation."

"So?" I beckon. "Let me see."

She sighs. "Okay, but if we're gonna talk temporal rifts, I want tea. Want me to make you some while you read?"

"Sure. Whatever you find that's not caffeinated is fine."

She opens her laptop and types in her password. "The document's in front. I'll be right back."

I open her laptop.

The document isn't in front. Her web browser is; she was looking up some resources on temporal paradox. I smile and minimize the window.

Her blogpost *still* isn't in front. What I see next is a spreadsheet. She's told me about this spreadsheet before; it's her job search spreadsheet.

Last I heard, there was one place she was waiting to hear from before she made a decision. Last I heard, she had an offer from a smaller firm in the East Bay, and a bigger one in San Francisco. She'd turned down the place in Sacramento, which is why that line is highlighted in gray.

The thing she didn't tell me was that she had an offer in New York.

I belatedly realize—after I've seen the name of the job, after I've read the pros and cons and seen the salary line that is three times larger than the San Francisco offer—that I'm violating her privacy. If she *wanted* me to know all the details, she would have told me.

Of course that leaves one burning question: Why didn't she want me to know?

I close the spreadsheet and start reading about temporal rifts.

Funny, how I can put my mind on autopilot. I can think about what she's written in some isolated chamber of my brain while the rest of me concentrates on something else.

I leave a note in the margin: *My back-of-the-envelope calculation suggests this will take more energy than the sun will produce in its lifetime. Explain?* My heart's not really in the nitpicking.

I can hear her in the kitchen—the click of closing cabinets, the low whistle of my teakettle as water slowly comes to a boil.

Hey, Em, I imagine saying when she comes back. *You want to tell me about this job?*

I can't see that turning out well. What would I be accusing her of, anyway? Keeping back information she has a perfect right not to tell me? And I know why she's doing it. She told me she needs places to hide. This is *hers.* If she needs it, she needs it. I'm not going to be a dick about it.

That doesn't mean it doesn't hurt.

I was in a half-serious relationship back when I was a postdoc at Harvard. To be specific, the serious half was Dave—in other words, the half that was not me. He wanted us to talk about coordinating our job searches. I didn't want to.

We had almost as many months of sniping sarcasm as we had good times. At the time, I was annoyed and frustrated. Who plans their entire life around someone you've only been dating a couple of months?

Not Maria, apparently.

I want her to. Oh, I want her to. But I shouldn't even know about that line I saw on her spreadsheet. If I asked her, I even know what she would say. She needs to have a place to hide, in case this goes wrong, and if that's New York, then she can have New York.

Still. She assumes this will end, and I want to be her enough.

I frown at her laptop, then close it.

I can hear her putting things away in the kitchen.

It's not a surprise that I'm more into Em than she is into me. Hell, she told me why just tonight. Good things freak her out.

She comes into the room, juggling two mugs and coasters. "Blueberry okay?"

I jump up and help her arrange the mugs. "It's fine."

She gets in bed, and I follow. She snuggles up next to me and opens her laptop. "Okay, so you took a look. What did you—oh." She reads my note. "Okay, let me think."

I can't make her fall in love with me. I can't make her trust me. Her forehead wrinkles as she ponders, and I reach out and smooth the furrows with my thumb.

But I know Em. She needs space and time, and crowding her close won't help matters. I can swallow that little sting that demands to know *why* and *how*.

I can't make Em trust me, but I can trust her. She'll give me the why and how when she's ready. And maybe, one day, I'll be enough.

"Okay," she says. "What about this?"

We hash out an alternate temporal rift—forty minutes for two lines in her post—and when we're done, I slide my arm around her.

She looks up at me. "Hey."

"Hey, yourself."

"What is it?" she asks.

I shake my head. "Just thinking that I'm going to miss you next week."

"You have a conference and a week with your coauthor," Maria says. "You won't have time to miss me."

I sigh. "And I haven't left yet, so…" I let my gaze linger on her. "In the meantime, I was wondering. Nice velociraptor invasion. Wanna fuck?"

Apparently, I've managed to hide how I feel. Because she smiles, long and slow. "I thought you'd never ask."

MARIA

I'm at lunch with Anj the next day, and she's ecstatic.

"It's all done but the super-picky formatting."

"Congratulations."

"And the defense, but whatever." She waves this off. "It's just a formality. Part of the hazing ritual, yada yada yada. Nobody actually *fails* their dissertation defense these days."

"Well, congratulations. Any thoughts on jobs?"

Anj gives me a perplexed look.

"Never mind," I say. "I forgot that salaries don't apply to you."

She blinks for a moment, as if she still doesn't understand. Then she goes on. "I'm having a party," she says. "You're invited. You and that new boyfriend you keep ditching me for."

"Ugh." I make a face. "*Once*. I ditched you for him *once.*"

"It's Sunday," Anj says, "and it's a costume party."

"Oh, no."

"Oh, yes! It's a chicken-or-shark costume party. Come as one or the other."

I stare at her in annoyed dismay. "Anj, I'm not dressing up as a chicken, not even for your dissertation party. I'm really sorry. I'm just not."

"Of course you aren't," Anj says with a smile. "You're coming as a shark."

Because I love sharks so much. Arguing with Anj is hopeless. I bite my lip.

"Are you bringing what's-his-name?"

"Jay," I say. "And no. He's going to be in Melbourne. Science stuff."

"Okay," she says. "Then I'll see you there."

After lunch, I'm already thinking of excuses to make to her when my phone rings. One glance at my caller ID, and I'm rushing to answer.

"Nana! Are you done with your trial?"

"Yes. Sort of."

"Sort of?"

"I spent the jury deliberations drafting a response to the expected motion for judgment notwithstanding the verdict," she says, "which I expect them to file in five days or so. But we won. For now."

"Yay!" I grin. "How long do you need to sleep?"

"Couple days. But come Saturday I may be temporarily human again. Come over?"

"Of course! We can celebrate your survival!"

"Urgh." She snorts. "Right now, I feel like ass...phalt."

"It's okay, Nana. You can say you feel like ass."

"I feel like a disgusting, tarry substance with potholes," she replies, "but I'll bounce back."

"Well, call me when you wake up, Sleeping Beauty."

No, I tell myself. It's probably for the best that Jay is out of town for a week. I can tell Nana about him and figure out how to avoid costumes.

It's probably for the best.

---

*I*t's probably for the best, I tell myself the next afternoon, after seeing Jay leave for the airport, because if I've neglected anyone, it's Tina.

She's had a rough couple of weeks herself.

We're sitting around, just like old times. I'm working on a blogpost. She's doing a problem set. And we only have a couple of months left as roommates, which is something I still have to discuss with her. But before we get there...

"Okay," I say to Tina, "so what sort of biological creature *could* I create with 3D-bioprinting if rodents won't work. Spiders?"

"What is this?" She shakes her head. "Ask Tina about bizarre bioprinting applications day?"

I sigh patiently. "I *have* to ask you about bioprinting. You said your boss would get a kick if bioLogica ended up in my blog."

Tina rolls her eyes. "He's not my boss. A, I don't work there right now. B, he doesn't really work there, either. Paul's an aging retired genius who doesn't even live in the US. He has crazy ideas that they asked me to test over the summer."

I look at her. "You're upset."

She sighs. "Not really. It's just an Adam Reynolds thing. He's acting weird and I don't know why. I should just ask him outright if he's on drugs again." She frowns. "And that'll go over *great* with Blake."

I do not envy her her boyfriend's family, that's for damned sure. I try to think of something positive to say. But while I'm fumbling to be supportive, my phone rings. It's my grandmother. She must have finally woken up.

"Hold on," I say. "I have to get this."

I answer.

"Hey, Maria." The sound of Nana's voice is familiar. The background noise—something like a PA system announcing something unintelligible—is not.

"Hey, Nana. Are you awake already?"

"So." She sighs. "About that. I don't want to freak you out, but…"

Her long pause is already freaking me out.

"I kind of went down to Saint Francis."

"You did *what?*" Saint Francis is the hospital near her house. My hands feel suddenly cold.

"Don't freak out," she tells me.

I'm freaking out. My hands feel unsteady.

"It's not a big deal," she continues. "I saw a doctor about it yesterday. It's just a little thing with my kidneys. They want to keep me in the hospital for a couple of days, but—"

"They're keeping you in the hospital?" I glance over at Tina.

Her mouth rounds in shock. Her eyes widen. *Oh, no,* she mouths. She stands up and puts an arm around me. My world seems to collapse to a couple of senses—the sound of Nana's voice on the phone, the feel of Tina's hand rubbing my back.

"I know," Nana says, sounding annoyed. "It's so stupid. It's just because I can't keep these stupid antibiotics down." She makes it sound like an inconvenience, like she left her keys at a coffee shop. "Also," she adds thoughtfully, "it might be because they think I'm stubborn. Maybe I didn't come in when I first realized there was blood in my urine."

"Nana." I say the word in absolute horror. "What are you *doing?*"

"Sitting here bored with an IV drip," she answers dryly.

"Fine." I stand up. "Good. I'm coming in, okay? Is there anything you need?"

"A bottle of wine."

I exhale. "That's going to interact with your antibiotics."

"Where's your sense of humor?"

"I seem to have left it somewhere around the word *hospital*. Maybe *kidney*."

"Be that way." She sighs. "If I'm not getting any alcohol out of you, stop by my house and get my Kindle."

"Okay." I'm glad to have something to do.

"And my cell phone charger."

"Sure."

"And my laptop." She sounds more hopeful as she says this. "I want to look over that response—"

"Nana, aren't you supposed to be resting?"

"I'm surrounded by doctors. If I'm going to collapse from overwork, I couldn't be in a better spot."

She's not helping. I can't tell from her tone if it's really serious and she's downplaying it, or if it's as minor as she claims.

Either is possible.

I look up at the ceiling. "You're freaking me out. Will you please take care of yourself?"

"Oh, fine," she says with bad grace. "I'll behave."

"I'll be there," I say. I'm already fumbling for my keys and my purse. "I'll be there as soon as I can."

25.

MARIA
---

*J*he BART across the Bay seems to take forever. It's rush hour, and it's standing room only all the way here. Between calling Gabe and ransacking Nana's apartment for her electronics, a small eternity passes before I arrive at the hospital.

The fact that I spent the entire train ride scouring the internet for kidney diseases, scaring myself with increasingly horrific medical scenarios, surely has not helped.

In reality, it's been three and a half hours since she called. The hospital staff signs me in as a visitor, and I find the room where she's staying.

She looks up as I come in. "Oh, thank god. My cell phone died thirty minutes ago."

I give her a dirty look and a hug designed not to disturb her IV. "Here." I plug the charger into the wall for her and hand her the business end. "Let me read your chart."

"Did you suddenly become a doctor?"

"WebMD," I say curtly. "I want to know what's wrong."

I look for the chart. I'm expecting some kind of unintelligible chicken scratch handwriting on a clipboard.

Instead, there's a computer in the corner of the room. I try to wake it up, but it's password protected.

"TV medical dramas have been telling me lies," I announce to the room at large.

"Or you could ask me."

"Fine." I pull up a chair and sit next to her. "What's going on, Nana?"

"Some kind of kidney infection that I can't pronounce."

"Pyelonephritis," I guess.

She snaps her fingers. "Yes. That sounds right. I'll be fine once the antibiotics run their course. I'm only here because the infection also makes me vomit, and I can't keep their stupid pills down. I just need a couple days on a drip IV and I'll be fine."

I look over at her. "Promise me there won't be any complications."

"Maria. You know I can't promise that. But the internist did say it was unlikely."

"Fine." I swallow panic. "Okay. Sure."

"Maria," she says more gently, "you know you're not really mad at me, right?"

I look into her eyes for the first time since I've arrived. She's watching me carefully, probably as aware as I am that I'm panicking for very little reason.

People are allowed to have minor health scares. People get sick. It's okay. She's not going anywhere.

I reach out and take her hand. Her skin is a little looser than mine over the knuckles, but she's still strong. I let out a breath, and try to release all the stupid medical knowledge I acquired on the way in as I exhale.

"I know," I say. "I'm such a basket case about these things."

"No," Nana says. "You're my strong girl."

We sit without saying anything. I try to shove my feelings into an appropriate channel.

"Hey." She interrupts me. "Stop blaming yourself."

"I wasn't."

"Yes, you were. You were telling yourself that you were a bad grandchild because you were making this about you, when I'm the one in the hospital."

I look back at her. Fine. I was.

"Tell me what you were doing while I was on trial."

I exhale again. "I seem to have acquired a boyfriend."

"Does he have a name?"

"Jay. Jay na Thalang." I swallow. "He knows Gabe from Harvard. He's a professor at Berkeley."

"Hmmm," she says.

"He's not in the country right now," I tell her. "He has a conference in Melbourne. And I'm kind of ridiculously glad he's not here for this."

"Why? Because you're afraid of how he'll react if he knows you occasionally freak out?"

I already know how Jay would react to that. He's witnessed it. I shake my head. I'm not entirely sure *why* I don't want him around.

"It would be weird," I say instead.

She doesn't say anything.

"It would be weird," I say, "to…you know. Lean on him. We haven't been together that long. It would be weird if I could trust him with something like this so soon."

"Weird," she repeats.

I know how ridiculous I sound. "Weird," I affirm. "It's better that he's not here."

And because she knows me, she doesn't push.

I walk out of her room forty-five minutes later, when a nurse gently suggests that visiting hours will be over soon and maybe my grandmother needs to rest.

Nana rolls her eyes at the suggestion that she may be human, but I leave.

It's been good to talk to her. I'm feeling better. Less anxious, and the damned medical diagnoses I had rattling around in my brain have finally quieted down.

I make my way out past the check-in desk.

As I do, I hear my name. "Maria."

My heart stands still for one moment, then it thumps, hard and fast. I turn around.

Jay is sitting in a plastic bucket seat. He has his laptop out. There's a blue plastic bag on the seat next to him.

My mind isn't working properly. I can't explain his presence. He's on a plane to Australia. It is not possible that he would be here.

"Jay?"

He shuts his laptop and slides it into his bag. "Hi."

It is apparently possible that he is here. I wrinkle my nose suspiciously. "How are you here?"

"Gabe texted me when I was still in LAX." He says this like it's some kind of explanation for his presence. It still doesn't make sense.

I try again. "*Why* are you here?"

He shrugs. "Your grandmother was in the hospital. Gabe was in Switzerland. *Someone* had to bring you soup." He gestures to the blue plastic bag. "I hope you like Korean."

I love Korean.

I try again. "But you were on your way to a conference."

"It's at the end of the week. I moved my flight back a couple of days."

"But you were going to spend time with your coauthor."

"I called Vithika and explained. She said it could wait."

"But why would you?"

"Seriously, Em?" He looks at me and I know the answer. I know the reason that I didn't want him here. I wasn't afraid that he would blame me or make fun of my anxieties. I wasn't even afraid of leaning on him.

I was afraid he would understand without my telling him.

"Come on," he says. "There's a cafeteria down the hall. Let me buy you a Coke and feed you dinner."

"But…you…" I trail off helplessly. "You're *here*."

"It's just work," he says. "Don't worry. It's not going anywhere."

"But…" I trail off uselessly.

He gives me a half smile. "Come on, Maria. Have some soup."

I let him feed me soup.

He was right about the Coke, too; I'd skipped dinner. Stress and low blood sugar, it turns out, really do not mix. It feels weird to let someone take care of me.

It feels weird that my grandmother's in the hospital, but it's only a minor thing. It feels weird that Jay would move his flight, lose time with someone he's doing research with. I don't have a better word for how it feels than *weird*. Unnatural.

He calls an Uber as we head out. We nestle together in the backseat, holding hands. I almost don't feel present in my own body.

The lights on the Bay Bridge strobe through the car windows, on and off. We're sitting thigh to thigh, my hand in his.

"What are you thinking?"

"Just how lucky I am. That this wasn't worse. That I have you."

All this luck is scaring me. Flip a coin, and have it come up heads, and it's no big deal. Flip it again, and heads still isn't a surprise. If you see Washington's profile nineteen times in a row, though…something's wrong with you. Or something's wrong with the quarter. Luck is lovely, until it keeps going and going and going. Until all you can do is hold your breath, waiting for it to run out.

Jay shrugs. "You're not lucky. This is just what life is like. Most of the time, it's not that bad."

I shake my head. He catches the movement, even though we are in a dark patch. He doesn't say anything, but he rearranges our fingers and squeezes my hand more tightly.

He doesn't speak again until we're in Oakland on the other side of the Bay. "I saw your job spreadsheet the other day. When you handed me your computer."

I look at him. My chest goes cold first, then my arms. I feel like ice all over. So. He saw that I have a job offer in New York. He knows I didn't tell him about it. I glance at our driver, who has been thankfully silent.

"This probably isn't the place to have this conversation," I say.

"Why?" I can't see his face.

I wish we were texting. Here in the dark, with my feelings wrapped around my throat, I can't tell if he's sarcastic. His voice gives me no clues.

His hand squeezes mine, hard. "Look. Maybe this isn't the right time for us. Maybe you need to go across the country. I looked up the company. They seem interesting."

Oh. My whole body feels light. *That's why this is happening. He's breaking up with me.* Finally something that makes sense.

"Maybe this isn't the right time for us," he says with a little more conviction, "but I'm pretty sure I just tipped my hand. You're the right person for me."

I blink. I turn to him. It takes me a moment to understand that he is not, in fact, breaking up with me. It takes me so long, in fact, that he keeps going.

"I don't know what this means, except that I'm all in. If you move across the country and I only get to see you four times a year, I'm still all in. If you go to New York and want to call it quits, I'm—"

He pauses. I can see his lip curl in a thin shaft of passing light.

"No. I'm not really into that. I'm too selfish for that. But I'll understand."

This is the point where a response of some kind is socially expected. The only word that comes to mind right now, though, is, "Oh."

Which has to be the worst response I could possibly give at the moment. It's a shitty response. *Such* a shitty response. I know it, and he knows it.

He exhales. "Fine. You don't want to talk about that. How about this? Your grandmother went to the hospital and you didn't even text me."

I shake my head. "You were on a plane."

"You didn't text me."

"It wasn't serious."

"Maria, don't tell me it wasn't serious to you. I know what she means to you and how much it would scare you to have her in the hospital. You didn't text me."

"I didn't want to bother you. I don't want to ask you for things."

He gives his head a short, sharp shake. "I'm serious about you, Maria. And I know you're not there yet, and I know this is shitty timing. But I want you to have expectations of me. I *want* you to ask me for things. I need you to believe that I can be enough."

I exhale. I can almost hear the echo of the words I sent him months ago. *Your boundaries are hurting me.* I can see that now. I'm hurting him, and I don't know what to do about it.

I use my one word again. "Oh."

Maybe he hears the shake in my voice, because he reaches out and touches my face.

"It's okay," he says. "I shouldn't have said anything. Shitty timing."

It's not okay. The car exits the freeway, and I'm still stunned.

I remember this time our childhood cat caught a crow. It landed in our front yard, and the cat didn't hesitate. He jumped on it. Crows are massive, but the surprise attack knocked it out, and the cat trotted it into the house. Where it proceeded to come to life and wreak havoc.

Jay can say that it's okay, but saying it doesn't make it so. If someone says "I love you," there's pressure. And I don't know what says *I love you* more loudly than rescheduling a transpacific flight just to bring me soup, and telling me I should be able to expect that from him.

I don't know how to expect that kind of care. I just understand that he needs me to expect it—just the way I need to go hide right now. Jay just attached a clock to our relationship. I can almost feel it ticking in time with my heart as the driver pulls alongside the curb of my house.

I don't ask Jay in. I don't ask him to spend the night. He changed a transcontinental flight for me, brought me soup, and told me he loved me. I should be delighted. Instead, I can't feel my own emotions. Just the vise grip of something fierce and relentless crushing my chest.

The best I can manage to say to him, as I exit the vehicle, is this: "Thanks."

He looks at me. He nods. This is the point where I should say something. Anything.

Instead, I don't let myself look back. I escape into the house.

26.

MARIA

"*Hey*." Tina is still awake and up, waiting for me in the kitchen when I arrive. "How are you? How's your grandmother?"

"Fine." I can hardly manage eye contact at this stage. "It's just a minor kidney infection. She's going to be fine."

"Oh, good."

I stand at the edge of the kitchen, not wanting to engage in conversation. My room is downstairs. I want to go hide.

Tina frowns at me. "Are you sure you're okay? You don't look okay."

"Fine."

"You've used that word three times."

I look over at her. She's watching me closely.

"Honestly," Tina says, "you don't look like anything like okay." She comes over to me and picks up my hand. My pulse is a rapid, staccato beat against her forefinger. "You look like you're in shock."

Huh. I consider this. My thoughts move at sloth speed.

"Come on. You're freezing." She pulls me into the living room and finds a blanket throw. I curl into a little ball underneath. She disappears for a moment, long enough for me to Google "symptoms of shock" and decide that Tina is wrong.

She comes back with a pile of blankets and a cup of tea.

"Look," I say, holding up my phone. "I'm not in shock. WebMD says so. Without any kind of trauma—"

She waves my phone away. "It's a figure of speech, not a medical diagnosis, genius. Come on. Tell me what's wrong."

Nothing's wrong. That's the problem. Nothing is wrong, and the thing about climbing to the top of the mountain is that it leaves you feeling exposed. Open. There's no protective tree cover, nothing between you and the sky.

Nothing is wrong. And so instead of telling her about Jay, I tell her about another thing that *is* actually wrong.

"Anj wants me to go to her costume party dressed as a shark."

Tina frowns. She looks at me. The best word I have to describe her is *nonplussed*.

"I don't want to go dressed as a shark." I'm aware that I am whining. "I *hate* her shark. *Hate* it. And if I don't show up with fins, she'll ask me why and I'll have to tell her."

"So. What if you tell her?"

I wring my hands.

Tina hands me the tea. "It's okay to tell people when you're upset."

"Fine," I snap out. "I don't want to be roommates next year."

She pauses. She looks at me again.

"You and Blake are together. Really together, and it looks like that's not changing. Adam Reynolds shows up at random intervals. I just feel…weird, like I don't even belong in here, and I *hate* feeling like I don't belong in my own living space."

Tina blows out a slow breath and hugs her knees on the couch. I didn't want to upset her.

I shake my head. "I shouldn't have said anything."

"Why?" she asks. "You'd prefer not to say anything and just be miserable instead?"

"I wasn't miserable. It's more like a low-level discontent. A two-point-five on the misery scale. I can live with that."

Tina looks at me. "But you don't deserve a two-point-five on the misery scale. Why would you think I'd want you to live with that?"

I blink. I don't answer. But deep down, I know the why. I just experienced it with Jay. I'm afraid to expect care. I certainly don't want to ask for it. I'm always afraid that one wrong move will disturb all the good things I've managed to find. Luck never lasts, and my friends are the luckiest part of my life. If I let them know what I need…

Maybe it won't all end.

I exhale and choose my next words carefully. "Jay met me at the hospital." It sounds like a non sequitur.

She blinks. Once. Then twice. "Isn't he supposed to be in Australia?"

"Gabe texted him during his layover. He took a flight back." My voice is trembling again. "His luggage is lost in limbo."

"Okay."

"He told me…" I almost can't say the words. They aren't bad; they're *great*. "He told me he was all in on the relationship. On me. The only reason I think he *didn't* say the l-word was because he could tell how much it was messing with my mind."

Tina doesn't say anything. How could she? *You're being a dramatic idiot* is not the kind of thing a supportive friend ever says.

"It's too soon," I say. "We've been together for like, a month."

"Kind of," Tina says. "I mean, you two have been talking for…how long now?"

At this point, it's been a little over two years. I wrinkle my nose.

"And you know," Tina says, "even if it were true that you'd only been together for a month, it's actually really believable to me that someone could fall for you in a month. You're really great."

I burrow into my blankets, hiding my face. "You're just saying that because you're my best friend."

"You get your grandmother groceries when she's on trial." Tina holds up one finger. "You fix your brother's PowerPoint slides. When I ruined my lucky sweater last year, you got it secretly dry-cleaned. You're funny and you're sweet and you care about the people you love so much. Anyone who *doesn't* know you and love you is an asshole."

I can feel my eyes stinging. A hint of hoarse congestion clogs my voice. "Shut *up.*"

"You're all in for everyone else," Tina says. "Always, all the time. I think you're freaking out right now because the only person in your life you *aren't* all in for is yourself."

I shake my head. But Tina doesn't go away. She holds me. When I start crying, she strokes my hair. She tells me I'm okay.

"I'm not okay. I'm a ridiculous idiot."

"Don't talk about yourself that way." She says it gently. "You're ridiculously smart, and if you feel like this, there's a good reason for it."

I stumble off to bed half an hour later, where I cocoon myself in blankets. I lie in the dark, looking up at the ceiling, trying to make sense of what Tina told me. After the shock, after the tears, I'm grateful for the dark of night and the weight of blankets. These are simple physical sensations. Uncomplicated. Impossible to misinterpret.

I try on sentences for size.

The thing about getting struck by lightning on the mountaintop is that your unthinking animal brain learns the wrong lesson. *Never go above tree line.*

There's a reason I don't want to test how much people care about me. There's a reason I'm pushing Jay away, why I'm waffling between jobs that leave me feeling fundamentally dissatisfied. I'm not all in on myself.

Maybe I deserve to be. I turn this thought over. It scares me, but I don't let go. Maybe this isn't luck. Maybe good things don't have to end.

It's easier to express that thought when I put a maybe in front, but as I turn over the *maybes* in my head, I discover something else.

I don't need the maybe.

I actually *do* deserve to be happy. I deserve to have people love me. I haven't fought this hard, and come this far, to settle for a tentative maybe. I deserve to be ecstatic. I deserve to have people care for me. I don't want to accept any less.

Most of the time I think of worst-case scenarios—the catastrophes that could come. Right now, I swallow my fear, and I let myself daydream the best case instead.

I don't want to drown in a job I don't love just in case it turns into another better one. I don't want to keep swallowing things that bother me while anxiety builds up in my stomach.

As for Jay... He's right. Expectations are hope. I don't know how to hope like this. I'm afraid to let myself believe that I deserve to have someone love me enough to change all his plans because he knew I'd be scared. But maybe, maybe... No, no maybe. I *do* deserve it.

I pull my laptop onto the bed. I look at my spreadsheet of jobs. I tried to reduce all of my worries and doubts and misgivings to numbers. I tried to put a price on how much I wanted to stay here so I could compare it to living in New York.

The truth is, I only have a spreadsheet because I'm not excited about any of my options. I'm letting numbers flip a coin for me. If I really, really wanted any of these, I would have already said yes.

Slowly, I select every line. My careful comparison of health care plans and salaries highlights in blue.

I hit delete, and every line disappears. My future is nothing but blank cells. It's scary, but for the first time, I feel a tickle of excitement about what's to come.

Just after midnight, I shed my blankets, get out of bed, and stub my toe on a chair while looking for my phone on its charger.

I had meant to send a text to someone else. But there's a message from Jay waiting for me.

I was wrong, the message reads. *Really wrong to expect this of you now. I keep waiting for you to tell me I'm enough, but tonight I had it backward. You were the one who needed to hear it tonight. You're enough. You are. And that isn't going to change.*

I shut my eyes. Let myself feel my own feelings—everything from the fluttering fear that says, *this will end* to that deep still place inside me that whispers, *maybe he's right.*

I read his message again, and I tell myself—firmly, because deep down, I'm still wavering—that I deserve someone who cares for me this much.

I think of my blank spreadsheet. I look at the blank space beneath this message. I don't know how to respond. But maybe it's okay to not know everything right away.

Thanks, I reply. *I needed to hear that.*

He's asleep, as he should be. He doesn't answer. And I have something else to do. I thumb through my contacts in the faint light from its screen. The one I'm looking for—Angela Choi—isn't far down. I send her a message.

Do you have any time tomorrow?

She should be asleep, but...no, this is Anj. *Sure. What do you need?*

I think about all the things I want. That I deserve.

Then I write. *I want to talk.*

After much deliberation, I realize I have one last email to send. For the last few months, I've ignored my anxiety. Told myself I'd work it out. That I was better, and that if only I was strong enough, I wouldn't need any more help.

But I don't need to fight anxiety with nothing but willpower and sleepless nights. I have better things to do with my willpower. So I write to my old psychiatrist.

I'm graduating from college right now, and things are changing really fast. I'd like to make an appointment to talk about renewing my prescription until things normalize.

Thanks,

Maria

---

*A*nj's apartment is all too familiar. It's not the same place we lived together, but it feels almost the same. That *almost* is because her cereal bowls are stacked in the sink, like she's an actual adult.

The living room is still half aquariums.

"Hey," says Anj. "What's up?"

I rearrange a stack of prototype batteries to make room for me on the couch and sit. "I don't want to dress up as a shark."

She raises an eyebrow. "O...kay. And you came here at eight in the morning to tell me that?"

I take a deep breath. "Thing is, Anj? I kind of hate Lisa."

Her eyes widen. She glances back at the aquariums, a worried look on her face. "Oh my god," she whispers.

"You know sharks can hear in the frequency of human voices, right?"

I shake my head. "I don't really hate Lisa. I hate the way she makes me feel."

Anj shakes her head in puzzlement.

"Our landlord said he was going to kick us out because of Lisa," I say. "I have issues with getting kicked out of places I live. I like stability and I hate surprises. Lisa gave me nightmares."

Anj blinks. She looks at Lisa. She looks back at me. "Oh," she says slowly. "Oh. I knew something wasn't right, but... Why didn't you tell me? I could have made my dad keep her."

I swallow. "I thought you might choose Lisa over me. And...if you were going to do that, I didn't want to know."

"Oh." She looks utterly dazed. I've never seen her so confused. I was never jealous of her money, or her startups—but I *am* jealous of the fact that she takes being loved for granted. "Oh." She's privileged, not stupid. She figures it out.

She shoves aside a stack of tech manuals and hugs me. "Oh, no," Anj says. "I'm sorry. I'm sorry I ever made you feel that way. I get stuck in my own head."

"I know." I hug her back. "I really—honestly—don't hold anything against you."

"I would have moved her," Anj says. "I love you and Lisa in totally different ways. But I love you just as much as Lisa."

I can't help myself. I start laughing.

"What?"

"No. It's nothing." I hug her back. And this time, it is.

"What else do you have going on today?"

I think of that blank spreadsheet. "Visiting my grandmother," I say. "Visiting a friend of yours."

"And?"

"And talking to a boy."

She wrinkles her nose. "Okay. Well. Have fun."

---

*T*he Bay Area's odd microclimates are such that the dark clouds and drizzle hovering over Berkeley have dissolved into brilliant blue skies and sunshine by the time I arrive in Palo Alto in the car I've borrowed from Blake.

Stanford University is almost exactly the opposite of Cal in every possible way. It's a private school, where Berkeley is public. There are huge expanses of green grass and not nearly as many students. Where Cal is a mishmash of opposing architecture, Stanford was built on a plan. Every building looks like it's part of a branded franchise of red roofs and sandstone arches.

I consult a map on my phone and make my way into a building. It's not hard to find the right door.

Professor Dan van Tijn yells at me to come in when I knock, so I do. He's grown out his beard since I last saw him in December. He shakes my hand, and asks me to sit down.

I hope that my hand isn't sweaty. I smile and try to look like I'm a reasonably intelligent human being.

"What can I do for you?"

I took Anj's name in vain in my introductory email. Reminded him that we met before. I was utterly shameless. And now I'm scared.

"You're on—" I cough, because my throat is suddenly dry. "You're on the admissions committee for the graduate program in Management and Engineering Science."

"Yes." He looks away.

"How flexible is the program on their admission deadlines?"

He frowns and glances at his laptop. I suspect he's checking his email.

"Um. Well. It would depend. We don't like making exceptions, but…" He frowns at his screen, types something in response, then drags his gaze back to me. "It's not the kind of thing I would do as a favor to a friend. Anj should know better." This comes out more firmly. "Exceptions would require exceptional circumstances. And an exceptional applicant."

I don't let myself choke. Not when I'm about to articulate something I've barely let myself think.

"I want to do worldwide risk assessment for companies attempting to adapt to changing circumstances." My dream, the thing I really want, feels massive spoken out loud. "Before anyone really lets me do that, I'm going to need a credential of some kind."

He doesn't notice. He's openly reading his messages. I can tell that his mind has drifted off to other spheres. "I'd be happy to advise you on your application next year."

"And we can wait a year, if necessary, for me to send out a full panel of applications everywhere." My heart is beating hard now. "I absolutely need more formal training."

"Okay." He's bored. He's not paying attention.

"But you asked me if I wanted to write a paper on cybersecurity risks with you last September. And I was…kind of hoping the offer was still open."

He blinks. He turns to me, no longer distracted by his computer screen. He frowns. "I did?"

"I write a blog under the pseudonym MCL."

He is the fifth person I've told. I'm not sure why I've kept it back. Part of it was wanting to keep my anonymity. Part of it was being afraid, back when I started, that my brother would make fun of my science. Maybe all of it is being afraid to take credit.

My heart beats wildly.

"It's my initials," I say. "Maria Camilla Lopez."

He stares at me. "Holy crap," he says slowly. "Holy crap! You are not like I imagined." He stands up and shakes my hand again, this time more vigorously. "I'm really excited to meet you."

I give him a half smile. "Hi?"

We stare at each other for a moment; him in bemusement, me, with my heart pounding. "So," I say. "Grad school?"

"Holy crap," he says again. "Yes. But—you're—"

"An undergrad."

"That wasn't what I was going to say." He looks upward.

I know what he was going to say. He said it when we crossed paths at the Cyclone party months ago. He thought I was a man.

"Well," he says. "I'm an idiot. Clearly. But since I have you here, look, I have a question about how you ran this network simulation."

Instead of talking about grad school, we talk about cybersecurity, and the model of the internet I built, and whether it's applicable to targeted malware delivery. He only remembers why I came half an hour later.

We hash out details and a plan. He makes me sign up to take the GRE from the computer in his office. When I leave, he's on the phone with admissions.

Before I head up to see my grandmother, I check my messages.

Tina has sent me good luck wishes; Jay texted a brief message saying that he hopes I'm feeling better, and that he'll be here in town for another thirty-six hours if I want to see him.

My friends sent me notes from the classes I missed this morning.

There's a text from Gabe, too. He took an early flight back, and has apparently just arrived in town. *Hey, I told Jay about Nana. I know he's kind of a shitty boyfriend, so I hope he didn't ignore it.*

I consider this perfidy. *He's fine,* I write tersely. *It was fine.* It was more than fine.

Gabe must still be jet-lagged, because he writes back almost immediately.

Okay, but don't be so defensive. He told me months before he started dating you that he was really into someone else. I'm trying not to be all aggro big brother about this, but I just don't want you to get hurt.

I exhale and pinch the bridge of my nose. *Look, little brother. First things first: You're seriously telling me this the day after Nana lands in the hospital? Your timing sucks.*

He doesn't respond.

Second, has it ever occurred to you that he was talking about me?

His response is not long in coming: *Wut?*

I look out the window. The clouds are still gathered over Berkeley, but they've dissipated somewhat. They're less gray now.

It's a long story. But I've known Jay online for years. I grin as I type. *And actually we get along really well. We just had to figure it out.*

I ignore his requests for more information. I'll tell him later.

I send one last text after that, this time to Jay. *Hey. I played hooky on classes all day. Heading over to visit Nana now. Will you have time around seven tonight?*

Yes, Jay writes back almost instantly.

Okay. Want me to meet you at home or at your office?

For you? They should just be words, pixels on a screen. They shouldn't convey warmth, acceptance, or belonging. Yet somehow they do. *For you, I'm at home.*

27.

MARIA

I knock on Jay's door.

I should be nervous; I was nothing but nerves last night and for less reason. Somehow, though, after today, I feel steady.

He opens the door. For a moment, we look at each other. He doesn't step forward. He doesn't reach out. He just looks at me, as if wondering what will happen next.

I step into him, hugging him as hard as I can. His arms wrap around me, strong, squeezing me until I can feel the air squeak from my lungs.

"You okay?" His voice is low.

"I'm doing…better. A lot better."

"Your grandmother?"

"Complaining up a storm. They're going to discharge her tomorrow, assuming everything is still on track."

"That's fantastic." He looks at me.

I pull away from him long enough to brandish the paper bag I have with me. "I brought you presents."

"Oooh." He looks at me. There's a hint of wariness still in his eyes. Just a tiny tightness around his mouth, the whisper of a wrinkle on his forehead.

I reach in and pull out the first package. "This is for your flight."

He takes the rectangle from me. He turns it around, frowning at it. He bends it.

"It's a book," he guesses.

"Oh my god. You're one of those. You have to guess everything."

He flashes me a smile. "I am totally one of those. I'm going to be even worse. It's *From the Mixed-Up Files of Mrs. Basil E. Frankweiler.*"

I make an outraged noise as he carefully unwraps his present—not ripping the paper, carefully parting every piece of tape, before removing the paperback I purchased for him.

It is, of course, *From the Mixed-Up Files of Mrs. Basil E. Frankweiler.*

"Oh, look," he says. "*From the Mixed-Up Files of Mrs. Basil E. Frankweiler.* How surprising."

I shake my head. "I may freak out when I'm nervous, but you're even worse. When *you* get nervous, you have to be right about things."

"Fine." He leans in and kisses me lightly on the cheek. "Thank you. I'm looking forward to reading it." Then he kisses me again, this time not so lightly. On the lips. It's the first time we've kissed since...

No, we didn't actually kiss at the hospital. Since I kissed him good-bye, thinking I wouldn't see him for a little more than a week when he left for Australia. It's a sweet kiss. A tender kiss. His lips ask the question that he himself has not.

Are we okay?

I pull away. "I have one more present for you."

"Oooh."

I give the paper bag a light shake. "Since you're going to be like that? Guess."

He glares at the bag as if he could see through it Superman-style. Then he looks at me. "I can't touch?"

"Nope."

He looks upward. "Shit. That makes it difficult. I don't know, it's a fancy pen?"

I look at him. He looks back at me, one eyebrow raised in question.

"Oh, look." I reach into the paper bag and remove his present. "It's a fancy pen."

It is not a fancy pen. It's a plant of trailing green-and-white striated leaves. We both look at it for a long, long moment.

"Maria," he says in a low voice, "I kill plants."

"I know." Now my voice does shake, just a little. "You told me. That's why I need to keep coming over. To make sure you don't."

Our eyes meet again. Slowly, ever so slowly, his face begins to light. I can see the realization of what I just said come over him like a sunrise. The corners of his mouth tilt upward. His eyes widen, and then blaze. His whole expression lifts, and I realize just how worried he really has been.

"I love you," I say. "I love you because you make me want to be my best self. I love you because even when you hated me, you still listened and still learned. I love you because we fit together so well that you scare me. I love you."

"Oh, good." He reaches in and takes my head in his hands. We nestle against each other, nose to nose, breath to breath. "I love you, too."

"Unfortunately," I say, "for the next handful of years or so, we're going to be long-distance."

He doesn't even flinch. "I like New York. Are you going to take temporary custody of my plant?"

"Not that long-distance," I say. "This is going to sound strange, but—while you're in Australia, I'm taking the GRE. And finishing an application to graduate school. I had a long talk with a professor at Stanford about cybersecurity. It's a long story."

"Good," he says. "I like long stories. I have time." Then he kisses me again—this time, harder.

"It's scary," I tell him. "It's scary to expect things. It's going to take me time to get used to it."

He pulls me toward him. "We have time."

"We do." I find myself looking into his eyes. Leaning my forehead against his. "I don't think I could ever have told you that you were enough until I believed I was, too. But maybe it's that simple. We're enough."

He doesn't respond. Not at first. Then he smiles, and his smile seems to envelop me in warmth. "Tell me all about it in an hour. For now, I have some other ideas as to how we should spend our time."

"I like other ideas," I say. "I like them a lot."

Then he kisses me again, and again, and again, until we're nothing but other ideas.

Thank you!

Thank you for reading *Hold Me*. I hope you enjoyed it.

- Would you like to know when my next book is available? You can sign up for my new release e-mail list at www.courtneymilan.com, follow me on twitter at @courtneymilan, or like my Facebook page at :

    http://facebook.com/courtneymilanauthor

- Reviews help other readers find books. I appreciate all reviews, whether positive or negative.

- *Hold Me* is the second book in the Cyclone series. It's preceded by *Trade Me,* and followed by *Find Me, What Lies Between Me and You, Keep Me,* and *Show Me.*

Is there anything else I can read about Jay and Maria?

A lot of times, when I delete scenes, there's really nothing to do with them—I delete them because they're stupid or they don't belong in the story. I don't want you to see them, now or ever.

When I wrote the first draft of *Hold Me,* I originally had flashbacks to Jay and Maria's first discussions on Maria's blog. I ended up deleting them because they interrupted the flow of the story, but you might still be interested. You can see the first time they exchanged comments, and why they call each other A. and Em. You can read them at:

http://www.courtneymilan.com/jayandmaria.php

What is the Cyclone series?

The Cyclone series is a set of stories loosely (or not so loosely) connected to Cyclone Technologies, a fictional computer company located in the heart of Silicon Valley.

What other characters are getting stories?

Blake and Tina's story started in *Trade Me,* and will be continued in *Find Me.* Kenji Miyahara, mentioned very briefly in this book, will be the star of *Keep Me* (alongside Ellie Wise—there's an excerpt from *Find Me* that introduces her right after this section). Angela Choi is the star of *Show Me.* And Adam Reynolds will be the star of *What Lies Between Me and You.*

When will these books release?

I'm not the fastest writer and I don't like making promises when I'm not sure I can keep them. I hope that *Find Me* and *What Lies Between Me and You* will be out sometime in 2017.

I don't want to wait that long! What can I do in the meantime?

Luckily, I have written many other books. If you haven't already done so, you can try my historical romances. I suggest starting with *The Governess Affair*— it's free on most platforms right now. There's humor, there's angst…there are no smartwatches, but in the course of the Brothers Sinister series, you will get primers (they go from A-Z), pretty gowns (and some intentionally hideous ones), pink snapdragons (except there is no such thing as a pink snapdragon), and exclamation points (necessary for proper pronunciation). Give them a try. If you've already read all my books, I have a list of recommendations for other authors on my website.

And if you're looking for more in the Cyclone universe, there are three shorts you can read. The first is from a few years before *Trade Me* starts, and it's a snippet of life at Cyclone from Adam Reynolds's point of view. You can find it here: http://bit.ly/afr-at-cyclone The second is a crossover story between the Brothers Sinister series and the Cyclone universe, set initially in the year 2020…until Adam accidentally time-travels back to Victorian England. You can find that here: http://bit.ly/afr-meets-free.

Finally, *The Year of the Crocodile* is a short story that takes place between *Trade Me* and *Find Me,* right in the middle of *Hold Me.* You can find it for sale on any vendor where you purchased this book, or you can get a free copy by signing up for my newsletter through this link: https://www.instafreebie.com/free/xTLPC

You can also read an excerpt from Find Me, the next book in the series, at:
http://www.courtneymilan.com/findme.php

Other Books by Courtney

The Cyclone Series
Trade Me
Hold Me
Find Me
What Lies Between Me and You
Keep Me
Show Me

The Worth Saga
Once Upon a Marquess
Her Every Wish
After the Wedding
The Devil Comes Courting
The Return of the Scoundrel
The Kissing Hour
A Tale of Two Viscounts
The Once and Future Earl

The Brothers Sinister Series
The Governess Affair
The Duchess War
A Kiss for Midwinter
The Heiress Effect
The Countess Conspiracy
The Suffragette Scandal
Talk Sweetly to Me

The Turner Series
Unveiled
Unlocked
Unclaimed
Unraveled

Not in any series
A Right Honorable Gentleman
What Happened at Midnight
The Lady Always Wins

The Carhart Series
This Wicked Gift
Proof by Seduction
Trial by Desire

Author's Note

*A*uthors sometimes talk about the book of their heart. *Hold Me* is the book of my gigantic unending nerdiness, more so than any other book I've written. It combines my love for technogadgetry with my love for science fiction, quantum mechanics, and my three years in the Berkeley chemistry department. Writing Jay and Maria was intensely, ridiculously fun.

For those who are wondering about the things mentioned peripherally in this book, most of the technology is real. Quantum computation is real (although in its infancy). Angela Choi's chickenosaurus really is happening (this is a link to more). There really are people talking about bringing back the wooly mammoth and other species (another link). To the best of my knowledge, I haven't found any sharks that have had green fluorescent protein spliced into their genes...but there have been glow-in-the-dark rabbits. And while we can't 3D bioprint spiders (yet) (shiver), we're getting to the point where we might be able to create organs. There is an impending helium shortage.

It is both weird and exciting to live in the future, and here I am—in mid-October of 2016—really hoping that we get to it.

A few notes on incredibly arcane things: I mentioned briefly the physics/chemistry dichotomy, and that what counted as "physics" in the UK would be chemistry here. This is drawn from something I learned as a graduate student. In Europe, much of statistical physics falls into physics departments. In the US, it falls in chemistry. The historical reason I was given for this (and I have never found a source other than word of mouth from people who were there at the time) was that the US got a ton of top-caliber scientists who fled World War II—so many, that the physics departments filled up on nuclear and quantum scientists. Those who fell in the statistical physics field ended up filling out chemistry departments.

So if you want to know Jay's full background, he got a PhD in theoretical statistical physics—one of the nonexperimental fields where you could legitimately manage a three-and-a-half-year PhD. (It would be unheard of in some other disciplines). Partway through this program, Jay attended a monthlong course run by the EU in Les Houches, in France, where he met Vithika Chaudhary, who at the time was another theoretical physicist up at Edinburgh. When they touched base at another conference, they started talking about quantum computation. Jay did a postdoc with someone who was doing laser work to nail down the experimental side of things. Vithika now does theory, and he does experimental verification.

I don't know how widespread the advice that Jay's former principal investigator gave him really is (do excellent research, adequate service, and passable teaching), but since I heard it from about five people in a much less research-oriented field, I assume that it would not be out of line based on where he was. The actual line

I repeatedly heard when I was in science (in the Berkeley Chemistry department, no less) was that it didn't matter if you taught badly because the good students would learn anyway. Not everyone believed that, but it was probably fifty-fifty.

Finally, I was originally going to give Jay an experience that I have not had, but that someone close to me had once had—namely, winning a MacArthur Genius Grant fellowship (not the real name). I did a little poking around, and decided that he was way too early in his career to be awarded one. It just wouldn't make sense. So I gave Jay another experience my older sister once had—being told that she'd get twenty percent of the grants she applied for, and then getting them all. Thanks, Tami.

$\mathcal{A}$ very tiny part of this book stems from something that happened to me as a first-year graduate student. Every new physical chemistry graduate student was drafted into teaching lab sections for the introductory chemistry class.

Chem 1A at the time was co-taught by a professor and a lecturer. They were experimenting with multimedia presentations, online components, and video clips to spice up the class. At one point in that first year, the lecturer showed a video clip from a James Bond movie where the Bond girl du jour was a nuclear scientist.

The lecturer made a comment to the entire class that this Bond girl didn't *look* like a scientist because of her boobs. (Sadly, I'm downplaying the crudity of the comment he actually made.)

The female graduate student instructors—there were quite a few of us—exploded. We told him in no uncertain terms that he'd messed up and needed to recant and apologize to the class.

The next day, that lecturer stood up and told the class that he apologized for sending the message that women could not be scientists. He had only said what he did, he explained, because he found it unbelievable that she could be a scientist *and* look the way she did. Women could be scientists, he said, and his only point was that scientists just wouldn't be the ones with big perky boobs who wore makeup.

I don't think he ever understood why this apology didn't help.

But... I actually needed to have that conversation myself. It sucked to hear those words. It was wonderful to have my fellow graduate students affirm over and over why women—all women, any women—deserved respect. And I listened and learned and discovered that I'd had my own internalized issues that I needed to address.

I   hope   I've   been   doing   better   since.

Acknowledgments

I'm going to forget a million people in this acknowledgments section, and I apologize in advance.

Lindsey Faber, Martha Trachtenberg, Rawles Lumumba, Eliza Stefaniw—thanks so much for everything you did to make this book better. Louisa Jordan stepped in and helped me with the most annoying part of book construction, and I owe her an eternal debt of gratitude. Thanks to Tami for reading my mind when I asked her to send me over a grant proposal, any grant proposal, because I needed to see how they were structured.

I'm deeply grateful to my many, many friends who have held my hand through good and bad times. Bree, Alyssa, Alisha, Rebekah, Tessa, Leigh, Carey, Brenna, Julio, all the Northwest Pixies who listened to me talk about this book when it was in its infancy, Rose and Olivia, who heard about the version of this book that eventually ended up vanishing... My list is endless and I'm so sorry if I left you off. It's because my memory is terrible.

Thanks also for Michael Nielsen's (sadly unfinished) (no, I'm really sad it's unfinished) YouTube course, entitled Quantum Computing for the Determined. If you want to take it, it's here. It's sadly incomplete, but got me up to speed enough to remind me of all the quantum mechanics I'd forgotten so that I could vaguely muddle through his book, which promptly ended up not showing up in this book at all, but oh well, I had fun.

Ali Fischer was my on-the-scene eyes and ears for all the things I did not remember, or did not know, about the Berkeley College of Chemistry's layout. She provided details, descriptions, and *so* many pictures.

Deirdre Saoirse Moen answered questions about what a product release cycle workload looks like behind the scenes for a company like Cyclone *cough* which is of course not like any other company on the planet, including any other company *cough*Apple*cough* that she might have worked for.

Denise Brogan-Kator…thank you for everything. My *everything* here encompasses so much that I'm not even going to try. But thank you.

To the ~~mathematicians~~ scientists who poured so much effort into shaping me—Adam, Mark, Jack, Bettye Anne, Bob—my undying gratitude. I left one of you off that initial list. For DNMNC—every so often, I think about where my life has gone since I left your lab, and I wonder what would have happened if I'd realized sometime around the summer of my second year that my persistent unhappiness and malaise was depression, not dissatisfaction.

I honestly don't know. But I think of everywhere I've been and everything I've done, and I feel incredibly lucky. The person who came to a grinding halt in the Pitzer Center basement is the same person who got to clerk for Sandra Day O'Connor and write romance novels and here we are, almost full circle. It's been the grandest adventure, and still, I look back on moving through the Little Green Book and the White Set of

Notes with affection. And, David, if you're wondering, and I am 100% positive you are not because how would you do that, Maria's computer model mentioned in chapter three is a modified Ising Model.

Of *course* it's an Ising Model. It's always an Ising Model. I came up with a computer simulation to model the diffusion of free speech for a class while I was in law school, and if anyone ever tells you that, I'm positive that you'll nod your head and agree that in fact, this should also be an Ising Model.

Finally, for you, my readers... Thanks for waiting. I hope it was worthwhile.